HARD SELL

Mandy slipped the thin straps of her nightie from her shoulders. It fell to her waist giving Joe an unfettered view of her luscious peaks. Hips swaying, she stepped close and wound her bare arms around his neck. Her breasts, the nipples as hard as bullets, pressed into his chest. Suddenly he was as stiff as a poker – he couldn't help it.

'So, you *do* want me,' she said triumphantly. 'What are you waiting for? Do you want to spank me first – is that it?'

She bent over the bed, baring the full moons of her curvaceous buttocks. Joe remembered just how much he had enjoyed slapping them last night . . .

Hard Sell

Felice Ash

HEADLINE
DELTA

First published in 1995 by
HEADLINE BOOK PUBLISHING

A HEADLINE DELTA paperback

10 9 8 7 6 5 4 3 2 1

ISBN 0 7472 4804 4

Phototypeset by Intype, London
Printed and bound in Great Britain by
Cox & Wyman Ltd, Reading, Berks

HEADLINE BOOK PUBLISHING
A division of Hodder Headline PLC
338 Euston Road
London NW1 3BH

Hard Sell

Chapter One

'You did what!'

Quentin's patrician features were rigid with shock and disapproval as he surveyed her across the dinner table.

'I took my panties off in the ladies and now I'm not wearing any,' repeated Sue in a low voice. 'I thought it would excite you,' she added, unable to conceal her disappointment.

'Excite me – that the lady I'm dining with has apparently lost all sense of decency,' hissed Quentin, glancing around to make sure that none of the other diners in the restaurant of the West End hotel had heard Sue's confession. 'Well it doesn't. It makes me think you must have taken leave of your senses to behave like some common little slut instead of the cultured professional woman I believed you to be. Go and put them back on immediately.'

Cultured? Wherever had he got that idea?

Rising to her feet so quickly that she nearly knocked over her chair the process, Sue stalked out of the restaurant.

No wonder Quentin was such a successful barrister. She could imagine him intimidating an entire courtroom just by raising one disdainful eyebrow – she found him pretty intimidating herself some of the time.

How could she have miscalculated so badly? When the idea of discarding her panties had occurred to her earlier in the evening, she'd been certain that it would get him hot and ensure that he wanted to screw her later.

How wrong could you be?

It was Quentin's birthday and their fifth date and she was treating him to dinner, hoping that after the meal they'd return to his pristine bachelor flat in Holborn and have wild, abandoned sex.

Or at least have sex.

Wild and abandoned weren't really character traits she associated with Quentin. But they'd been seeing each other for over three weeks and Sue thought she'd go mad with frustration if he didn't make a move on her tonight. She'd spent all day in a fever of erotic anticipation and now it looked as if she'd blown it.

Or Quentin had, depending on which way you looked at it.

She was starting to think that the new leaf she'd resolved to turn over wasn't such a good idea after all.

Shortly after she and her partner Gemma had opened their own advertising agency six months ago, she'd decided that she needed a more mature approach to life, one in keeping with her status of creative director of Covent Garden's newest agency.

Gorgeous, sexy and impulsive, Sue seemed to have spent most of her adult life in a disorganised, chaotic mess, ricocheting from man to man, opening her legs as easily as she opened each morning's post.

But she'd decided that it was time for all that to come

to an end and when she'd met Quentin, a successful barrister, at a party she'd thought he might be the one to keep
her on the straight and narrow path of monogamy. He was
very attractive and seemed to imbue all the qualities she
now felt she needed in her life.

Except he'd made no attempt to take her to bed.

Heading towards the ladies, her blonde head bent, Sue
was only dimly aware of some shouts coming from the hotel
foyer behind her. She was startled to hear an unfamiliar
noise, like a series of sharp cracks, and even more startled
to be seized by the wrist and dragged to the floor behind
a potted palm.

The world had suddenly gone crazy.

One moment people were strolling decorously through
the hotel's lavishly appointed foyer and the next the air
was rent by screams and people either froze with shock or
dived to the floor.

'Wh ... what's going on?' she stammered, looking wildly
around and trying to free her wrist from the grip of the
man who'd dragged her down next to him.

'He's got a gun – keep down!' he replied tersely.

Lifting her head, Sue glimpsed a man in a balaclava at
the far end of the foyer, holding a gun straight-armed and
two-handed in front of him, just the way she'd seen on
television. She heard two more cracks and drew the unwelcome conclusion that he'd pulled the trigger again – twice.

'When I say "go", crawl behind that sofa as fast as you
can, keeping your head well down,' ordered her companion,
nodding in the direction of a large chintz-covered sofa in
an alcove about a dozen yards away. She registered that he
was dark, perhaps in his early thirties and that he had a

grip of iron in the hand still encircling her wrist.

As if he'd read her mind he released her. Behind the sofa definitely looked like a desirable option compared to the scanty cover afforded by the potted palm, so Sue got onto her hands and knees and waited for his signal.

Unfortunately, a few moments before he gave it, she remembered her current knickerless state.

She was wearing a short black evening dress with a tight skirt and knew beyond a shadow of a doubt that her state of undress would be immediately obvious as she crawled across the carpet.

'Go!'

Sue remained where she was, weighing up the mortification of a total stranger thinking her the sort of woman who habitually went out without underwear, against the very real possibility of being shot.

'What are you waiting for? A bus? He's looking the other way – now go!' Sue's companion gave her a none-too-gentle push and, against her better judgement, she somehow found herself scrambling across the thick carpet.

Covering the dozen or so yards seemed to take forever and she was humiliatingly aware that her tight skirt had ridden up and she was undoubtedly presenting him with a clear view of her curvaceous backside, bare except for a black satin suspender bisecting each buttock.

At long last she reached the sofa and crawled behind it, lying on her stomach in the narrow gap between the back and the wall. It was set in an alcove so she felt relatively safe – or as safe as anyone could feel with some psycho with a gun rampaging around fifty yards away.

Before she had time to pull her skirt down, her companion from the potted palm shot around the sofa at speed and threw himself on top of her.

'Sorry!' he gasped as his weight made her involuntarily expel all the air in her lungs. 'There's not much room behind here, but try and look on the bright side – if there are any bullets flying around, I'll stop them before they get to you.'

It only took a few moments for Sue to realise something very disconcerting.

He had what felt to be a massive hard-on wedged in the cleft between her buttocks.

Her face, already pink, flooded with even hotter colour and she closed her eyes briefly before saying in as cool a voice as she could manage, 'Would you mind raising yourself so I can pull my skirt down?'

'Do I have to?' His tone was lascivious in the extreme.

'Please.'

Sighing, he reluctantly took his weight on his elbows for a few seconds while she dragged her skirt down and tried to turn onto her side. She was only partially successful in the confined space and they ended up with his lower body still lying across hers in a tangle of legs, but at least his erection was now digging into her hip rather than her backside.

'Can I ask you something?' he muttered hoarsely.

'What?'

'Do you often go out without knickers?'

Sue tried to think of something humorous to say, but failed and found herself replying truthfully, 'No, never. Anyway I didn't go out without them – I just took them off in the ladies – they're in my bag.'

'Why did you take them off?' he asked with interest.

Sue was aware that the conversation had taken a dangerous turn, but there was something about the enforced intimacy of lying behind a sofa with a man who'd arguably saved her life – she'd still be standing frozen with shock in the corridor now, a sitting duck, if he hadn't intervened – which made her confide in him.

'I . . . I wanted to excite the man I'm with.'

'And did you?'

'No. He was very disapproving and told me to go and put them back on.'

'He must be mad. I wouldn't have been able to finish my meal if you'd said that to me. In fact I'd have been hard put not to ravish you on the the table in front of everyone.'

Sue giggled at the idea of the strait-laced Quentin behaving in such an unlikely way.

'In fact,' he continued, 'I'm hard put not to ravish you right now. It isn't every day I find myself lying on top of a gorgeous woman who I know isn't wearing any panties. I could barely get my legs to work to follow you, I was so stunned to see the most fantastic bum I'd ever laid eyes on, wiggling away from me. I'm sure you've already noticed what effect it's had.'

Joe had always had a one track mind and it was a dirt track. One of his ex-girlfriends had once described him pretty accurately as being a libido on legs.

He could never look at an attractive woman without imagining what it would be like to screw her, preferably in some particularly lewd position. And he couldn't be alone with one without actually trying to. And that was when she was fully clothed.

Sue's provocatively naked backside had lit his blue touchpaper and made him feel his dick was about to explode.

Sue blushed again. She could smell his light cologne and feel the weight of his lean, hard body pressing against hers, particularly his cock which felt as if it was trying to wear a ridge in her hip.

'I don't even know your name,' she murmured.

'Joe.'

'I'm Sue.'

Incongruously, in the dim light they shook hands. Sue had to proffer her left hand because the other was trapped underneath her.

'So, how about it?' he asked cheerfully.

'How about what?'

'Shall I ravish you? It looks like we're going to be here for a while and it would pass the time.'

Sue giggled again. 'I don't think Quentin would like it.'

'Sod Quentin – he sounds like a cold fish to me. Is he?'

'Some people think so,' she replied cautiously.

'Do you?'

She didn't respond because the only truthful answer would have been in the affirmative, and that wasn't something she wanted to think about just at that moment.

Joe began to stroke her bare shoulders above the tight-fitting bodice of her dress, making her uncomfortably aware that she was aroused and getting more so by the second.

A sudden surge of heat through her body as he intensified the caress made her catch her breath.

'What . . . are you doing?' she faltered.

'Mmm? In what way?'

'Touching me.'

'I can't help but touch you – we're crammed together in a space not big enough to swing the proverbial cat.'

His hand slid down her back, smoothing over the silk of her dress and his face nuzzled her neck, making her spine turn to jelly and a feeling of moist heat prickle between her legs.

Sue's natural recklessness, determinedly suppressed in recent months, suddenly rose to the surface and made her throw caution to the wind. She moaned softly and rubbed her hip against his hard-on, making it grow even bigger.

She knew that there was now no chance of Quentin screwing her that evening – not after his shocked reaction to her removing her panties and then having his birthday dinner rudely disturbed by the advent of a balaclava'd gunman.

So what the hell?

She was fed up with feeling frustrated.

And anyway her body had just gone into enthusiastic pre-fuck overdrive – she could already feel a trickle of her female lubrications on her inner thigh.

Reaching out, she stroked Joe's sleek dark hair, then slid her hand down his back until it reached his firm, muscular buttocks.

He groaned and muttered. 'Shall I take that as a yes?'

'Yes.'

His hand slipped up her skirt and caressed her naked backside, while she tried to get her own hand between them so she could reach his cock. It wasn't easy in the confined space, but somehow she got his zip down and pulled out his member, which felt like velvet-covered steel in her slender hand.

She gasped and moaned when he slipped his fingers into the outer crevices of her floss-covered delta from behind, exploring the warm stickiness he found there. She parted her legs as widely as she could and felt tremors of sheer sexual sensation jolt over her body.

When he pushed two fingers deep into her and stroked the walls of her wet cavern, Sue thought she would pass out from pleasure. Anxious to have him inside her she stopped squeezing and stroking his cock and tried to guide it towards her pussy.

'Hang on,' he muttered, then manoeuvred himself so he was in the right position, poised above her as she pushed her backside impatiently upwards. He dragged her skirt up out of the way, then she felt the head of his cock nudging into her soft, slippery folds before he entered her in one smooth thrust.

It was a fast and furious fuck which left her hot, sticky, breathless and panting for more – particularly after a period of reluctant celibacy.

The first time didn't last very long – they were both in the grip of too urgent a need – but he was hard again almost immediately.

This time he pulled her onto her hands and knees so he could free her hard-nippled breasts from the constraining bodice. She felt the palm of his hand, warm and dry, skimming over the engorged points, then closing fervently over one full, round orb. He caressed it, gently kneading and fondling the creamy flesh, before gathering both breasts into his hands as they humped frantically away.

Their groans of pleasure were punctuated by cries and screams from the hotel foyer and the whine of more bullets, but they were oblivious to it, the additional adrenalin pumping through both their bodies only adding to the depth of arousal.

At last, after another urgent climax which left her sated – at least for now – Sue collapsed onto the dusty carpet with Joe on top of her, his cock still buried deep into her honeypot, his hands on her breasts.

Her thick, wavy blonde hair had come loose from its tight French knot and now tumbled down around her bare shoulders. Joe buried his face in it, breathing in the scent of shampoo and perfume.

'It suits you down,' he murmured inconsequentially. 'Why do you pull it back like that? Don't tell me – Quentin? I'm liking him less and less, and I didn't like him very much in the first place.'

'You haven't met him,' Sue pointed out, rotating her pelvis slightly so his cock moved within her.

'No, but I saw you together going into the restaurant. I wondered then what a gorgeous girl like you was doing with a pompous ass like him.'

Quentin, true to form, had given the head waiter a hard time because there had been a few seconds delay in seating them.

'I don't want to talk about Quentin – in fact I don't want to talk at all.'

Rotating her pelvis had caused a renewed hardening of Joe's cock and Sue was more than ready for him to put it to good use again.

This time he screwed her so vigorously that she found herself travelling along the carpet until her head and shoulders were jammed uncomfortably against the wall of the alcove.

Some time during their final ecstatic moments, something must have happened in the hotel foyer because when they came back down to earth, Joe was the first to realise that the situation had changed. After listening for a few minutes, he slid reluctantly out of her in time to see policemen swarming all over the hotel and no sign of the gunman.

'I think it's safe to come out,' he told her, pushing the sofa forward so there was room for them to sit side by side and adjust their clothing. 'I think our friend with the gun has made good his escape. Pity – particularly since I'm supposed to be in charge of security tonight.'

Sue only half heard what he was saying, she was too busy gazing around to see if anyone was hurt.

When she was satisfied that no one seemed to be injured she turned to look at him and liked what she saw – which was probably just as well considering that she'd just let a total stranger fuck her without even having had a drink with him first.

It would have been awful to find him repellent now.

As it was, he was attractive in an understated way with blue eyes, sleek dark hair worn short and very white teeth. He was grinning at her engagingly in a way which made his eyes crinkle.

'The party seems to be over, so is this a good time to ask for your phone number?' He stood up then bent down to help her to her feet.

At that moment, Sue spotted Quentin engaged in some sort of argument at the reception desk and ducked hastily down behind the sofa again.

'I don't want to see him at the moment,' she gasped. 'Let me know when he's gone.'

'He hasn't gone, but he's got his back turned.'

Peering huntedly over the top of the sofa, Sue saw that he was busy laying down the law to a receptionist, two waiters and a policeman.

'It was lovely,' she said to Joe, 'but I've got to go.' Ignoring his protests, she bolted down the corridor and into the ladies, then stopped dead when she saw herself in the full-length mirror.

She looked terrible.

Her hair was falling down in an untidy mass of tousled blonde waves, her face was streaked with dust from the carpet and her eye make-up was smudged around her wide-set, almond-shaped brown eyes.

She did her best to repair the damage, but it wasn't easy with her black silk dress irrevocably crumpled and her stockings in holes around the knees.

She threw them in the bin and, as an afterthought, she pulled her panties out of her bag and stepped into them. Her hairpins must still have been on the carpet, so she dragged a comb through her hair and left it down.

Taking a deep breath she left the ladies and prepared to reluctantly rejoin Quentin, hoping he wouldn't be able to smell Joe on her, though she'd cleaned herself up as best she could with a handful of damp tissues and sprayed herself liberally with scent.

To be honest, she didn't know why she was bothering – Quentin would definitely have to go.

He might be extremely handsome, charming and successful, but he was obviously a non-starter when it came to sex.

There was no sign of him in either the foyer or the restaurant, but as she stood uncertainly in the doorway a waiter greeted her with every sign of relief and promptly handed her the bill for their meal.

So that's what Quentin had been arguing about – he didn't want to get stuck with paying for an aborted meal. She'd done her best to ignore his meanness, his pomposity and his bossiness, but she was damned if she'd ignore his lack of sex drive too.

Bye Quentin – you're history, she told herself as she handed the waiter her Amex card.

'Was anyone hurt?' asked Gemma the following day, after Sue had told her about the gunman and her subsequent sojourn behind the sofa with Joe. She'd omitted any mention of the sex they'd enjoyed together, but she could see Gemma was intrigued.

'Thankfully no – though they took a couple of people to hospital suffering from shock.'

'And you've ditched Quentin?'

'Definitely. He didn't even hang around to see if I was okay.'

She'd already told Gemma about Quentin's reaction to her dispensing with her panties.

'Pity,' had been her partner's comment, pushing back a lock of glossy sable hair. 'He was *very* good-looking, but he's obviously got ice-water for blood, which makes him a big no-no. What did you think of the hotel?' she added, changing the subject.

One of the reasons Sue had taken Quentin to that particular hotel was that it was one of a luxury chain whose account they were currently pitching for.

'Somewhat dusty behind the sofas and a bit stiff for my taste, but pretty well run – they were serving meals again in the restaurant within minutes of the gunman running out.'

'How's the Fitted-Kitchens pitch coming along?'

'Not bad. If you have time this afternoon we could go through it.'

'Okay. See you later.'

Gemma left the room and returned to her own office, pausing to remove the tailored jacket of her well-cut scarlet suit before sitting down and swinging her long legs behind her desk.

In her mid-thirties, Gemma was several years older than Sue. A tall, slender brunette, she had a delicate, high-cheek-boned face with dark blue eyes and a full, well-shaped mouth. Her apparent fragility hid a will of finely tempered steel, as anyone who'd ever crossed her found out too late and usually to their cost.

The phone rang just as she was opening the first of a pile of files in front of her.

'Hello,' she began, then stopped as the unmistakable sound of a man's heavy breathing greeted her from the other end of the phone.

'What colour knickers are you wearing?' asked a deep, hoarse voice.

Gemma slid her skirt up her shapely thighs and looked at her ivory satin camiknickers.

'Ivory,' she told the caller hesitantly, 'ivory satin.'

'Is that just your knickers, or anything else?'

'My slip and my suspender belt are ivory satin too.'

'A suspender belt, eh? You must be a sexy little number. What about your bra?'

'I'm not wearing one.'

'You must be a bit of a tart then – am I right?'

'Possibly.'

'Well then, you little tart, I'll bet you're the sort of slut who's always hot for it. I'll bet there's nothing you like better than a good hard cock inside your pussy. I'll bet if I was there now you'd be dropping your knickers and spreading your legs for me. Wouldn't you?'

He didn't wait for her to reply but continued in a thickened voice. 'Is there anyone else there?'

'No, I'm alone.'

'Good, because I want you to touch yourself. Go on, put your hand inside your knickers and touch yourself.'

Gemma hesitated, then slowly slid her fingers beneath the thin strip of satin covering her private parts. She stroked the silken floss of her bush, diffidently at first, then more confidently. She felt a slight stirring, then her clit, which was currently nestling well inside the warm folds of her labia, began to harden and swell as she increased the pressure.

'Keep going, make yourself good and wet until your knickers are soaking and your cunt's itching for a big, thick cock inside it. Are you doing it?'

'Yes ... yes I am.'

'How does it feel?'

'Good. It feels good.'

'Is it turning you on?'

'Yes – it's making me hot – very hot.'

Gemma opened her legs wider and dipped her fingers into the moist entrance to her honeypot, spreading the juices gathering there around the pointed little sliver of flesh which was her clit. She began to rub it rhythmically, slipping backwards and forwards over the slick shaft until it had swollen into a pulsing nub of sensation.

While she worked on herself, the hoarse voice continued to talk to her obscenely, urging her on to greater efforts until she felt the hazy wave of heat which indicated she was about to climax. She cried out as she came, her breath coming in little gasps.

There was silence at the other end of the phone, then the caller said, 'You enjoyed that didn't you, Gemma, you sexy little cat?'

Despite the fact that she was still trembling, Gemma managed to say calmly, 'Hello, Rob, when did you get back in town?'

'I flew in from LA yesterday afternoon and crashed straight out before I'd even had a chance to unpack.'

'How's the project coming along?'

'Great. The money people are on the point of signing.'

Rob was an independent TV producer, her long-term casual lover and the only man she'd ever allowed to dominate her – at least sexually.

'I'm only in town for a couple of nights – I could get round to your place around nine,' he continued.

'Make it ten – Sue and I are having dinner with a client,' said Gemma reluctantly. She wouldn't have said no if he'd suggested coming round right away and screwing her on the desk – that's how hot he always made her feel – but business was business and tonight's dinner was too important to postpone or cut short early.

'Okay. And sweetheart . . .'

'Yes,'

'I'm going to want to get my dick in your pussy the

16

second I walk through the door – so don't be wearing much.'

Chapter Two

After putting the phone down, Gemma straightened her clothing and then rang for a cup of coffee.

So Rob was back, albeit briefly, come to disrupt her carefully ordered life with the insatiable, and often perverse, sexual demands she could never resist.

And goodness knows she'd tried hard enough.

She could really do without him around at the moment. The agency was doing brilliantly to say it was only six months old, but it took all her time and energy to keep it on track.

Tish, the Australian receptionist, brought her coffee and then left, leaving Gemma to sip it thoughtfully.

She didn't know why she was addicted to sex with Rob.

When he was away she could manage without him for weeks at a time without too much of a problem, but as soon as she saw him, or even heard his voice on the phone, she was like an addict desperate for her next fix.

The problem was that she couldn't control him – unlike the other men in her life – and that wasn't a situation she was happy with. She'd tried to stop seeing him but it was impossible; she felt her willpower ebbing away in his presence, until she was helpless under his wolfish gaze.

It couldn't just be that he was spectacularly attractive – which he undoubtedly was. He was six foot of pure male animal with thick blond hair, piercing blue eyes and a lean, firmly muscled body.

Not to mention his huge, ever-ready cock.

Gemma squirmed slightly on her seat as she visualised it, towering massively up between his thighs, heavily knob-bed and a deep, dark red.

She'd been to bed with better-looking men and even ones with bigger cocks – though not many – so it wasn't just that.

No, it was his will to dominate her and his ability to get her to do things she wouldn't have contemplated with other men which set him apart. He could make her nipples harden and her private parts lubricate just by looking at her.

They'd been seeing each other for over three years and in that time she'd tried to accommodate their strange and erratic sex life so it spilled over into her professional life as little as possible. She was more or less successful, though there were times when it was difficult.

She didn't fool herself for one minute that she was the only woman in Rob's life but, as he certainly wasn't the only man in hers, she didn't let it bother her.

Which reminded her – she'd arranged to see David tonight after the client dinner. She'd better phone and cancel. He definitely wouldn't be pleased and, as the head of the company which was the agency's biggest client, she needed to keep him happy if he wasn't to take the account elsewhere.

'This is great – I think they'll love it,' commented Gemma,

when she and Sue had finished going over the pitch
together. Her partner had done it again – the campaign
she'd come up with for the fitted-kitchens company was
brilliant.

'I'm quite pleased with the way it's come together, but
to make it really effective we need to increase the budget,'
stated Sue firmly.

Gemma sighed and said evasively, 'Let's see how it goes
down before we get onto that, shall we?'

In an ideal world Sue wouldn't have been her choice
of business partner – however much she liked her – but
nevertheless she undoubtedly delivered the goods time after
time.

The only problem was that, although Sue was unarguably
highly creative, she never quite seemed to grasp the bottom
line – which was that they were in business to make money.

Winning awards was all very well and it undoubtedly
helped to bring in new clients, but as far as Gemma was
concerned it wasn't the agency's primary aim.

Sue was always trying to up the budget for the creative
side of campaigns – even if it meant taking a cut in profits,
which it usually did. Which was why Gemma dealt with the
financial side of the business herself – the less involvement
Sue had with that, the better.

When Gemma had first planned to start up on her own
and leave Detroit's, the large, well-established agency where
she was account director, she hadn't intended to invite Sue
to join her as head of the creative staff. The idea of having
her as a partner had never entered her head, particularly
as the younger woman had no capital to invest.

But fate took a hand when, within the same week,
Gemma's potential partner had a heart attack and decided

to pull out and Sue won a considerable sum of money with some premium bonds an aunt had bought her over twenty years ago.

So far it had worked out reasonably well, but Gemma had never wavered in her determination to keep a firm hand on the reins.

'What time is it?' asked Sue, stretching and yawning so demonstratively that the top button of her tight-fitting daffodil-yellow blouse popped open, revealing a generous amount of creamy cleavage.

'Five-thirty,' Gemma told her after glancing at her watch.

'What time are they due?'

'Six. I've estimated just over an hour to do the pitch, then I've booked us a table at Raimondo's for seven-thirty.'

'Yum. Don't you just love taking clients out for meals?'

'There are worse ways to earn a living,' admitted Gemma. 'I think I'll just go and tidy up before they arrive,' she added pointedly.

Sue beamed at her. 'And you think I should do the same. Okay, point taken.'

When Gemma had left the room, her high-heeled shoes making no sound on the thick black carpet, Sue went over to the mirror and began to pull a comb through her tangled, wavy blonde hair. She wished she always looked as effortlessly well-groomed as Gemma, but her hair was virtually uncontrollable and her clothes always looked untidy.

After tucking her blouse back into her dark fawn skirt and fastening her top button, Sue pulled on a loose black jacket and inspected herself critically. Was that a mark on her skirt? No, thankfully it was just a piece of fluff.

She went down to Gemma's office where the meeting

was to be held and marvelled at how neat it was. Clients were never allowed to see her own chaotic office – it always looked like a bomb had hit it and tended to be littered with piles of paper, stacks of magazines she kept for reference and half-finished cups of coffee.

'Drink?' offered Gemma, busy removing a cork from a bottle of red wine.

'Yes please.' She took a seat on a small easy chair covered in rough black cotton and put her feet up on the coffee table. 'Thanks,' she murmured when Gemma passed her a glass. At that moment there was a knock at the door, a sharp rat-a-tat-tat which made Sue jump and spill the wine down the front of her blouse.

She leapt to her feet as Paul, the art director, appeared in the doorway holding a set of transparencies.

'Shit!' wailed Sue. 'My blouse is soaked.'

'Let me see,' said Gemma calmly, adding to Paul, 'just leave them on the desk, thanks.'

Sue peeled off her jacket to reveal a blouse with a large red stain down the front.

'I'll have to go out and see if I can buy something,' she said wretchedly. 'I can't wear this.' Underneath, Gemma could see she was wearing a beige bra which was also stained.

'There isn't time – they'll be here any moment. Let me think.'

After a moment's hesitation, she slipped out of her scarlet jacket and white silk blouse to reveal a plain ivory satin slip tucked into her skirt. She pulled it swiftly out of the waistband and dragged it over her head.

'Put this on under your jacket,' she ordered, standing

naked to the waist, displaying small, pointed breasts with toffee-coloured, crinkled nipples. Sue had never seen her partner undressed before and found it hard to tear her eyes away from the oddly alluring sight.

'What beautiful breasts you have,' she heard herself saying, watching them disappear as Gemma deftly buttoned up her blouse again.

Gemma raised one arched, dark eyebrow before saying, 'I think most men would prefer yours.'

Sue's own breasts were now revealed in all their cream and pink glory. Large and firm, they jutted proudly out over her tiny waist, the nipples a deep rosy hue.

She drew the satin slip over her head and fastened her skirt into position over it. Her breasts strained at the fine fabric of a garment which was patently designed for a less voluptuous woman and could barely contain them. Even with her jacket on and the buttons fastened, she was still showing a stunning expanse of cleavage.

Gemma shook her head. 'No, that won't do. You'll have to wear my blouse and *I'll* wear just the slip under my jacket.'

About to exchange clothes again, they were interrupted by a knock at the door, then Tish showed their potential clients from the fitted-kitchens company, all male, into the room.

Making a mental note to reprimand Tish, who should have phoned through first to check it was okay to bring them down, Gemma resigned herself to making the best of the situation and stepped forward to greet them.

Throughout the pitch, the three men were like rabbits in the glare of headlights, paying far more attention to Sue's cleavage than they did to the storyboard she was showing them.

It was even worse in the restaurant. Not only did their dining companions seem unable to hold any sort of sensible conversation, but all the waiters vied with each other to serve their table, crowding noisily around until Gemma nearly lost her temper.

What was it about a glimpse of a pair of breasts which made otherwise rational males go gaga?

Admittedly Sue's were worthy of admiration, but surely not to this extent?

When at long last the men took their regretful leave at around nine-thirty, leaving the two women to settle the bill, Sue drained her glass of Tia Maria and smiled sunnily.

'How do you think it went?'

'If they remember the first thing about the campaign I'll be very surprised,' replied Gemma crossly. 'On the other hand the memory of your cleavage will undoubtedly fuel their erotic fantasies for many a day. I'm amazed you could eat your pasta – there was so much pepper and parmesan on it by the time each of the waiters in turn had finished giving you some.'

'I like pepper and parmesan – restaurants are usually fairly stingy with them so I didn't mind,' returned Sue. 'The question is – will they go for the campaign?'

'We'll know soon enough,' said Gemma, signing the credit card slip. 'Okay – I've got to go. See you tomorrow.'

Gemma had no trouble getting a cab and arrived back at her small town house in Camden Town at around nine forty-five.

She hurried upstairs and undressed before diving into the shower, being careful not to streak her make-up because she didn't have time to redo it.

She was just fastening her flimsy amethyst silk robe when the bell went. She went downstairs, opened the front door and stepped back. Rob slammed it behind him and she gasped as he dragged down his zip, lifted her into his arms and thrust himself into her with no preamble.

With anyone but Rob it would have been a disastrous coupling. But all the way home in the cab and then under the shower, her body had been producing copious female lubrications in anticipation and his huge member slipped easily inside her, right up to the hilt.

She wound her legs around his waist and her arms around his neck as they fucked wildly in the narrow hallway. Her silk robe drifted open exposing her pert little breasts and he bent his blond head and took one pointed, puckered nipple in his mouth.

There seemed to be a direct line from that caramel-hued nipple to her well-filled honeypot as he sucked hard then flicked the tip of his tongue backwards and forwards across the taut peak, plunging frenziedly in and out of her all the while.

She climaxed twice in the time it took him to build up a similar head of steam and erupt into her in a great scalding flood.

Still holding her, his large hands gripping her small backside, he took several steps forward then lowered her onto the fourth step of the stairs, lifting her off his cock as he did so.

'Have you missed me?' he asked.

She tilted back her head and looked at him from beneath her thick, dark lashes.

'Probably about as much as you've missed me.'

He grinned at her and knelt on the bottom step, covering her breasts with his hands and fondling them casually. Gemma could feel his juices trickling out of her onto the carpet and her excitement mounted again.

She leant forward and lapped delicately at the swollen head of his cock with the tip of her tongue, like a cat with a bowl of creamy milk. His huge organ had subsided to some extent but at the touch of her tongue it stirred expectantly.

She licked her way down the shaft and it leapt back into ramrod hardness while he buried his hands in her glossy dark hair and guided it into her mouth.

Gemma was good at this.

She had long ago mastered the knack of getting all of a cock into her mouth – however large it was – by letting the end slip partially down her throat, breathing through her nose all the while.

She heard Rob grunt as she took it in, sucking hard. Then she let it slip slowly out until only the glans remained between her lips. She held it in position with her hand while circling it teasingly with her tongue.

For a long time she sucked, licked and manipulated his hot, heavy organ until at last he reluctantly withdrew, then kissed her hard on the mouth, entwining his tongue with hers.

She felt his hand slide up her thigh, then he parted her legs and slipped his fingers into her sticky, wet warmth, his thumb finding her clit. All her nerve endings shrieked with

27

renewed pleasure as he manipulated it skilfully for a few moments.

'Turn round,' he ordered her. Shrugging out of her robe Gemma obeyed, kneeling on the step she'd been sitting on. She didn't need telling to keep her legs wide apart.

'You're dying for it again, aren't you?' he muttered, roughly parting her buttocks, then stabbing his tongue between them in a way which made her squirm with lust. 'Aren't you?' he repeated.

'Yes,' she moaned as he plunged his large tongue into her vulva. She cried out as it made fleeting contact with her clit then withdrew.

'Bring yourself off,' he said softly. Gemma slipped a hand down over her short, silken bush and began to rub herself. It only took a few seconds of direct stimulation for her to climax, her back arching and her head falling back.

At that moment he seized her by the waist and plunged determinedly into her again, prolonging her climax as her internal muscles convulsed around his huge cock.

Pushed forward onto the stairs by the force of his thrusts, Gemma moved her smooth-skinned derrière backwards rhythmically to welcome each piston-driven motion.

As he approached another orgasm, the thrusts became less deep and more rapid, his balls slapping arousingly against her buttocks.

She felt his release when it came and it triggered her own. Her moans of pleasure echoed around the hallway as he erupted inside her, filling her up with all the force of a dam bursting.

As usual Gemma arrived at work early the following morning, walking rather gingerly. Rob had shown his usual stamina and most of the night had been passed in hot, urgent couplings, leaving her feeling slightly stiff and sore but *very* satisfied.

She half regretted and was half relieved that he was only in town for a couple of days. Part of her would like nothing better than to have him always on hand to screw her into a gasping, panting, sex-sated daze. But her more rational side knew it would be bad news as far as the rest of her life was concerned.

Thinking of which, she'd better start considering ways to placate David – he'd obviously been annoyed that she'd cancelled their late-evening rendezvous yesterday, but it shouldn't be too difficult because he was besotted with her.

The head of a large family-owned company which supplied bread to half the supermarkets in Britain, David took a great personal interest in the company's advertising. She'd met him when she'd been account director at Detroit's, her old agency, and was soon handling more than just his account.

When she'd decided to start her own agency she'd managed to take his company's business with her, along with several others – something which had not exactly endeared her to her ex-employers. But David's account was by far the largest and she was well aware that without his backing the venture would probably have been impossible.

She knew she wouldn't be able to see him tonight – Rob had told her he was arranging something special – but she'd better find time to phone him again and arrange a date for tomorrow night.

No, not tomorrow – she'd need at least one night off sex after two with Rob.

After giving it some thought, she picked up the phone

and dialled his number. He was predictably cool with her, but when they'd had a brief discussion about a new series of print ads, she changed the tone of the conversation.

'Do you know what I wish we were doing, instead of talking on the phone?' she purred.

'What?'

'I wish we were in your office fucking on your desk.' She heard his sharp intake of breath and continued, 'And that's *after* I'd given you a long, slow blow job.'

She described it in great detail. David loved her to talk dirty because he'd never before been with a woman who did. And because he found it a huge turn-on to have a beautiful, coolly-controlled woman talk about sex in such crudely explicit detail in her mellifluous middle-class voice.

At the end of the conversation she added, 'By the way – I'm biking the visual for the wholemeal bread ad over for you to take a look at. Open it when you're alone.'

'Why?' he asked.

'You'll find out. Bye, David.'

She hoped he'd find the pair of silk panties she'd put in the package enough to keep him happy until she saw him again.

'We've got it!' crowed Sue happily, bursting into Gemma's office just after she'd put the phone down.

'Got what?'

'The fitted-kitchens account!'

'That's great, absolutely great,' said Gemma. 'The whole works?'

'Yep. TV, radio and print – we *are* going to be busy. They

want us to go ahead and start work on the print ads first, so as soon as I've finished the copy for David's stuff I'll get right onto it.'

'The question is, did we get the work because of your brilliant pitch, or your traffic-stopping cleavage?' speculated Gemma.

Sue giggled. 'Who cares? I certainly don't. I can't believe how well we're doing. I thought there was a very good chance we'd go under within a few months and I'd be crawling to Detroit's begging for my old job back.'

'You wouldn't have got it. The knives are out for us after we poached so much of their business. There's nothing they'd like better than to see us fail.'

'I think I'll go shopping sometime soon to celebrate – I need some new clothes.'

Sue was wearing a black silk shirt tucked into a black leather miniskirt which made Gemma blanch. She wouldn't have been seen dead in something so unashamedly tarty. The smooth glove leather clung alluringly to the curvaceous contours of Sue's bottom, making her look drop-dead sexy.

'Did you bring my slip back, by the way?'

Sue had already forgotten she'd borrowed it and when she'd got in last night she'd flung it on the floor to join most of the other clothes she owned.

'No, I'm going to wash it first,' she improvised hastily, hoping she'd remember. 'Better get back to it – see you later.'

She practically skipped out of the office, fizzing with delight at the prospect of so much work. She stopped short in reception and her almond-shaped brown eyes widened when she saw who was standing there patently flirting with Tish.

Joe. Her partner in the fast and furious fuck behind the sofa.

The air suddenly seemed thick with sexual heat.

'Hello. What are you doing here?' she asked.

'Tracked you down at last,' he greeted her. 'Nice place you've got,' he added, taking in the black, grey and white decor.

'Thanks. Do you want to come down to my office? Can you bring coffee please, Tish?'

'How did you find me?' she enquired, once she'd cleared a space for him on her small sofa, carelessly brushing the clutter on it to the floor.

'A lucky break really. When I realised you'd gone, I asked the hotel receptionist and the head waiter, but they didn't know you. Then later I was talking to the PR man who'd seen us emerging from behind the sofa together and he said you were a partner in an agency currently pitching for their account. He told me where I could find you.'

'How come you were talking to him?' Sue was curious to know.

'My company was supposed to be in charge of security that evening – there was a political dinner being held in a private room. I'm not exactly flavour of the month with the hotel at the moment – my men didn't manage to stop our friend in the balaclava running amok.'

'You've got your own company? Tell me about it,' she invited, trying unsuccessfully to block out images of the two of them humping behind the sofa.

'We advise on and provide security for hotels and various

other businesses. That night was a disaster – we slipped up and it'll take a lot of hard work to convince the hotel that they shouldn't stop using us.'

'Do you advertise?' she wanted to know, scenting the prospect of more work. He grinned at her, his blue eyes crinkling.

'We don't need to – at least not at present, though if word about the recent cock-up gets around we may find ourselves needing to.'

'Well, remember us if you do.'

'Are you any good?'

'The best.'

'Convince me.' He sat back on the sofa, his arms folded, imagining her on her knees in front of him with his dick sliding in and out of her hungry, pouting mouth.

Sue felt a sharp tug of pure sexual response to his presence, particularly as his eyes kept travelling appreciatively over her body. She crossed her legs and studied the pointed toe of one high-heeled shoe, trying not to give in to it.

'I don't have time I'm afraid,' she returned, glancing at her watch. 'Duty calls – I've a lot of work to do.'

She rose reluctantly to her feet, took a step towards the door, then tripped over the pile of clutter she'd brushed onto the floor before. She would have fallen over completely if he hadn't grabbed her and pulled her back onto the sofa, so she was half lying across him.

Her stomach was across his groin and she felt the immediate hardening of his member as she clutched at him. She tried to pull herself into a sitting position but only ended up with her full breasts pressed into his chest.

His arms tightened around her and she felt a heady wave

of lust flood her body. Without considering the consequences of such an action she wriggled against him, then felt his hand running over what she realised belatedly were her scarlet panties – her short leather skirt had ridden up her hips as she sprawled over him.

He caressed her well-rounded backside over the tiny scrap of scarlet silk, then the smooth skin above her stocking tops. He'd just slipped his hand under her panties and was delving arousingly between her legs when there was a brisk tap at the door and Gemma stepped into the room.

She stopped dead, her eyes met Sue's, then she said, 'Sorry,' and went out again.

Sue scrambled hastily to her feet and dragged her skirt down over her thighs, blushing fiercely. 'Oh dear – I seem to make a habit of displaying my bum to you.'

'You can display it to me any time you like – it's the most gorgeous bum I've ever seen.'

Fleetingly, he imagined her squatting over his dick with her back to him, lowering herself slowly until his aching member vanished between the full moons of her buttocks and into her moist cavern. Shit. He was desperate to screw her again – but it obviously wasn't on at the moment.

Sue's body was also clamouring for more and it was with great difficulty that she ushered him from the room, when all she wanted was to throw him to the floor and tear his clothes off. In reception he picked up one of the agency's cards.

'I'm going away for a few days – can I ring you when I get back?'

Sue's hormones leapt at the idea.

'Sure,' she said happily.

Chapter Three

It was a warm evening but showery, which made the air uncomfortably damp and humid in central London.

'I thought we'd go for a drive in the country,' Rob said to Gemma when he came to pick her up. He ran his hand possessively over her mound as she settled into the passenger seat.

'Fine – it'll be good to get out of the city.' She could tell from the gleam in his eye that it wasn't going to be a normal drive in the country and her private parts prickled in anticipation.

After an hour's drive they reached a quiet country lane and Rob stopped the car, got out, then came round and opened the door.

It was high summer and the Kent countryside looked lush and green after the recent rain. On the other side of a hawthorn hedge a grassy, tree-strewn knoll rose towards the cinnamon-and-pink-streaked horizon and the air hung heavily around them, sultry and still. They were parked next to a chestnut tree, the leaves a deep, dark green dripping with warm moisture.

Gemma was practically dripping with warm moisture herself.

Whatever Rob had planned, she knew she probably wouldn't like it, but she would undoubtedly find it lewdly arousing.

She swung her long silk-clad legs onto the grass verge and looked at him enquiringly.

'Strip,' he said succinctly.

'Wh ... what?' she stammered, as a car drove past them.

'You heard.'

'Here? There are cars driving past.'

'Only occasionally. You'd better be quick before the next one comes along.'

Gemma hesitated, biting her lip, while he watched her impassively. It was no good – she couldn't resist the carnal determination in his deep blue eyes.

Slowly, she undid the buttons on her plain black linen dress, then pulled it open to reveal her black satin camisole, camiknickers, suspender belt and sheer black stockings.

She glanced nervously around, but there was no one in sight. She slipped the dress off her shoulders then put it on the back seat of the car.

'And the rest – no, on second thoughts, keep the stockings and suspender belt on.'

'Rob – please.' She made one last attempt to sway him.

'Now.'

Trembling, she pulled the camisole over her head, then turned to face him with her small, high breasts bared, the toffee-coloured nipples already swollen with anticipation below the single strand of pearls she wore.

She threw the camisole in the back of the car, then hooked her fingers in the elasticated top of her camiknickers. She slid them slowly over her hips then stepped out of them, revealing the neat damp triangle of her sable bush.

Rob ran his hand over her naked backside, idly caressing the pert globes of her provocatively jutting rump. He took the camiknickers from her hand and buried his face in them.

'You've got the sexiest smelling pussy I've ever fucked,' he told her.

To Gemma's horror, she heard the unmistakable sound of a vehicle approaching. She would have dived into the car but Rob was blocking the way, so instead she ducked behind the tree and flattened herself against it, praying she was invisible from the road.

He followed her and pressed her against the tree trunk with his lean body, pushing his denim-covered dick into her stomach so she could feel how hard it was. She moaned as he covered her breasts with his hands and fondled them, while at the same time he kissed her passionately, his tongue sliding into her mouth.

Two more cars passed while Gemma half hoped he would screw her up against the tree right away and half hoped he wouldn't in case anyone saw them.

After a few minutes of kissing her he stepped back and said, 'Time to move on – here, put this on.'

'This' was a light black silk summer mac which he must have taken from her closet. She pulled it thankfully over her semi-nakedness, tied the belt, rolled up the sleeves as a concession to the heat and got back into the car. Once she'd fastened her seat-belt he pulled the front of the mac apart below the waist so her mound and stocking tops were visible.

'Open your legs.'

She did as she was told, spreading them so the delicate point of her clit peeped out from within her parted labia.

He kept his left hand between them as they drove along, removing it only long enough to change gear, keeping her in a state of red-hot arousal without ever rubbing her clit long enough for her to climax.

Gemma prayed that a lorry wouldn't pass them. She was perfectly decorously dressed as far as anyone passing in a car was concerned, but a lorry driver would get a bird's eye view of the proceedings.

Thankfully there were no lorries on the road, but all the same it was a relief when Rob stopped the car at an old thatched pub. The car park was overhung with trees from a neighbouring field which were leaving sticky deposits on the cars parked beneath them and casting deep shadows in the damp pre-dusk.

Rob took her hand and led her into the pub. Her knee-length mac fell back around her thighs hiding her nakedness but Gemma was aware that the fine fabric showed off the prominent points of her distended nipples.

Rob climbed onto a barstool at the ancient, pitted-oak bar and waited for her to climb onto the one adjacent – no easy feat as she was trying not to let her mac fall open enough to show she wasn't wearing anything underneath.

She ordered a gin and tonic and gulped it gratefully, while Rob perused a menu with every appearance of interest. Gemma couldn't have been less interested – she was far too keyed up to think about food.

'I think we'll eat here,' he remarked, passing her the menu. 'What do you think?'

It was a fairly limited choice offering typical English pub

food – steak, chicken or fish with chips plus a few dishes like shepherd's pie, also with chips.

'If you want to,' she returned indifferently, absent-mindedly crossing and uncrossing her legs, then making a frantic grab for the edges of her mac as they threatened to fall apart and give the local drinkers an intoxicating flash of her private parts. 'Can't I at least go and put my knickers on?' she demanded in an undertone.

'Not a chance – it's far too much of a turn-on for me to know you're virtually naked under there.'

A waiter conducted them to a battered table between two old high-backed church pews overlooked by a leaded window. Every available surface around them seemed to be crammed with antiques, dried flowers and other artefacts. Gemma preferred her restaurants smarter and more sophisticated, but she mentally conceded that it had a dusty charm.

'Can I take your coat?' asked the waiter sullenly, his eyes nevertheless lingering on the small points of her heavy-nippled breasts.

'No thank you.'

'Why don't you let the waiter take it, sweetheart? You'll be too warm like that,' Rob suggested, grinning.

'No, thank you, I'm fine,' she repeated firmly, glowering at her lover.

She slid into the pew and Rob slid in next to her, his thigh pressing against hers. He ordered their food and a bottle of claret, then began to talk to her in a low voice.

'It would only take one yank and the whole pub would be able to see what a little tart you are. I think I'm going to make you eat your meal in just your suspender belt and stockings – no one would say anything – they'd all be too busy copping an eyeful. You'd like that, wouldn't you? You'd like them to see what a hot, over-sexed slut you are, despite that cool, touch-me-not air of yours.'

Gemma kept her eyes lowered and gulped down another mouthful of her drink, conscious of the hot flush covering her body.

Damn Rob.

Damn him to hell.

There wasn't another man in the world she'd have let talk to her like that – so why did she put up with it?

Because it made her molten inside, that's why.

Because it made her pussy feel like it was on fire, throbbing and itching for the one thing which could assuage the heat consuming it.

Rob's cock deep inside her.

'After they've all had a good look and we've eaten our meal, I'm going to throw you on the table, spread your legs and fuck you in front of them all. Fuck you until you're writhing under me and begging me for more, not caring who's watching. Then after that I might even let them all take turns with you . . .'

They were interrupted by the waiter who slapped the plates containing their starters down in front of them, then vanished again.

Gemma ate her melon without tasting it, while Rob, between mouthfuls of battered mushrooms, continued to talk to her in a similar vein.

They were sitting side by side facing into the pub, but the high back of the pew opposite blocked Gemma's view of their fellow drinkers and diners.

She made a start on the claret, wished she didn't keep wanting to bear down on the seat to stimulate her quivering clit. She gasped in horror when Rob suddenly pulled the front of the mac apart, baring her sweat-slicked breasts.

'Are you crazy!' she exclaimed, trying to pull the mac closed again.

'Leave it! No one can see you, you're completely hidden by the pew opposite.'

'Not if anyone walks past, I'm not. The waiter will be back at any moment.'

'Don't pretend you're not loving it.' His hand delved roughly between her legs and slipped around in the copious wetness he found there. 'You're not creaming yourself because you're finding it such a turn-off.'

'*Rob*! Stop that!' she hissed frantically.

He withdrew his hand and let her pull the mac closed again, and not a moment too soon as the waiter appeared bearing their plates of food.

Gemma toyed with hers unenthusiastically – she was far too worked up and far too hot to want a huge plate of chicken and chips. She kept gulping down claret in the hope of subduing the impatient clamouring of her overheated honeypot.

Rob ate his steak hungrily, tearing at it with his even white teeth in a way which made her shudder. When he'd finished he refilled both their glasses, then pushed his hand inside her mac and began to idly caress her breasts.

Gemma's cheeks burned and she seriously considered plunging her fork into his thighs. How could he treat her like this? Touching her so intimately in a public place.

She could kill him.

But even while she seethed she could feel her copious juices soaking into her expensive silk mac – she'd probably never get the stain out.

Again, he removed his hand just a few seconds before the waiter slouched over to collect their plates. It dawned on her belatedly that being taller than her, Rob could see over the top of the pew if anyone was approaching.

Something he hadn't bothered to tell her.

She rose abruptly to her feet.

'I'm going to the loo.'

He angled his knees to one side to let her pass.

'Don't be too long,' he muttered, fondling her bum under her mac as she pushed past.

Once in the rather dingy cubicle of the ladies, she sank onto the toilet seat, opened her legs and began to masturbate. She climaxed swiftly and sat there trembling, waiting for the waves of heat to abate.

She felt a little better – at least it had taken the edge off her frustration – but she was still molten inside. If he didn't screw her soon, she felt like she'd explode.

Back in the pub she didn't sit down. Instead she walked past him and outside, leaving him with no option but to pay the bill and follow her.

He caught her up in the humid twilight of the car park.

'Did you bring yourself off in there?' he asked interestedly.

'Yes.'

'You couldn't wait, huh? You wanton little slut.' He felt between her legs, provoking a renewed flood of moisture. She bore down against his hand, opening her legs so he could bury two fingers deep inside her. 'You want it badly, don't you? Tell me how badly you want it.'

When she didn't answer, he intensified the pressure of his fingers. 'Tell me what you want, you over-sexed little trollop.'

'I ... I want you to fuck me.'

'Say it again.'

'I want you to fuck me.'

'Again.'

'*I want you to fuck me!*' she practically screamed at him.

He picked her up and swung her onto the bonnet of the car, throwing open her mac as he did so.

'Not here!' she gasped. 'For goodness sake, anyone coming out will see us – let's climb into that field.'

In reply, he unzipped his jeans and without further pre-liminaries plunged into her.

Gemma was immediately caught up in the hot urgency of their coupling as he thrust energetically into her again and again, sending her into a frenzy of white-hot arousal.

She wound her long, stocking-clad legs around his waist and her arms around his neck, meeting each movement with an equally vigorous one of her own.

She didn't know how long they were going at it, or even whether anyone saw them; all she cared about was the gasping, choking climax she was working towards.

She let out a strangled cry as she came, her whole body going rigid, then being convulsed by a series of spasms. Rob erupted into her at that moment, flooding her stream-ing pussy with his own hot fluid.

Gemma came slowly back to reality, realising that her entire body was drenched with sweat and sex-juices. Even her hair was wet, and it took her a few moments to realise it was actually raining as well.

She unwound herself slowly from his body and slid to

her feet, her legs were trembling so much they could hardly support her.

At that moment a group of people emerged from the pub, laughing and talking noisily. Rob unlocked the car and she scrambled hastily in, dabbing at her streaming hair with a tissue.

Back at her house, Gemma was appalled by the state of her expensive silk mac which was soaked, ripped and covered in bits of sticky tree fibres.

'It's ruined,' she groaned, holding it aloft. Rob took it out of her hand and tossed it to the floor. 'I'll buy you another tomorrow,' he promised, unzipping his jeans.

Sue was in her flat working on headlines for the wholemeal-bread ads when Quentin rang.

'I'd expected to hear from you by now,' he said stiffly, after greeting her coldly.

'Did you?' she asked, her mind still on her work.

'Yes. What happened to you on Tuesday evening, may I ask? You didn't come back.'

'I was lying behind a sofa being terrorised by a crazy gunman. After that I went to the ladies and when I came out you'd gone. You didn't hang about for long, did you?'

There was a pause, then Quentin continued as if she hadn't spoken.

'I've thought about it and I've decided to overlook your behaviour that evening,' he told her pompously. 'You've obviously been subjected to the wrong sort of influences in the past by the men you've chosen to associate with. Your unfortunate background is also probably partially to blame.'

Unfortunate background?

Sue made no secret of the fact that her father was a plumber and her mother a school cook, but she'd never in her life considered her comfortable, working-class background to be unfortunate.

'You're badly in need of firm guidance,' he continued. 'You've already shaken off a good deal of your low origins, but you've still a lot to learn. If you'll give me your word there'll be no repetition of your *vulgar* behaviour in the hotel, we'll put it behind us.'

Sue could hardly believe she was hearing this.

She took a deep breath and said sweetly, 'I'm afraid you'd be wasting your time, Quentin, and I'd hate you to do that. Let's face it – I'm as common as shit and always will be. Goodbye.'

She put the phone down.

Joe had a problem.

Five foot two of petite, voluptuous, eyelash-fluttering female, with a face and figure which regularly reduced otherwise hard-bitten men to gibbering idiots.

Her name was Mandy and she was his eighteen-year-old cousin.

Until a couple of weeks ago, Joe had felt that his life was well on track. At thirty-four he owned a security company which he'd built up from two employees, an alsatian and a walkie-talkie into one of the best in its field. He had an XJS, a wharfside service apartment overlooking the Thames and a series of stunning, sexy girlfriends.

Then along came Mandy.

They were both from the same small Cheshire town which Joe had left at seventeen and now returned to only infrequently. Mandy had been a baby then and he'd been an occasional baby-sitter, simply because his aunt's sofa provided a more comfortable venue for screwing his various girlfriends than the back of his car – and he got paid.

Unfortunately, baby Mandy had an annoying knack of toddling downstairs and coming into the room at the most inconvenient moments, then screaming her head off when he tried to take her back upstairs.

After he moved to London he rarely saw her. His last memory of her before she'd turned up on his doorstep, had been of a nauseatingly precocious thirteen-year-old in a sugar-pink frock with a matching bow in her hair, performing an embarrassing song-and-dance routine at a family gathering.

He'd been in his apartment one evening a fortnight ago, enjoying the later stages of foreplay with a gorgeous air hostess called Lynn, when the intercom buzzer went.

He didn't answer it, but a few minutes later there was a ring at his own front door which indicated that the caller had somehow managed to gain entry to the building and was obviously determined to ruin his evening.

Sighing, Joe disentangled himself from Lynn's slender, tanned limbs, then they adjusted their clothing before he opened the door.

'Joe!' shrieked a small, curvaceous and very young blonde girl, who then promptly flung her arms around his neck.

Normally this wouldn't have fazed him, but with Lynn watching he hastily unwound her arms and held her away from him.

'Who're you?' he asked blankly.

'Joe! Don't you know me? I'm your cousin Mandy.'

She had baby-blonde hair, round baby-blue eyes and a gorgeous baby-face.

But there was nothing babyish about her voluptuous figure, which gave the impression of being about to pop the buttons on her skimpy tee-shirt and tight, faded jeans.

'What are you doing here?' His tone wasn't exactly welcoming. As he spoke, he glanced huntedly over her shoulder into the luxuriously carpeted hallway to see if any other stray members of his family were lurking there.

'I've come to stay with you,' she announced, smiling beguilingly.

Completely taken aback, Joe glanced at Lynn to see how she was reacting to this – not very well judging by the stony expression on her face.

He could hardly blame her, she'd been well on the way to her first climax when the buzzer went.

He was just wondering how to tell Mandy that this was a long way from being even a remote possibility when she slipped past him, leaving her battered suitcase outside the door, and went to join Lynn on the sofa.

'Hello. Are you Joe's girlfriend?' she asked ingenuously, adding, 'Is there anything to eat? I'm starving.'

Reluctantly, Joe lifted her case over the threshold and closed the door.

'I'm sorry, but you can't stay here,' he said firmly.

Her softly pouting lower lip trembled and two large, shimmering tears gathered in the corners of her eyes.

'But where will I go?'

'Try a hotel,' suggested Lynn crossly.

'But I don't have any money.'

'How come my aunt and uncle let you come down to

London without any money?' asked Joe, with an uneasy feeling he wasn't going to like the answer.

'Oh, they don't know I'm here.'

'*What!*'

'I'm eighteen – I can do what I like,' she replied sulkily.

'Where do they think you are?'

'No idea. I just packed by bag and left this afternoon.'

From the moment he'd opened the door, Joe had been hoping to get rid of the caller fast, so he could take up where he'd left off with Lynn.

He now suspected that this wasn't going to be possible.

His dick, which had been gradually losing its rigidity, subsided into flaccid mode as he realised that this was a situation which was going to take some sorting out.

Lynn must have realised it too, because she rose to her feet, saying icily, 'I'll leave you two to your family reunion.' Then she picked up her bag and jacket and left.

'She wasn't very friendly, was she?' commented Mandy. 'Now, how about something to eat?'

'How about you tell me what's going on?'

Mandy pouted again. Her full, rosebud mouth was painted a shiny, sugar-pink. 'There's nothing going on. I decided it was time to leave home and left. That's all.'

'Why didn't you tell your parents?'

'They would have tried to stop me – they treat me like a child. This is a great place you have here.'

She jumped to her feet and began to explore. Her first stop was the kitchen where she opened a couple of cupboard doors and then pounced triumphantly on a packet of crisps, tearing it open with her small white teeth and consuming the contents within half a minute. Joe followed her.

'Just what are you planning to do in London?' he asked.

'Is that all you have to eat?' she said, ignoring his question. She began opening other cupboard doors and then the fridge, but didn't find anything else she considered edible. 'You've got to feed me – I'm starving.'

Sighing with exasperation, Joe rooted in the freezer and brought out a pizza, which he shoved in the oven and then set the timer. He took her by the arm and returned her to the sitting room, pushing her down onto the sofa.

'You must have some idea of what you're planning to do down here. Tell me about it.'

'I'm going to be an actress. Just films though – doing the same boring old play night after night would be deathly.'

'And how do you plan on getting into films?'

'Oh – you know. Going to see people and so on,' she said vaguely.

'I thought you didn't have any money.'

'That's right – I don't.' This didn't appear to cause her any problems.

'So what are you planning to live on?'

'I thought I might stay with you for a bit and get a part-time job or something until I land my first film role. How many bedrooms does this flat have?'

The phone rang at that moment and he picked it up automatically. It was one of his supervisors phoning to say that three of the men due on duty hadn't turned up and he couldn't get through to the control office.

While he was talking, Mandy vanished from the room, taking her case with her.

When he hung up ten minutes later he found that she'd already unpacked by simply emptying her possessions over

49

the bed in the spare room and that she was now locked in the bathroom.

He returned exasperatedly to the sitting room just in time to hear the timer go in the kitchen. When she still hadn't come out twenty minutes later, he went and banged on the door and shouted, 'Your pizza's going cold.'

She emerged inadequately wrapped in a black towel and looked around.

'Where is it?'

'In the bloody oven.'

She went to get it and sat munching hungrily, covering both the carpet and sofa with large fragments of crust and glutinous dollops of anchovy and cheese.

The towel revealed more than it concealed and although she kept pulling it impatiently over some naked bit of flesh, another part of her glorious anatomy invariably popped swiftly into view.

Joe made a half-hearted attempt not to look, but it was breaking the habit of a lifetime. Trying not to imagine oiling her breasts then putting his dick between them and sliding it up and down, he reminded himself she was his cousin and spoke to her firmly.

'Right. Let me make a few things clear. You can't stay here. When you've finished eating, you're going to phone your parents, tell them you're staying overnight with a friend, then you'll get dressed and I'll take you to a hotel. I'll give you the money for the room and your train fare. Tomorrow you're going home and if you've any sense you'll forget any half-baked ideas of being a film actress.'

Mandy continued serenely consuming her pizza.

'What do you do anyway – as a job I mean?' he asked,

when he'd waited in vain for her to reply.

'All sorts of things. I've worked in a shop and an office and a café – but they were all dead boring, so now I'm going to be an actress.'

Joe resisted the temptation to shake her.

'Get dressed,' he said shortly when she'd finished eating. She yawned, showing small, even white teeth and a flicker of pink tongue.

'I'm tired – I think I'll go to bed.'

Before he could say anything, she left the room. He followed her and was just in time to catch a glimpse of a temptingly well-rounded backside before she leapt into bed, leaving the towel on the floor.

'You are not staying here tonight or any other night,' he told her through gritted teeth. She clutched the sheet to the distracting swellings of her full breasts and her eyes filled with tears again.

'I'll be frightened in a hotel all on my own. It might not be safe.' The tears trembled above her lower lashes then overflowed and spilled down her cheeks. 'I thought you'd look after me as we're cousins and everything,' she sobbed.

His hands clenched in impotent fists, Joe heard himself saying, 'Alright – you can stay, but just for one night. Tomorrow you go home.'

Two weeks later she was still there.

He'd tried everything.

The morning after she arrived, he gave her the train fare, dropped her at Euston and went off to work, congratulating himself on being firm with her.

That evening when he arrived home she was curled up outside his door reading a magazine.

51

He had another date with Lynn. It had taken him twenty minutes and the promise of an expensive dinner to persuade her to see him again. He'd assured her that Mandy had gone, but she'd obviously not been thrilled about their aborted evening.

Without bothering to argue, Joe bundled Mandy and her suitcase into the car, parked on a double yellow line outside Euston and waited with her until the next InterCity arrived. He put her on it himself and thought it almost worth it when he returned to his car to find it had been wheel-clamped.

He was late for his date, but by exerting his considerable charm and spending a substantial amount of money, he arrived back at the apartment at midnight with Lynn in tow, looking forward to the night of hot, dirty sex he'd been cheated of yesterday.

Mandy was asleep outside his door again.

She'd got off the train at Watford and come straight back.

Lynn left without a word.

The following day, although it was very inconvenient and he had to cancel three meetings, he put her in the car and set off up the M1, intending to deliver her to her parents and tell them just what she'd been up to.

She gave him the slip at Scratchwood, having insisted she needed to use the ladies, and arrived back at his apartment before he did, after hitching a lift from a travelling salesman.

He telephoned her home and spoke to his aunt. To his horror she seemed disinclined to come and retrieve her erring daughter. In fact, he suspected she was relieved to be passing over the responsibility for her to someone else for a while.

She seemed to think that Mandy would return home soon enough when she found it more difficult than she anticipated to break into films. Joe's protests that he didn't actually want his cousin staying with him, went unheeded.

'I'm sure you'll look after her, Joe love, and make sure she doesn't get into any trouble,' were his aunt's parting, and blood-curdling words.

It wasn't as if Mandy was the ideal house guest.

She was messy and untidy and the previously immaculate flat was soon strewn with her possessions. She never put anything back where she found it and she was constantly borrowing his things without permission.

It was worst in the bathroom.

Whenever she bathed she left every towel soaking wet and in a heap on the floor. Everything was covered in a thick layer of talc and the bath had a permanent ring around it from the bath oil she used. After skidding and falling on the slippery surface getting in, Joe limited himself to showers. His cleaner only came twice a week and had already voiced her dissatisfaction with the situation, although he'd assured her it was only temporary.

Mandy's constant presence in his life was a nightmare from which, certainly for the foreseeable future, there seemed to be no awakening.

Chapter Four

'It would be great if we won this account,' said Sue, enthusiastically poring over a brochure depicting all the luxury hotels in the group. 'There's one in Jamaica, Hawaii, Sydney, Rio ... in fact just about everywhere I've ever wanted to visit. We might get a freebie out of it.'

'Don't get over-excited. Even if we do get the account we'll probably never see anything more than the conference room of the London one,' replied Gemma.

She lowered herself gracefully into a chair then winced. She'd be slightly stiff and sore for days after last night's marathon session with Rob. It was almost a relief he'd gone – now she could give her undivided attention to work.

Unfortunately David had phoned last night while Rob was there and, although Rob was aware that he wasn't the only man in her life, he obviously hadn't liked being reminded of the fact. Afterwards, as if to put his scent on her, he'd screwed her insatiably until she was saturated with the smell and taste of him.

Gemma was trying very hard not to remember sitting in the country pub, virtually naked under her mac, while Rob fondled her furtively. She felt a renewed surge of moisture steadily soaking her white lace panties and crossed her legs uncomfortably.

She had all the self-control of a three-year-old, not being able to put the wild sex they'd enjoyed out of her mind while she was at work.

But it was so hard not to think about his huge cock moving steadily in and out of her slippery, appreciative pussy – particularly when he'd been screwing her over the car bonnet.

A flush of heat rose over Gemma's normally porcelain pale complexion, causing Sue to look at her curiously.

'Are you okay?' she asked.

'Yes, thanks. Just a bit hot,' replied her partner, giving herself a mental shake.

'It *is* warm today. I know what – let's go and have coffee in Covent Garden while we think about this pitch.'

Normally Gemma would have vetoed the suggestion, but she was desperate for anything to distract her from thoughts of sex.

The two women strolled down Floral Street and into the old market place. They took a seat at a table under an umbrella and ordered coffee.

The area was thronging with tourists and locals, all enjoying the hot August sunshine. Sue often came here for lunch – she loved the cosmopolitan atmosphere.

'Didn't you say that your friend Joe handled some of the security for the hotel group?' asked Gemma.

'Uum?' Sue was idly watching a handsome youth strut past them in a plain white tee-shirt and a pair of tight-fitting jeans. Hmm – definitely her type. There was something about sunshine which got the juices flowing and she followed him with her large, dark eyes until he was out of sight. She became belatedly aware that Gemma had asked her something.

'Sorry – what? Oh, yes, Joe. He does handle some of their security though I gather he blotted his copy book somewhat on Monday night.'

Gemma hadn't made any reference to finding them groping each other on the sofa in Sue's office. In retrospect Sue was quite embarrassed. She couldn't imagine her partner behaving with such undignified abandon.

'Will you be seeing him again? Anything he could tell us about the hotel group's structure could be useful. Maybe he even knows who else is pitching – it wouldn't do any harm to ask anyway.'

'He's away for a few days. He said he'd ring me when he gets back. If he does I'll find out anything I can.'

Joe was enjoying himself.

He was in Manchester on business and had a couple of hours to spare before his meeting. He'd forgotten his sunglasses so he strolled down King Street looking for another pair – it was hell driving without them in sunny weather. With his jacket slung casually over his shoulder, his tie loosened and his sleeves rolled up, he ambled along admiring the scantily clad women.

He found a pair of sunglasses he liked and wore them out of the shop. He was just wondering whether to buy a couple of shirts when a sultry-looking dark-haired woman suddenly took his arm. He turned to look at her enquiringly and was pleasantly taken aback when her crimson lips curved into a seductive smile.

He immediately imagined them hot, wet and hungry, sliding up and down his dick.

'I wonder if you would do me a favour?' she asked. Her husky voice had a slight foreign inflexion.

'Sure – if I can sweetheart.'

'Would you mind kissing me passionately – as if we were lovers I mean.'

Joe didn't mind at all.

She pressed her soft, ample bosom against his chest and wound her bare arms around his neck. His dick leapt into immediate rigidity as he was enveloped in a wave of exotic, musky perfume.

Her lips felt soft and pulpy as she opened her mouth beneath his and they kissed lengthily. When at last she pulled away and smiled up at him, her eyes were smoky beneath their heavy lids. He kept his arms around her, his hands smoothing over her ripe, womanly hips.

'Thank you,' she murmured.

'My pleasure – but do you mind telling me what this is about?'

'My husband is watching us – I want to make him jealous.'

Joe's eyes flickered wildly around but he couldn't see anyone looking at them. He fervently hoped it wasn't the bloke built like a brick shithouse, loitering a few yards away. No – he was obviously part of the team of builders currently banging out the interior of one of the expensive shops.

The woman took Joe's arm and began to walk along the pedestrianised street, her hip brushing his with every step.

'Tell me – is he likely to try to inflict physical violence on my person?'

The woman laughed contemptuously. 'No – he's a coward. A fat, loathsome coward.'

'Why do you want to make him jealous?'

'Because I've just found out he's been having an affair with my best friend. Fifteen years married and he's been poking her behind my back. Me – the mother of his children. And I have been completely faithful. Always,' she ended dramatically.

He placed her accent now as Italian.

'I told him this morning that I too have a lover, so he followed me. He thinks I have not spotted him, but I have. He can see that you are young and virile; not a fat old pig like him and he will be very unhappy.'

She was wearing a sleeveless black, grey-and-white-striped dress which clung to her gorgeous curves like a second skin and stopped several inches above the knee. Her shapely legs were encased in sheer stockings.

At least Joe hoped they were stockings – like most men he heartily disliked tights.

She was elegantly shod in black suede high-heeled shoes and carried a small matching bag.

They crossed Deansgate and walked down the side of Kendals.

'Where are we going?' he asked.

'I thought you might be very kind and walk me to my car. If you get in with me, he will think we're on our way to make love somewhere. I'll drop you a couple of streets away as soon as he's out of sight.'

Joe tried to glance over his shoulder to see if he could spot the erring husband, but his companion gave his arm a painful squeeze and hissed, 'Don't look round. I want him to think I've not seen him.'

They walked on for a few minutes. Joe thought he'd add realism to the situation by putting his arm around her waist and letting his hand drop down to caress the firm, voluptuous curves of her upper buttocks.

'Yes,' she said approvingly. 'That is good. Do it some more – let him see how hot for each other we are.'

Joe obligingly fondled the large globes of her rump over her dress.

That was definitely a suspender belt.

He'd like to see the best friend if the straying husband found her more attractive than this sultry beauty.

Although he knew that that really had nothing to do with it. It was probably just the usual 'grass on the other side of the fence' syndrome.

Whatever it was, he wouldn't mind grazing awhile himself.

He decided that once he was in the car with her he'd suggest going to a hotel and giving it a bit of sauce for the gander. He'd be doing her a favour – not quite as big as the one he'd be doing himself – but a favour nevertheless.

They turned into the entrance of a multi-storey car park and stopped by the lift. She immediately wound her arms around his neck and kissed him again. He grasped her backside in both hands and pulled her hard against him so she could feel his straining erection. His fingers slid into the cleft between her buttocks and she rubbed her mound against his thigh in a way which made him groan.

The lift arrived and they stepped into it. It had a heady aroma of urine and mould, but he hardly noticed it and once behind the privacy of the graffiti-scrawled doors, they clung together, their hands straying urgently over each other's bodies.

Joe slipped his hand up her short skirt and caressed the soft, bare flesh above her stocking top. Her legs parted invitingly and he probed the damp crotch of her panties with exploring fingers.

When the metal doors rattled noisily open to reveal a couple of teenagers waiting to descend, they sprung guiltily apart.

The sun was beating down on the top level of the carpark, making the tarmac shimmer in the heat. There were only a few cars parked there and no one in sight. She led him over to a scarlet Mercedes and unlocked the door.

He caught an intoxicating glimpse of olive-hued cleavage as she bent forward, then he pulled her into his arms again, covering one heavy orb with his hand. She began to pant as he fondled it gently. He undid the three buttons on her dress to reveal a steel-grey satin bra, struggling to contain two luscious, satin-skinned breasts.

He undid the front fastening and they spilled juicily out like firm, ripe melons. Joe gave one his full attention with his hand and the other with his mouth. He squeezed, kneaded, sucked and nuzzled until his dick felt like it was going to burst his zip.

The sudden sound of an engine made them jump apart again and she slid hastily into the Mercedes as a car nosed up the ramp and parked opposite them.

Joe got in beside her, breaking out in a sweat as the ferocious heat inside the sun-baked car hit him. She touched a button and the sun-roof opened silently above them.

They sat side by side looking straight ahead as the driver

of the car opposite fiddled about with his keys, transferring something from the back seat to the boot. Out of sight below the dashboard they were greedily exploring each other's private parts.

Joe groaned with relief to feel his zip go down and his swollen dick being released from his briefs. It sprang eagerly out and she caressed it, rolling the tip between her finger and thumb, before tightening her hand around it and beginning an up-and-down motion which threatened to have him erupting almost immediately.

He had his own hand up her skirt, buried in her crotch. He worked his way feverishly under the tight elastic of her panties at the top of her legs and found a satisfying amount of hot stickiness awaiting him.

She arched her back and spread her legs as he pushed two fingers deep inside her. Glancing down, he saw the olive flesh of her thighs above her stocking tops and two lace-trimmed suspenders emerging from her flimsy grey panties.

The man opposite them finally left his car and vanished down the flight of stone steps. Immediately, Joe's companion lifted her backside from the leather seat and dragged her panties down her legs.

Joe tried to help her, but it was difficult in the confined space. They caught on the heels of her shoes, but eventually he managed to free one foot and impatiently left the tiny scrap of silk wrapped around her other ankle.

She turned sideways, half reclining against the driver's door, her head just below the level of the window. She dragged her skirt up above her waist, revealing a thick, luxuriant dark bush, then grabbed his head and pushed it down between her thighs.

Somehow, she managed to get her left leg up along the back of his seat and her right over the gear stick and into the passenger seat foot space.

With his face buried in her hot, musky pussy, Joe went at it with a will, trying to ignore the fact that he could hardly breathe. It was stifling in the car, even with the sun-roof open and his companion felt like she was approaching boiling point.

He plunged his tongue deep into her simmering honey-pot, exploring her overlapping folds of heated flesh, then flicking over the throbbing nub of her clit.

He could feel sweat trickling down his back and his trousers were sticking to his legs from the heat striking up from the leather seats.

He was grasping her thighs above her stocking tops with his hands and he could feel how wet they were, but whether from perspiration or from her own female lubrications, he wasn't sure.

Rearing up from his groin like a periscope, his dick was telegraphing an urgent message that it was keen to join the fray. Joe tried to raise his head, only to have it shoved back against her pussy so forcefully that his entire face was drenched in her juices.

He redoubled his efforts against her clit, trying to give her the satisfaction she sought as quickly as possible before he suffocated. He was rewarded when a few moments later she emitted a piercing scream which seemed to go on for ever, echoing ear-splittingly around the interior of the car.

As soon as she relaxed her grip, he sat up, gulped down some much needed air and glanced hurriedly around to make sure no one was within earshot. Happily the car park was still deserted.

More than ready to plunge his aching cock into her honeypot, he tried to manoeuvre himself on top of her, but found it impossible in the confined space – there was nowhere to put his legs unless he opened the door and let them hang out.

His companion wasn't helping.

Having achieved her own satisfaction she seemed to have slipped into a coma.

They weren't going to get very far if she didn't actively co-operate.

The simplest method of screwing her would be if she sat astride and facing him. The arousing thought of her rising and falling on his cock, made him break out in a renewed flood of sweat. Of course, there was always a possibility that her head might stick up through the sun-roof, but at least that way she'd be able to see if anyone was coming.

He shook her gently.

'There's more where that came from, sweetheart – climb aboard,' he said, indicating his rampant member. He removed her left leg from the back of his seat and pulled her into a sitting position saying encouragingly. 'Just swing your right knee over me.'

She remained unresponsive, staring rather coldly at his eager cock.

'You cannot put that inside me,' she announced. 'I have never been unfaithful to my husband.'

Presumably being brought to a climax by the tongue of a total stranger didn't count.

'You've got to be joking!' he exclaimed. 'It's a bit late to be saying that, now you've had *your* fun. What am I sup-posed to do with this?'

As if to bear out the urgency of the situation, a large drop of seminal fluid gathered on the end of his cock, then rolled slowly down the shaft.

'You could at least return the favour,' he told her.

'I don't do that. It is for whores.'

Joe was beginning to see why her husband might have strayed.

'A hand-job then,' he suggested hopefully. It might not be what he'd had in mind, but it was better than nothing.

She considered for a moment. He suspected she was weighing up the chances of getting rid of him without *some* sort of consolation prize.

Eventually she nodded.

'Very well.' The weary sigh with which she accompanied her words caused his dick to droop perceptibly, but it perked up again when, after delving into her bag for a handful of tissues, she grasped it firmly.

After glancing at her face and seeing the distaste there, Joe thought it better to focus on her melon-like breasts, still hanging lusciously out of her unfastened clothing.

Particularly when they began to jiggle erotically, in response to the swift movement of her hand.

He was tempted to try and hold back and make her continue the stimulation for the maximum amount of time, but he suspected she'd call a halt if he didn't come soon.

With a strangled groan, he ejaculated forcefully into the air. She made an unsuccessful attempt to catch it in the tissues but instead it spattered copiously onto the windscreen. She wiped her hand, grimacing all the while, then tried to mop the glass but only succeeded in smearing the thick liquid several inches in each direction.

Joe tucked his cock back in his trousers and made no attempt to help her.

'It was nice meeting you,' he said, reaching for his jacket and opening the car door.

'Wait! You can't go now – my husband must see us drive off together.'

'Sorry – I'm late for a meeting.'

'I'll take you wherever you want to go – but please stay in the car.'

He was very tempted to ignore her plea and get out anyway, but he was due at a meeting in ten minutes and he would get there much quicker if she drove him.

'St Peter's Square then.'

She dropped him outside the office block where his meeting was being held. He wondered if she'd remember that she still had her panties draped around one ankle before she got out of the car.

He went inside and looked hastily about for the gents. His face and hands were still covered in her female juices, so he was in desperate need of a wash. Unfortunately there certainly wasn't one in the foyer. He was just wondering whether there would be one on the first floor, when to his horror he saw one of the men he was meeting enter the building.

'Joe!' the man greeted him amiably, holding out his hand.

'Hi William,' said Joe, shaking it automatically. He immediately wished he hadn't when he saw the man's expression upon feeling how sticky it was.

'Hot day,' he offered, trying to retrieve the situation. 'I was just looking for the gents as a matter of fact.'

'There's one outside the conference room,' William told

him, his expression becoming incredulous as he took in Joe's disreputable appearance.

The lift arrived and they stepped in together and began to ascend. Unfortunately it was about the size of an upright coffin and in the enclosed space the strong smell of female secretions and male sweat was almost overpowering, a fact which William obviously registered.

Joe bolted into the gents and washed his hands and face, but the mirror told him that his appearance was still a long way from that acceptable at a business meeting, particularly one where he was trying to get his company work.

He combed his hair, which was standing up all over his head, and straightened his clothing, but his shirt was sweat-soaked and wrinkled and his trousers were spattered with whatever semen hadn't reached the windscreen. He did his best with damp paper towels, but he still looked – and smelt – like a tramp.

When he entered the conference room, conversation was immediately suspended and he knew that William had been talking about him.

It would have been the understatement of the year to say that the meeting didn't go well. Despite his wash and the fact that several windows had been opened, a strong smell of sex still hung over the room like an invisible but malodorous cloud.

Needless to say, he didn't get the work.

Chapter Five

By the time Joe got back to London he wasn't in a very good mood.

The drive back had been a nightmare of contra-flow systems, long tailbacks of stationary traffic and homicidal maniacs in lorries trying to kill him. It had also been very hot.

He unlocked the door to his apartment, looking forward to a long, cool shower and several cans of beer; he'd only been away three days, but it felt much longer.

His eardrums were immediately assaulted by the sound of deafening heavy-metal music and he belatedly remembered his uninvited house-guest.

But why the hell was the music coming from his bedroom?

The sitting room was deserted. It also looked like a bomb had hit it. It was strewn with discarded clothing, dirty plates and what looked like the entire contents of his CD collection, all out of their cases.

He threw open the door to his bedroom and was greeted by the sight of Mandy lying in his bed with an unknown and vacant-looking youth. They were watching a music video on his VCR and eating a take-away Chinese meal, most of which seemed to be on the quilt cover.

He stopped the video and roared, 'What the hell do you think you're doing? And who the fuck is that?'

'Hello – have you had a good time?' was Mandy's unruffled response.

He grabbed the foil tray she was eating from and threw it in the bin. Then he took her arm and would have dragged her from the bed if he hadn't realised she was naked. He turned to the youth who was cowering back against the pillows.

'Get out of my bed!'

The youth yelped and leapt out from beneath the quilt. He grabbed an armful of clothing and retreated behind the open closet door where he began to dress feverishly. He was skinny with big feet, a scrawny neck and a spotty backside.

'How dare you entertain strange men in my bed? Who is he?'

'He's the delivery boy from the local Chinese restaurant,' Mandy told him calmly, picking up a beansprout and nibbling it. Even in his rage Joe wondered fleetingly why the boy wasn't Chinese. 'Don't be so cross – we were just watching the video. My room doesn't have one,' she added accusingly.

'It isn't your room!' he exploded. 'It isn't your room, or your flat, or your CDs which are lying all over the floor out there. Get out of that bed you little slut and pack your bags. You're leaving!'

The youth, who had finished dressing, edged nervously past Joe and bolted. Mandy meanwhile, leant back against the pillows and looked at him reproachfully.

One naked breast peeped distractingly at him from the

folds of the quilt. He tried not to look at it, but couldn't help but notice how white and firm it looked with a tiny pink puckered nipple surrounded by a large, paler pink aureola.

'There's no need to take it out on me just because you've come home in a bad mood. And there's no need to yell at me either,' she said, pouting.

'Yell at you! You're lucky I don't shake you till your teeth rattle – you've turned my apartment into a pigsty. It doesn't even look as if Deidre has cleaned it – didn't she come today?'

'Yes she did as a matter of fact, but she won't be coming again.'

'What! Why the fuck not?'

Deidre was the building's cleaner-cum-caretaker who could also be prevailed upon to take Joe's shirts to the laundry, his suits to the dry cleaners and stock up his fridge and freezer. Her charges for performing these services were fairly extortionate, but she kept his domestic life on an even keel so he was prepared to pay through the nose.

'She was rude and unpleasant so I told her not to come again. You smell sweaty by the way – why don't you take a shower?'

Joe's already thunderous face became practically black with rage. He advanced on his cousin threateningly and she slipped a little further beneath the covers, taking the naked breast with her.

'Are you getting out of that bed, getting dressed and leaving, or am I going to throw you out?'

Mandy's lower lip began to tremble ominously. 'You're a beast sometimes, Joe.'

As she still showed no signs of getting out of bed, he

grabbed her and picked her up quilt and all, then carried her to the front door, deposited her outside and slammed it hard. Then he threw her clothes in her suitcase, closed it, hurled it out through the front door and spent the next hour trying to restore order to his flat.

His temper wasn't improved by finding bills for several deliver-to-the-door meals from the various take-aways in the area he had accounts with. She'd obviously charged them all to him.

When he'd cleaned up, changed the bed and had a long cool shower followed by several beers out on the terrace, he felt slightly better – but only slightly. At around eleven his phone rang.

It was Mandy.

'I was just ringing to tell you that I've found somewhere else to stay – so you needn't worry about me any more.' Her voice was slurred.

'I wasn't worried,' he snapped.

It obviously wasn't the response Mandy had been hoping for.

'Don't you want to know where I am?' she demanded petulantly.

'Not particularly.'

'I'll tell you anyway. I'm staying with the man in the penthouse – he says I can stay as long as I like – and his flat's much better than yours.' She hung up on him.

Joe groaned as he put the phone down.

The penthouse was owned by a man he knew only by sight and reputation. He was a South American in the import-export business and Joe had his own reasons for believing him to have connections with drug trafficking. The man was undoubtedly not someone he wanted his young cousin hooking up with.

He hesitated, picked up the phone, put it down again, then began to pace the room.

Damn the troublesome little bitch to hell.

After struggling with his conscience, Joe left the flat – the quilt was still outside his door – took the lift up to the penthouse and rang the bell. After a long pause the South American opened the door on the chain.

'Yes?'

Through the crack Joe could see Mandy, naked to the waist, sitting on the sofa with her head thrown back and her eyes closed.

'That's my sister and she's only fifteen,' he greeted the man with no preamble. 'That means she's under-age and she's coming home with me now.'

The South American's eyes narrowed. 'She told me that you'd thrown her out and she had nowhere to go.'

'We quarrelled – that's all,' replied Joe shortly. 'Either she comes back with me now or I phone the police.'

Their eyes locked but the other man obviously wanted no trouble because he shrugged and took the chain off the door.

'You should take better care of your family.'

Joe stepped past him and pulled Mandy to her feet. She opened her eyes and looked at him hazily – she'd obviously been drinking. At least he hoped it was drink.

'Come on,' he growled. 'And cover yourself up.' Again, he found his eyes drawn to her naked breasts as she fumbled with the buttons on her blouse. As soon as she was decent he asked the South American, 'Where are her things?'

The man nodded at her case, standing by the wall. Joe picked it up and left, dragging Mandy behind him. In the lift she sagged against him. He shook her roughly until her eyes fluttered open again.

'Did he give you any drugs?' he demanded.

'Jus' vodka. Vodka and orange.' He wanted to believe her.

Once back in his apartment he threw her case into the spare room.

'Go to bed,' he ordered her tersely.

Instead, she stood in front of him, swaying gently, and began to unbutton her blouse.

'I know why you're so cross with me,' she slurred. 'It's because you found me in bed with someone else and you want me yourself. Well, that's okay – you can have me.'

She pulled open her blouse and her tiny pink nipples nodded perkily at him as she let it fall to the floor. Joe closed his eyes tightly then opened them again.

'You're drunk,' he told her. 'Go to bed.'

She opened her round, baby-blue eyes wide and smiled at him, then the tip of her pink tongue appeared and she licked her pink lipsticked lips.

'You know you want me,' she said drunkenly. 'I've seen you looking at me.'

Joe's dick was already taking a keen interest in the proceedings and was urging him not to look a gift horse in the mouth. He closed his eyes again and with a huge effort of will conjured up the picture of her as a precocious thirteen year old doing her nauseating song-and-dance routine.

When he opened them again she was holding her own breasts and caressing them, smiling at him inebriatedly.

Joe was a man of flexible integrity and in his time had taken cheerful and unashamed advantage of more than one woman who was the worse for drink and under most circumstances he wouldn't have needed asking twice.

But Mandy was his eighteen-year-old cousin whom he remembered as a baby and the idea seemed as incestuous as if she were his sister.

He hesitated, images of screwing her vigorously and satisfyingly flitting tantalisingly across his mind. He was keeping her after all and she'd caused him endless trouble – didn't he deserve something in return?

It wouldn't be as if he'd seduced her – she was the one who'd issued the invitation.

He took a step towards her just as her eyes closed and she slumped slowly onto the floor. Cursing furiously, he dragged her into her room and threw her on the bed. He stood over her, thinking that her luscious breasts would fill the palms of his hands nicely. He stretched one out towards her, the other hand on the buckle of his belt, then stopped.

What the hell was the matter with him? How could be even consider fucking her – drunk or not?

He was worse than a dog on heat.

One thing was for certain – she had to go before he did something he'd regret.

Sue and Gemma had been summoned to meet the head of the fitted-kitchens company. The meeting took place at seven-thirty a.m. in the boardroom of the company's head office in Slough. Not a time either of them would have chosen, but the big boss apparently liked to make an early start.

Phil Jenkins was a short, balding man with a strong Geordie accent and a lamentable taste in suits. He also had several annoying mannerisms, which included prodding whoever he was talking to when emphasising a point. Sue ran him through her ideas for the campaign while he puffed on a cigar, dropping ash down his tie and on her visuals.

He interrupted her half way through to say abruptly, 'How much is this going to cost me?'

'I haven't finish—' began Sue, Gemma interjected smoothly.

'Your accountant has the figures – we can go over them when my colleague has finished her presentation.'

He held out his hand to the accountant, who extracted a sheet of paper from the stack in front of him and handed it over. Phil Jenkins whistled when he saw the total.

'Just what is it I'm getting for this?' he demanded. Gemma began to tell him but he interrupted again. 'You're a pricey pair of lasses, aren't you? I'll bet I could get it done for a quarter of this amount if I shop around.'

'Undoubtedly,' Gemma assured him coolly. 'Whether the results would be what you wanted is another matter altogether.' He glared at her but she remained unruffled.

'For this money I'll expect guaranteed increased sales.'

'No reputable advertising agency would guarantee you any such thing. What I can promise is that our campaign will raise your profile and move you upmarket. Now, may my partner continue?'

Sue finished her presentation with no further interruptions. There was silence when she'd stopped speaking. Phil Jenkins ground out his cigar in an onyx ashtray and assaulted one of the visuals with a stubby forefinger.

'Well, I suppose you know what you're doing,' he said grudgingly. 'There's just one thing that I think's missing.'

'What's that?' enquired Sue politely.

'Me. I've thought about it and I've decided that what it needs is for me to be in all the ads – particularly the TV one.'

Gemma kept her face carefully blank of the dismay she felt. What was it with clients that they often wanted to front their own products? She could only think of one campaign like that which had worked. And, as this brief had been to move well upmarket, if Phil Jenkins appeared in the ads it would be completely counter-productive.

She was just formulating a diplomatic reply when Sue burst out, 'That's the most ridiculous suggestion I've every heard! I was briefed to come up with a slick, stylish campaign which would take you upmarket – not down. If you're in the ads the whole concept will be completely ruined!'

She stood up as she spoke, her hands on the boardroom table in front of her, her cheeks pink with indignation. Before she could get into full spate, Gemma kicked her hard on the ankle.

'What my colleague means—' she began. She was interrupted by Phil Jenkins.

'What she means is that she doesn't want my ugly mug spoiling her pretty pictures. Well I don't care what either of you want – *I'm going to be in my own ads*!' He emphasised his words by stabbing Gemma on the upper arm with his blunt forefinger.

'Then you'll have to use another agency,' blazed Sue furiously.

Gemma resisted the temptation to bury her head in her

hands. Instead she spoke calmly.

'What we need to do now is go away and have a rethink. I'm sure there must be a way to involve you if we use a slightly different approach. Don't you think so, Sue?'

Sue glared at her. Without giving her partner a chance to reply Gemma continued, 'We'll work on it and get back to you.'

She held out her hand and he shook it automatically. 'So nice to have met you. Ready, Sue?'

Joe had a disturbed night, tossing and turning in the humid August air. It wasn't until dawn that he fell deeply asleep, sprawled on his back with only his legs below the covers.

The nature of his dreams changed and became sexual.

He was in a circus ring and a gorgeous woman standing on the back of a cantering pony was riding round and round him.

She was naked except for a pair of thigh-high soft black leather boots and she carried a whip which she kept cracking over his head. Her legs were apart and he could see the deep pink tip of her clit protruding provocatively from a soft moss of downy pubic hair.

He was naked too and was gripping his dick in his right hand. As the woman cantered dizzyingly around him he masturbated fiercely, his arousal mounting as she rode faster and faster.

Then he was flat on his back in the sawdust-strewn ring and she was climbing astride him, sinking gracefully onto his cock and enveloping it in the warm folds of her sex.

His eyes flew open to find that a woman had indeed just mounted him – but not a mysterious bareback circus rider.

Instead he was greeted by the confusing sight of Mandy bobbing up and down on his cock as if she were on a merry-go-round.

'What . . . aah . . .' he grunted, his sleep-misted eyes riveted on her voluptuous breasts.

His hands automatically found her small waist and adjusted her position as she smiled at him, her baby-round face flushed with triumph.

'See. I knew you wanted me,' she gloated, tightening her internal muscles so that he groaned.

Somewhere at the back of his mind Joe knew that this was a terrible mistake and one which he would undoubtedly pay for later, but the thought only half-flitted across his brain, blotted out by an atavistic urge to gain his own satisfaction as soon as possible.

He was as incapable of stopping the proceedings as he was of stopping the Thames flowing past the apartment block a long way below.

His hands closed on her breasts and he fondled them roughly, rubbing her small nipples with his thumbs until they stood out like tiny ripe berries.

Years of dance lessons had made her extremely supple. He could feel the hot urgency of his approaching climax when frustratingly she stopped moving up and down. Instead, she bent her body back in an arc, letting all but the head of his cock slip out of her, pulling it away from his body at an angle he felt was never intended.

He grabbed her by the waist intending to jam her back down hard, but his cock plopped out of her slippery pussy. He tried to get her to sit on it again, but she eluded him, sitting instead on his stomach and wriggling her clit against his belly.

She pouted down at him with her rosebud mouth as he wondered what the hell was going on.

'I don't think I'm going to let you finish,' she said in a little girl voice. 'After all – you haven't been very nice to me, have you?'

Joe felt this was really no time to start a conversation. Still half asleep and in an advanced state of arousal, he didn't bother to reply. Grunting, he rolled her onto her back, shoved his knee between her thighs and thrust into her again. She wound her legs around his waist and moved under him, making little mewing noises of pleasure deep in her throat.

He came in a deeply satisfying, long-drawn-out surge of release and collapsed onto her, already wishing he'd had the strength of mind to resist.

About to drift off to sleep again he heard her say. 'Now you'll have to let me stay.' Then she wriggled out from beneath him and left the room with a dismissive twitch of her well-rounded backside.

Chapter Six

'Scotland?' echoed Sue. 'A company with luxury hotels in exotic locations throughout the world – and they want me to visit the one in Scotland!'

'It's still a free trip,' pointed out Gemma. 'Quite frankly, I wish I could spare the time – but, as you'll be the one writing the brochure, it's more important that you go.'

'But Scotland,' moaned Sue. 'It's all lochs and heather – I'll be like a fish out of water. Why couldn't it have been Rio? I've got eleven bikinis, but absolutely no kilts, tweeds, or anything even remotely suitable for the country.'

Today she was wearing a short wrap-over cream skirt which was reasonably decorous when she was standing, but positively indecent when she was walking or sitting. It was teamed with a scarlet off-the-shoulder top which kept threatening to slip right down her arms, leaving her naked from the waist up. As far as Gemma could see, her partner wasn't wearing a bra.

The two women had had a heated argument on the way back from Slough after their meeting with the fitted-kitchens king, Phil Jenkins. At least it had been heated on Sue's part – Gemma had maintained her composure with some difficulty.

When they'd both worked at Detroit's, it had been general policy to keep Sue away from the clients as she couldn't be relied upon to handle them with the degree of tact necessary in their precarious business.

When they'd set up the agency together, Gemma had impressed upon her the need to remain diplomatic whatever the provocation – obviously to no avail. She never let her partner see clients alone and was now seriously considering preventing her having any future contact with them at all.

Unfortunately, no one did a better presentation than Sue – she could make a hard sell look a soft sell and her flair and enthusiasm usually carried everyone along with her in a way Gemma knew she could never hope to emulate.

At first, Sue had been adamant that there was no way Phil Jenkins could appear in his own ads without rendering the campaign meaningless. Gemma had thought she was going to have to bring in a freelance creative director to take over the account, but Sue had suddenly come up with the goods.

With some deft rearrangement she'd given the ads a tongue-in-cheek humorous slant, while still emphasising the quality of the product. Phil Jenkins had been pleased and the account was secure – at least for now.

But Gemma had decided that Sue, having created the concept for the campaign, had better have no further involvement with the actual production. She could tell that Phil Jenkins would want to keep poking a stubby finger in every pie and would probably demand changes to each individual ad. Sue would only fly off the handle again. Paul, the art director, could deal with it while Sue concentrated on the brochure and print ads for the Scottish hotel.

The invitation for her to stay there for a few days to immerse herself in the atmosphere was very well timed. Gemma could have gone herself, but she chose not to – she'd stay in London keeping a tight rein on things.

'How will you get there?' she asked. 'Are you going to hire a car?' Sue had a licence but didn't own a vehicle. She preferred to take cabs around London and trains elsewhere.

'Not likely,' was Sue's reply. 'Driving's so boring. No – I'll take the InterCity to Edinburgh, then have someone meet me.'

She decided that travelling overnight on the sleeper would be the most time-effective method of travel as she had so much work to do. She could read up about the area where the hotel was situated over dinner, then go to sleep and wake up at her destination without wasting any time.

The train was half empty, but even so an overweight middle-aged man joined her at her table in the dining car. He didn't ask if it was okay to squeeze his huge bulk opposite her, just assumed that as a woman alone she'd welcome his company.

Although she was obviously working he insisted on talking non-stop and spoilt what would otherwise have been a pleasant meal. Sue downed more wine than she would have usually, trying to blot out the sound of his voice as he told her all about his problems with his wife.

It soon became obvious that he was hoping to enjoy a little extra-marital fling, which made Sue giggle. How the hell did he think they'd both fit in one of the narrow bunks?

She said a pointed good night and went back to her compartment. As she was about to let herself in, she saw

83

that he'd followed her. She didn't want to have him rattling at her door all night, so she hastily passed on and continued into the next carriage.

Damn. How was she going to lose him so she could return to her compartment without him seeing her? Luck must have been with her because a door opened and a young man stepped into the corridor. He only looked to be about twenty, tall and athletic with red hair, fair skin and blue eyes.

Without a moment's hesitation she launched herself into his arms saying, 'Alistair – I've been looking all over the train for you!' She raised her face to his, wound her arms around his neck and kissed him.

The kiss was very enjoyable and went on much longer than she'd intended. So long, in fact, that she almost forgot why she was kissing him in the first place. They only stopped when a guard needed to pass them in the corridor, then he drew her half into his compartment, keeping his arms around her.

'I feel it's only fair to tell you that I'm not in fact Alistair,' he said in an appealing Scottish accent.

'I know,' she admitted sunnily. 'Sorry about that – there was some ghastly man following me and I wanted him to think I was with someone – but I think he's gone now.'

She poked her head out of the door and checked the corridor, but there was no sign of him.

'Don't apologise – it was my pleasure,' he told her, not relinquishing his hold on her. 'Since you're here – why not stay for a drink?'

Sue hesitated. She really should be getting an early night. But one drink couldn't do any harm – could it? Sensing her indecision he produced a quarter bottle of whisky and a tooth mug.

'I'm afraid we'll have to share,' he said, sloshing a generous measure into the glass.

His bunk was already made up so they climbed aloft and sat side by side with their legs swinging. Sue was wearing a tight, bright blue dress with scooped neckline. It was also very short, so short in fact that she could barely get it to cover her stocking tops and kept having to tug it down.

'Alistair' turned out to be called Rory, a student on his way home after visiting relatives down south for a couple of weeks.

He didn't waste any time. After telling her that, he pulled her into his arms and kissed her again. Sue felt her stomach muscles contract with lust as he slid his tongue expertly into her mouth.

She really shouldn't be doing this. Her resolution to stop her life of insouciant promiscuity still held firm. Admittedly she'd lapsed when she'd enjoyed the fast and furious couplings behind the sofa with Joe – but that had been under exceptional circumstances.

It was a pity that Quentin hadn't been the man she'd hoped for – someone who could keep her on the straight and narrow path of sexual fidelity. But that was no reason to return to her old ways. She was absolutely *not* going to let this attractive boy screw her.

He seemed very experienced for his age. She noticed with surprise that he already had his hand inside her dress and was caressing her breast over the flimsy lace of her bra. How had he managed that?

Another warm hand was stroking the smooth skin above

her stocking tops, particularly her inner thigh which Sue had always found to be a major erogenous zone. Delicious tremors of pleasure were washing over her body, making her feel hot and breathless.

She'd better call a halt before they passed the point of no return.

She tried to sit up – they were now both lying sideways on the bunk, their legs still dangling over the edge – but in attempting to do so she somehow found herself lying beneath him, the weight of his hard body pressing arousingly against her. He smelt engagingly of talcum powder and healthy male flesh. It was a long time since she'd had a man so young – was her memory playing tricks or did they really have twice the stamina of older men?

It was definitely time to call a halt before she got carried away.

She pressed her hands against his chest and tried to roll from underneath him. He took the opportunity to slide his hand inside her panties and located her clit with practised ease.

Sue gasped and her legs parted in a movement which was quite involuntary. As two fingers found their way inside her warm, pulsating private parts she sighed and relaxed on the narrow bunk.

She couldn't have stopped him now if she'd wanted to – and she didn't. The sensations he was evoking were just too delicious.

He stopped circling her clit with his forefinger and knelt above her. He slipped his hands up her skirt and began to pull her beige lacy briefs down. She raised her hips to help him, then sat up and dragged her blue dress over her head, tossing it carelessly onto the floor. Her bra followed. She left the flimsy suspender belt and stockings where they were – men usually preferred that to nakedness.

While she was undressing he wrenched off his T-shirt and then his jeans – not easy in the confined space of the narrow bunk. He had a smooth boyish chest, lightly tanned to a pinkish brown. His huge hard-on looked as if it had been carved from rock and reared up impressively from between his thighs.

'You're beautiful,' he breathed, taking in her cream and gold beauty.

'So are you,' she replied truthfully, grasping his cock in her hand and squeezing it experimentally. If possible it became even harder. She half expected him to ram it straight into her – her memories of younger men were that they might have the stamina but often lacked finesse.

Not this one.

He stroked and caressed her, lingering on her breasts, teasing her nipples with his tongue, while keeping up an insidious manipulation of her clitoris.

She slid her hand under his balls, savouring the weight of them, then returned to his cock. She was more than ready for him. She guided his throbbing rod to the entrance of her honeypot and gasped as he slid it smoothly in.

Screwing on the narrow top bunk of a train compartment wasn't the easiest thing in the world; Sue was convinced that at any moment they might roll off and land in a heap of tangled, and possibly broken limbs on the floor.

They started slowly, both trying to keep themselves under control, but within minutes they were humping frantically, the rhythm of the train adding urgency to their movements.

It was short and sweet. The bunk began to beat a loud tattoo against the wall as it rocked vigorously under them.

It sounded deafening in the confined space.

Whoever was in the next compartment obviously found it deafening too, because there was an angry banging on the wall, barely audible beneath the noise they were making.

Rory came with a loud, strangled cry and slumped to one side of her. Sue had come herself only moments before. They both burst out laughing, then tried to stifle it as the banging on the wall redoubled.

'We might as well be doing it in the corridor for all the privacy there is in here,' commented Sue, as they attempted to rearrange their limbs so they could lie facing each other on their sides. It was impossible. Her breasts were squashed against his chest and her backside was hanging precariously off the edge of the bunk.

'One thrust and I'll be thrown off,' she whispered. He was still inside her and she could already feel a definite hardening of his cock. He made an experimental movement with his hips, holding onto her waist as he did so. She slid half off, then he pulled her back on.

'I don't think whoever's next door is going to get much sleep tonight,' he said, slipping his fingers into the cleft between her buttocks and exploring the taut bud of her anus, 'I'm just about ready again.'

'We'll have to do it on the floor or something,' she muttered, 'or they'll come a knocking at the door and put us off.'

'Do we have to?' he asked, already sliding in and out of her well-lubricated pussy.

'Yes,' she said firmly. They separated reluctantly and

climbed down. There wasn't enough room for them to do it actually lying on the floor – Rory's legs were too long – so they tried various other positions. But it was hard with the carriage swaying beneath them, making it difficult to keep their balance as they tried it standing up and leaning against the door.

'This is hopeless,' breathed Sue, as his dick was wrenched from her by a particularly wayward movement of the rocking train.

In the end she got on all fours on a pillow and he took her from behind in a carnally satisfying coupling which left her breathless and perspiring, her hair tumbling in her eyes and her breasts swinging heavily.

They tried to do it quietly, but without much success if the hammering on the wall was anything to go by.

Sue was struck by an idea. 'Let's try my compartment – I don't think there's anyone on either side of me,' she suggested, wishing she'd thought of it before.

They pulled their clothes on and lurched hand in hand along the corridor. Sue's bunk seemed to be better anchored to the wall and their next session was carried on without interruption.

For Sue it was a night to remember.

After the first couple of times, Rory seemed to be able to go on for ever and she lost count of the number of climaxes she sustained.

'Where did you get so good at this?' she asked drowsily as they lay pressed closely together taking a breather. 'Most men of your age have barely learnt to locate the clitoris – and there are many who never do. Did you start early?'

It was just getting light outside and a faint headache was

reproaching her for having mixed wine with whisky.

'I suppose I did start fairly young,' he admitted. 'Shall I tell you about it? It was the sort of introduction to sex all teenage boys should have.'

'Mmm, yes do,' she murmured, taking his hand and laying it on her breast.

'I was fourteen and had been noticing women for a while, but hadn't a clue what to do about it. We lived in a small village where there wasn't much going on and there were very few lasses of my age. At weekends I used to help in the garden of a big house where a man who worked for one of the major oil companies in Aberdeen lived with his wife.

'He was away a lot and I knew she was bored and lonely. She used to come wandering out into the garden with a drink in her hand and talk to me sometimes.

'I always fancied her, but at that age you fancy practically any woman between fourteen and fifty if they have the right number of limbs. It never occurred to me she might be interested in the callow wee laddie I was then. One day she asked me to go inside, saying she wanted something moved in the bedroom. I followed her upstairs, watching the swaying of her lovely bum and felt myself getting an erection just at that – the slightest thing could set me off – still can.'

'So I see,' said Sue, feeling his member hardening against her thigh. 'Go on.'

'She was wearing a kind of kimono thing – you know, like a dressing gown – and when we got upstairs I saw that it had come loose at the front and I could see some black lace and a lot of cleavage. It was heady stuff for a boy –

my face must have turned red because she asked me if I was too hot. I don't remember what I said, but she told me she was very hot herself and slipped out of the kimono.

'Underneath she was wearing a black satin teddy. I didn't know then it was called a teddy – it was just some intoxicating bit of female underwear, but I was so excited that I nearly came in my trousers. She lay down on the bed and asked if I found her attractive. I stuttered something along the lines that I did and she told me her husband had another woman in Aberdeen and never made love to her.

'I managed to blurt out that he must be mad and she just lay there looking at me and trailing her hand along her thigh. She was wearing black stockings – I've had a thing about them ever since – and I started to think I was going to explode. My cock felt like a live grenade ready to go off.

'I saw her looking at my hard-on, then she said, "Would you like me to show you what to do with that?" I must have been purple in the face by then and I just nodded. She beckoned me over to the bed and unzipped my jeans. As soon as she touched it I came all over her hand.

'I thought she'd be disgusted and throw me out there and then, but she didn't. She said something about me having a lot to learn and pulled me down next to her. She was a hard task mistress – she'd never let me inside her until I'd brought her off at least once. We used to do it for hours at a time, until my cock was raw and I could hardly walk.

'I couldn't think about anything else at home or at school. Luckily the school holidays started soon afterwards and I told my parents I was working on the garden there every day. We hardly ever got out of bed. By the end of the summer I knew more about lovemaking than men twice my age.

'We continued to see each other regularly, although it was difficult when her husband was at home. She used to take the dog for walk and meet me in a wood near the village. They moved away the following year, but after that I never had any trouble getting girlfriends – it was as if they knew, you see. I don't think a week's ever gone by when I haven't had sex since then,' he ended somewhat smugly, 'but I've always had a thing for older women – I prefer them to lasses my own age.'

'I suppose I am an older woman to you,' said Sue. 'Funny, I've never thought of myself like that. Just as long as I'm not old enough to be your mother. How old are you anyway? Twenty? Twenty-one?'

There was a silence.

'Well, come on – tell me. Nineteen?' In the dim light she could see that he was grinning at her. A terrible suspicion gripped her. 'Don't tell me you're younger than that? Eighteen?'

'Keep going.'

'Seventeen? Rory – please tell me you're kidding.'

He continued to grin at her. Sue let out a low moan.

'Sixteen?'

'I could lie to you but I won't. I'll be seventeen in a couple of months if it makes you feel any better.'

'I *am* old enough to be your mother!' wailed Sue. 'Give or take a couple of years. You told me you were a student! How could I let myself be seduced by a sixteen-year-old boy!'

He slid his hand up her thigh.

'I really am a student,' he assured her. 'I start at sixth form college in September.'

'That doesn't count! How will I ever live this down? I'm a cradle snatcher!'

He began to smooth his fingers soothingly over her damp, curling bush, petting her as if she were a cat.'

'Shsh. What does it matter? You enjoyed yourself, didn't you?'

'That's what makes it so terrible.'

With the tip of his forefinger he began to stroke her clit, causing a renewed surge of moisture.

'We can't do it again – not now that I know,' protested Sue weakly. He intensified the pressure on her clit, parting her thighs further with is other hand, before delving into the folds of her swollen labia.

She felt the insidious build-up of heat which signified that her tired pelvic muscles were readying themselves for yet another climax.

After the number of times they'd already done it, she supposed one more wouldn't make any difference.

'Come on then,' she muttered, reaching for his cock, 'but this is absolutely the last time.'

Sue was groggy from lack of sleep as she stumbled down the platform at Edinburgh station.

After that last feverish coupling she's sent Rory back to his own compartment and managed to fall into an uneasy doze. She was half horrified, half amused that he'd turned out to be so young.

What really stunned her was the realisation that he was

the youngest man she'd ever slept with. She'd had her first full sexual encounter at seventeen, but her partner had been twenty-one. In fact, thinking back, eighteen had been as young as they got and she'd been the same age herself then.

Still at least it was legal – but only just.

She smoothed one hand down the front of her crumpled dress, hoping there would be time to shower and change before meeting the PR woman at the hotel. She had other clothes with her, but they all needed ironing.

When she'd come to pack her case, she hadn't been able to find anything both clean and pressed and couldn't be bothered to get the ironing board out and start then. She'd thrown a few things into her case straight from the washing machine – if the hotel was as posh as it promised to be there'd be maid service. No point in doing it herself.

But, now as she tottered along the platform in her high heels, she wished she'd at least had one crease-free garment to change into. She knew she looked a mess.

But it was too late to worry about it now.

Maybe if she was really lucky there'd be time to sleep for a couple of hours, but she doubted it.

She really was falling back into bad ways, picking up a man on a train and spending the night screwing. This was absolutely the last time she succumbed to her promiscuous streak.

At least she was unlikely to meet anyone who tempted her up in the wilds of Scotland.

Chapter Seven

'Happy birthday, David,' said Gemma, kissing him lightly on the cheek and handing him a gift-wrapped present.

She'd driven out to the massive bakery to discuss the latest series of print ads. She'd been forced to cancel their date a couple of days after Rob had left because of a crisis at work. It was regrettable – it was the second time that week and David had made no secret of the fact that he was annoyed.

She knew she had some ground to make up. He was a major client and if she started taking him for granted and treating him in a cavalier fashion, she might risk losing the account. She knew he was contacted fairly frequently by other agencies hoping for some work – she'd better make him a priority for a while.

He greeted her coolly, settling his tall frame back behind his desk after holding out the chair in front of it for her. That was a bad sign – business between them was usually conducted at the other end of the office where there was a sofa and several easy chairs drawn up around a coffee table.

She smiled at him and crossed her legs seductively.

'Aren't you going to open your present?' she asked him.

'Later,' he said dismissively. 'Coffee?'

She nodded, mentally gearing herself up to charm him into a better mood. They discussed the ads and she made a note of the couple of minor changes he wanted. While they talked she allowed the skirt of her charcoal-grey, pin-striped suit to ride gradually up her thighs until there was just a hint of stocking-top visible.

David was in his mid-forties and had dedicated his life to building up the family bakery into the big business it was today. He was attractive enough in an unremarkable way, with dark, grey-flecked hair and pleasant brown eyes usually hidden behind horn-rimmed glasses.

A disastrous marriage in his twenties had made him wary of women – particularly after his ex-wife had walked off with all the money in the joint accounts. Gemma got the impression that since then, other than a couple of short-lived flings, she'd been the only woman he'd seen on a regular basis.

They began to discuss the budget for a forthcoming photographic shoot. Gemma passed him a sheet of figures, then undid the top button of her jacket as if she were too warm.

He glanced at her and she was gratified to see his eyes lingering on the decorous amount of cleavage she'd revealed. While he studied the figures she deftly undid the rest of the buttons and let the jacket fall open.

When he looked up he started visibly, then pushed his glasses back up his nose as he took in what she was wearing.

Beneath her severely tailored suit she was dressed in a tightly laced pearl-grey basque, trimmed with black lace.

He glanced nervously towards the door. His office opened

onto that of his secretary and the woman was clearly visible through a glass panel around the door, sitting at her desk typing.

But Gemma had her back to her so that only David could see her perfect breasts, pushed up by the tight lacing to form an enticingly deep cleavage.

He flushed and cleared his throat.

'That's lovely. I haven't seen it before, have I?' It was in fact a recent present from Rob, but Gemma saw no need to tell him that.

'No, it's new. I thought you deserved a treat on your birthday. Talking of which, I thought I'd take you out for dinner tonight – if you'd like that.'

He nodded, his eyes still drinking in the stirring sight she presented. Gemma didn't have to look to tell that he had a hard-on and he was wishing his secretary a hundred miles away.

'Where would you like to go? You can choose anywhere – I'd like to make this evening particularly special for you.'

'Your house,' he told her. 'I'd like you to cook dinner for me at your house – and I'd like you to wear that when you serve it.'

Gemma kept a smile on her face but inwardly she was nonplussed by his suggestion. She'd often had him round for drinks before they went out, or back for coffee after they'd eaten, but never dinner.

He'd hinted a few times that he'd like to be asked, but she'd ignored him. Just when did he think she had the time to shop and cook? She would gladly have taken him to the most expensive restaurant in London rather than be presented with this unwelcome request.

Her fridge, if she remembered correctly held champagne, white wine, gin, vodka, mineral water, milk and fruit juice. There might even be half a carton of yogurt, but that was about it. There was virtually nothing in the cupboards and the freezer was in desperate need of stocking up.

'I think I can do better than that,' she replied. 'What about the Venezia? My cooking isn't up to much I'm afraid.'

He shook his head stubbornly.

'Your house,' he repeated. 'You said I could choose – I'll bring the wine.'

'Okay then,' she said, reluctantly bowing to the inevitable. 'Shall we say about eight-thirty?'

Gemma swept into the agency, saying to Tish, 'Would you come into my office please?'

Once in there she spoke rapidly while removing her jacket and switching on her computer.

'Could you get on the phone and find some catering company that can provide dinner for two at my house tonight. When you've found one, put them through please.'

The receptionist nodded and left the room. Gemma began to amend a budget on screen but she was feeling too irritated by David's annoying determination to eat at her house to concentrate properly.

If he hadn't been adamant that she cook it, she would just have got caterers in and let them cook, serve and clear up afterwards. But he obviously wanted her to wait on him personally. Anyway, she supposed she could hardly have anyone else there if she was only wearing a basque.

When Tish put her through to a company she'd found which specialised in upmarket dinner parties, Gemma was relieved to discover they could help her – at a price.

She returned home at just after seven and an efficient young woman called Saskia arrived a few minutes later.

While Gemma showered and washed her hair, Saskia set the table, arranged the flowers she'd brought and laid everything out in the small kitchen.

When Gemma came downstairs, her basque decorously covered by a silk robe, everything was ready. She'd emphasised that she didn't want to spend half the night in the kitchen, so the meal was simplicity itself.

To start, there were fresh summer fruits in a raspberry coulis which Saskia had placed in the fridge to chill, together with a crisp green salad to accompany the main course. In the oven a rich beef casserole simmered and several small jacket potatoes were just beginning to bake. To follow there was a chocolate mousse and a cheeseboard.

All Gemma had to do was bring things through at the right time – her cleaner could load the dishwasher tomorrow. She saw Saskia out at about eight-fifteen and opened a bottle of champagne. She thought she deserved a quiet few minutes so she poured a glass, put on some soft music and curled up on the sofa.

For once she didn't particularly feel like sex, which wasn't wildly convenient as David would undoubtedly want to spend a good part of the evening screwing.

Better do something about that.

Gemma drank most of her glass of champagne, then slipped her hand between her thighs under her panties. She rubbed herself gently and thought about the last time David had fucked her. It had been good and the memory, together with the insidious stroking of her clit, brought her to a climax within a few minutes.

Just in time.

The doorbell went and a glance in the hall mirror as she passed it, assured her that her eyes were glittering and her pale cheeks suffused with a light flush of arousal.

As soon as she'd made David comfortable with a drink and opened the bottle of burgundy he'd brought so it could breathe, Gemma slipped out of her robe.

The grey satin basque was lavishly trimmed with black lace and pushed her small breasts upwards so they spilled wantonly out of their cups. Tight lacing made her already slim waist even slimmer and her long legs looked endless in their black seamed stockings. She was wearing a matching pair of tiny grey satin panties which barely covered her bush.

David was obviously finding the sight of her extremely exciting and she wondered if they'd make it through to the end of the meal.

'You look gorgeous,' he complimented her, 'good enough to eat in fact.'

'Thank you,' she murmured demurely.

He sniffed the air appreciatively as he noticed the delicious savoury smell coming from the kitchen. 'Talking of which – something smells good. What are we having?'

'Beef casserole – are you hungry?'

'I thought I was, but the sight of you in that lacy thing is making me lose interest in food.'

'Then maybe we'd better eat soon – I'd hate to have gone to all this trouble for nothing.'

Gemma had decided to give David a birthday to remember. She wanted him to be so strongly in her sexual thrall that he'd forget about her recent neglect.

She bent close to him when she placed his first course in

front of him, letting him catch a heady whiff of her expensive scent and get a close-up view of her satin-skinned breasts.

When she removed the plate she passed her hand fleetingly over his crotch and felt his already hard cock leap excitedly.

'I just can't wait to have you inside me,' she murmured.

'We could . . . we could go upstairs now,' he offered.

'Food first,' she purred, twitching her small, pert backside provocatively as she was leaving the room. The tiny panties were cut high on the thigh exposing a good part of her bottom and she could feel his eyes boring into it as she left.

'You've been hiding your light under a bushel,' he commented as he ate the delicious, perfectly cooked casserole. 'It must have taken you ages to make this.'

'Not really,' she returned sweetly. 'Make the most of it – this is a never-to-be-repeated experience. I really don't have time to cook.'

When she'd cleared away the main course she casually unlaced the top of the basque so her firm high breasts were revealed. He swallowed and glanced towards the stairs.

'Shall we . . .?'

'Not yet,' returned Gemma softly, the tone of her voice low and seductive. 'I want to think about what we're going to do together first. Before you fuck me, I want to unzip your trousers, draw your cock out and take it in my mouth – slowly, very slowly, until it's in as far as I can take it. Then I'm going to suck and suck until you're nearly ready to come. When you think you can't hold back a moment longer I'm going to . . .'

Her cultured voice husky with sexual promise, Gemma continued to talk to him, describing the pleasures to come. A thin film of sweat gathered on David's brow and he began to shift uneasily on his chair.

When Gemma judged him unlikely to be able to hold back much longer she dropped to her knees in front of him. She unzipped his trousers and his cock sprang out like a phallic jack-in-a-box, heavily marbled with purple veins.

He groaned when she slid it into her mouth and began to fondle her delectable boobs, teasing her toffee-coloured nipples until they jutted out and strained against the palms of his hands.

She turned fellatio into an art form, exploring his member thoroughly, leaving no part of it untouched by her wickedly flickering tongue.

David had a very conventional approach to sex and Gemma delighted in introducing him to new pleasures. When his hands tightened on her breasts and she judged he was on the verge of ejaculation, she withdrew her mouth so that he came all over her breasts.

The hot creamy liquid trickled over her creamy orbs and she took his hand and encouraged him to rub it in until she was glistening with his potent juices.

She returned to her chair opposite him and asked casually, 'Chocolate mousse?'

He wiped his hands on a handkerchief, removed his glasses and wiped them too then gasped, 'Not just yet – not until I've calmed down a bit.'

He lurched to his feet and went upstairs to the bathroom. When he came back down Gemma was sitting on the sofa with her breasts still exposed and glistening and her panties off. She was sipping a glass of burgundy with one leg tucked under her and the other bent at the knee, revealing the neat triangle of her sable bush and an intoxicating hint of her soft pink labia.

David gulped and sat down on the armchair at right angles to her. She started a casual conversation but his replies were disjointed, particularly when she slipped her hand between her legs and began to stroke herself until the deep pink, blunt arrow of her clit became visible.

'Chocolate mousse?' she asked again.

'I'd rather go upstairs,' he said, his eyes still riveted to her private parts.

'Not until you've finished your meal,' she told him sweetly.

Only when he'd spooned down the delicious concoction and drunk two cups of coffee did she lead the way upstairs. He stripped off his clothes and lay down on the bed. Gemma straddled him, her moist private parts engulfing his engorged cock.

'This is going to be a night to remember,' she promised him.

Sue didn't much like Scotland.

For one thing it was noticeably colder than London and she hadn't brought any warm clothes and for another she felt distinctly uncomfortable in such a rural environment.

The hotel was set in an area of great natural beauty – or so the old brochure told her. But there was a heavy mist hanging over it the day she arrived and all she could see were some occasional glimpses of a lot of barren hills – or were they mountains? – and a depressing-looking lake.

She didn't much like the hotel either. The mounted heads of various wildlife paid mute testimony to the area's favoured recreational pastime. She found it unnerving to keep coming across them every time she turned a corner, their large glass eyes silently reproachful. Any spare bit of wall not covered in decapitated heads was hung with ancient weaponry and assorted coats of arms.

She didn't like all the tartans either. Each of the bedrooms was decorated in a different one and she took a particular dislike to the one in her room – a rather nasty combination of dark reds and greens. As if that wasn't bad enough, all the public rooms were similarly done out.

The other guests made her feel like she'd popped down from Jupiter for a brief visit. Her clothes, perfectly appropriate for the watering holes she frequented in London (at least she thought so – Gemma might not agree) marked her out as different. All the guests seemed to wear green quilted things, big ugly pullovers and sensible shoes – and that was just the women.

She hadn't exactly taken to the hotel's PR woman Fiona, who'd been detailed to look after her. On her first day she was given an extensive tour of the hotel which lasted until mid-afternoon. Completely exhausted, she excused herself saying she wanted to make some preliminary notes, then returned to her room, crawled into bed and fell asleep.

She was awakened half an hour later by Fiona bringing her some more literature. The other woman made it quite clear that she took a dim view of people who napped in the afternoon instead of working.

It hadn't taken Sue long to discover that Fiona had written the hotel's old brochure and didn't see any need whatsoever to have it rewritten by some hack from a fancy London agency.

The fact that the hotel had just been bought out by a luxury group and was to be included in a huge, high profile advertising campaign seemed to cause her problems. Perhaps she was worried she was going to lose her job, but whatever the reason she seemed antagonistic and difficult.

When Sue went down to dinner that evening in a hot pink minidress, she was mildly disconcerted to see that Fiona was still in her dowdy tartan business suit. She didn't let it bother her unduly, although she wished she could eat alone rather than with someone who obviously disliked her.

She was looking forward to a couple of drinks in the bar before going through to the restaurant, but when she suggested it, Fiona looked down her long, red nose and said coldly, 'I never drink when I'm working.'

'Really?' replied Sue amazed. She considered that she did some of her best work under the influence of alcohol. As soon as the waiter proffered menus she ordered a vodka and tonic. If Fiona thought she was going to spend the evening sipping mineral water, she had another think coming.

The restaurant had a good reputation and her mouth watered as she read the menu. When the waiter came to take their order Fiona turned to her with an unpleasant smile.

'You'll be wanting to try all the local specialities our chef is renowned for.' She then ordered several dishes, most of which Sue knew from the menu to be made from the more disgusting parts of various animals. She'd always thought haggis was a joke and it was a shock to discover it really existed. Even a delicate accompanying sauce couldn't reconcile her to dining on such horrible sounding food.

Even worse, Fiona ordered a delicious chicken dish for herself.

Sue let her order then smiled sweetly.

'That all sounds wonderful. And as well as that I'll have the avocado salad followed by the Angus steak, medium rare, in the port and stilton sauce with vegetables of the day. Oh, and half a bottle of the house claret.'

'You can't possibly eat all that!' spluttered Fiona.

'I have an enormous appetite,' Sue told her, unperturbed.

They ate in chilly silence broken only by Sue exclaiming over the local specialities, pushing them around her plate a bit then leaving them. The food she'd ordered for herself was excellent and she enjoyed every mouthful. When it came to the puddings she looked enquiringly at Fiona.

'Is they anything in particular I should try?' The other woman shook her head, realising that Sue was quite capable of ordering the dessert she wanted as well, if Fiona's choice didn't please her.

Fortunately Fiona excused herself as soon as the meal was over and Sue retired to the bar where she contentedly tried a couple of single malt whiskys before going back to her room for an early night.

She woke up feeling mildly depressed, although she was pleased to see that the mist had lifted and a watery sun was shining over the bracken – or was it heather?

Fiona smirkingly suggested that she go for a walk and familiarise herself with the surrounding countryside. She made it sound like an order, but Sue was happy to get away from the hotel for a while and raised no objections.

She wondered why Fiona was smirking and decided that it must be because she was hoping that she'd get lost.

She needed to take a few photos anyway, to help her both write and design the brochure when she got back to London. She went up to her room to collect a jacket, wondering how soon she could head back home.

She looked doubtfully at her shoes, trying to decide which pair were the most suitable for a country walk. Her sandals had the lowest heels, but her feet would get wet. In the end she kept her red high-heels on, thinking she wouldn't be walking far after all and they did match her dress.

She was just strolling through the entrance hall when she heard a male voice behind her.

'Sue!'

'Joe! What are you doing here?' she asked, surprised but nevertheless delighted to see a familiar face. He was just as attractive as she remembered and she was immediately aware of a faint frisson in her pelvic region as she recalled lying across his knee in her office, oblivious to everything except purely carnal sensations.

'Working. How about you?' Walking behind her before he'd realised who it was, Joe had been admiring the provocative roll of her hips and imagining how she'd look naked, squatting on his prick, with her back to him.

'The same.' She remembered now that Joe handled security for the London hotel – and obviously this one too.

'Where are you off to?' he asked.

'A walk. I'm supposed to soak up the atmosphere so I can write about it. I'd rather be in the bar soaking up whisky, but it's a bit early yet.'

'I'll come with you if you like – I've a meeting this

afternoon, but until then my time's my own.'

Joe had hoped to resolve the Mandy problem before ringing Sue, but he'd been unexpectedly summoned to Scotland before he could deal with it. He'd phoned her at the agency and left a message with Tish, saying he'd be away longer than expected. Running into her like this in the back of beyond seemed like a gift from the gods.

They wandered through the hotel grounds and out to the lake. Although the sun was shining, Sue still felt cold in her thin jacket. At least the water looked clean, but when she dipped her hand into it, it was icy.

'I don't think I'll be swimming,' she shivered. 'And this is August – I'd hate to feel it in January.'

She realised for the first time that Joe was as inappropriately attired for country life as she was. His expensive suit and suede shoes shouted 'city dweller', just as surely as her own scarlet dress and matching shoes.

They tramped rather unenthusiastically up the lower slopes of one of the neighbouring hills and Joe sat on a rock while Sue took a few photos. The hotel looked pretty impressive from up here – she could see how inviting she could make it look in the brochure, even if she'd never choose to holiday there herself.

Bumping into Joe had cheered her up immeasurably. Hopefully they could dine together tonight and then retire to the bar and get cheerfully pissed.

Or to bed, murmured an insidious little voice in her head.

The memory of their hot, exciting sex behind the sofa in the London hotel brought her out in a mild sweat. Or maybe it was the unaccustomed exercise. The sun was fully out now and although there was still a chilly wind blowing, the sun's rays were warm, even on an exposed Scottish hillside.

They slowly circled the hotel, Sue making mental notes all the time and taking more photographs. She took a couple of Joe as if they really were on holiday.

They were just struggling through some waist-high, damp undergrowth which Sue suspected was bracken, when the heel on her delicate shoe broke. She stumbled and fell, landing on her back.

'Are you okay?' asked Joe, sinking to his knees beside her.

'I am, but I don't think my shoe is,' she replied ruefully, taking it off to inspect the damage. The heel had snapped in two and was beyond repair. She sat up and was just wondering how she was going to get back to the hotel, when the silence was suddenly rent by the terrifying and unmistakable sound of gunfire.

'*What the fuck!*' yelled Joe, throwing himself on top of her. Sue screamed but it was lost beneath the deafening retorts of what sounded like a battalion firing at the enemy.

Chapter Eight

Flattened against the ground on a bed of wet bracken, her eyes closed and her ears ringing, Sue clutched at Joe's shoulders and shouted, 'This must be an army training ground! They could have warned us! Shit!'

At that moment strange objects began to drop out of the sky all around them, falling like stones to the ground and beneath the noise of the guns she could hear a strange, unfamiliar squawking. She opened her eyes to see lots of large birds flying frantically up from the undergrowth only to be hit and plummet downwards.

'They're grouse!' exclaimed Joe. 'We're being shot at by a fucking hunting party!'

'I've just remembered what date it is!' shrieked Sue, verting her eyes from the spectacle.

'What the fuck does the date have to do with it?' demanded Joe.

'It's the twelfth. The glorious twelfth. The first day of the hunting season or something like that.'

The noise abated somewhat as the more unfortunate grouse were hit and the fortunate ones flew out of range.

Sue realised that something large and very hard was

pressing into her hip and was seized by a sense of *déjà vu* which made her burst out laughing. Joe was obviously struck by the same thought at the same time and began to laugh too.

'What's going on?' Sue gasped. 'If I'm going to find myself under fire every time I see you, this relationship is destined to be *very* short-lived.'

Despite the cold chill striking up through her clothes and the very real fear of being shot, a surge of pure unadulterated lust washed over her.

She looked at Joe's face and saw the same there. Slowly, very slowly, he undid the top button of her scarlet dress. Sue shivered with anticipation as she felt his fingers on her bare skin. He undid the second button, then the third, continuing until he'd unfastened them all and could pull her dress apart to expose her black lace slip.

It was very short and had ridden up when she fell, so he could see her black ribbon suspenders and the tops of her cream stockings. She wasn't wearing a bra and the sharp points of her nipples were trying to thrust their way through the holes in the lace. Her deep creamy cleavage was sprinkled with tiny goose bumps as the chill breeze played over her firm flesh.

Joe groaned as he drew one shoulder strap down and pulled the slip aside to bare one full, straining breast. His mouth closed moistly over it and he circled the hard, eager nipple with his tongue. Sue ground her pelvis upwards against his, positioning her mound directly beneath the ramrod hardness of his cock.

They rubbed against each other while he continued to suck and tease her nipple. He bared her other breast and covered it with his hand, squeezing and kneading it gently.

Sue could feel hot moisture trickling into her black lace panties and an urgent throbbing deep in her pussy. She spread her legs and Joe's hand slid down over her gently rounded stomach to graze the contour of her hip, then cup her mound over two layers of black lace.

He pushed the heel of his hand upwards and she pressed hard against it, feeling her labia pulsing and a tiny tingling in the nub of her clit. He could feel how wet she was through the flimsy material and rubbed harder.

The friction of the damp black lace against her clit was making Sue gasp and waves of heat washed over her previously chilled body. Where there had been goose bumps on her exposed skin, now there was a fine film of perspiration as she realised she was about to come.

The heel of his hand moved faster and faster, then with a sharp intake of breath she spiralled over the edge and began the dizzying fall into a whirling abyss of pleasure.

Joe was surprised but pleased that she'd come so quickly. He dragged her panties down to her stocking tops, then unzipped his trousers and thrust eagerly into her. He was immediately engulfed by the hot folds of her honeypot as her internal muscles closed welcomingly around his granite-hard cock.

She tried to wrap her legs around his thighs, but was hampered by her panties. Joe hooked his hand into the side and jerked, tearing the flimsy material from her.

With her slip around her waist and her heavy breasts pressed pleasingly against his chest, Sue moved beneath him, milking every ounce of pleasure from the fast and furious fuck.

She forgot she was lying on a bed of wet bracken, her jacket and dress soaked through at the back. She was only aware of each strong thrust as Joe screwed her vigorously on the windswept Scottish hillside.

He could feel his own climax approaching fast and adjusted his position, taking the weight on his elbows so he could see her luscious breasts and penetrate her more deeply. Sue unclasped her legs then hooked them around his waist, her hips moving urgently against his as they hit the home stretch.

She came again, crying out as her body spasmed into a renewed burst of pure, erotic pleasure. It was too much for Joe, he pumped his juices into her like a man possessed, his body jerking above hers as he gasped and groaned his release. Sue came slowly back to earth, feeling the weight of his body as he slumped on top of her.

There was a loud panting in her ear and a blast of foul breath wafted across her face. She opened her eyes, startled, but Joe's face was buried in her shoulder.

She turned her head to be met by the unexpected sight of a dog, its tongue lolling out of its mouth, wagging its tail delightedly. At that moment, Joe's eyes flew open.

'*Fucking hell!* he exclaimed, then they both burst out laughing. Another dog appeared through the undergrowth, a dead grouse clutched between its jaws.

'Get lost! Go away!' he urged them as yet another dog appeared and began to sniff at their private parts. They separated abruptly and Joe lurched to his feet, shooing the dogs away. In the distance he could see the hunting party, their backs to him as they tramped across the moor in search of more wildlife to slaughter.

Sue stumbled to her feet and pulled her slip down, then began to fasten her dress.

'Where did my panties get to?' she asked, looking around, but there was no sign of the scrap of black lace. One of the dogs turned and looked back at her. In its mouth was what was unmistakably the remains of her panties. They both burst out laughing again.

'What are they going to think when Fido goes back with a torn pair of damp female panties instead of a grouse?' gasped Sue.

'I dread to think,' returned Joe. 'I don't think they would have been much use to you anyway – I tore them getting them off.'

'Let's get back to the hotel – the next thing on my agenda is a soak in a hot bath with some coffee and whisky.'

'That's funny – that's exactly what I had in mind too.'

Dinner that night was a much more enjoyable event than the one the previous evening. Sue, Joe and Fiona were joined by Craig, the head of security and Derek, the manager, who'd just got back from a meeting with the hotel's new owners.

Sue had donned a condom-tight cream silk dress with a plunging neckline for the occasion. She'd just spent another couple of hours in bed with Joe and her dark, almond shaped eyes and creamy skin were glowing with sexual satisfaction.

It was obvious that both Derek and Craig were smitten by her. Derek took one look and immediately ordered a bottle of champagne. Throughout the meal they vied for her attention, until Fiona, who'd been seeing Craig for several months, was practically puce with rage.

He'd never once looked at her the way he was looking

at that over made-up slut. How dare she come to what was, after all, a business meeting, with her boobs spilling out of her dress? And when were they going to get onto business? So far it had all been pointless chit-chat.

And everyone seemed to be drinking heavily – they were already onto their third bottle and they hadn't even finished the main course yet. Her thin lips pursed and her long red nose turned a mottled magenta, Fiona was ready to explode.

Sue was quite well aware what was going through the other woman's mind, but she felt that Fiona should have warned her that she was liable to find herself on the wrong end of a large number of shotguns, when she'd suggested she go for a walk that morning.

Sue had discovered that the hotel organised shooting parties for those with pretensions to belonging to the huntin', shootin' and fishin' set. They'd all obviously enjoyed a good day's sport and were now busy getting noisily drunk.

She pushed back a lock of tousled blonde hair and glanced around the crowded restaurant, wondering which of them had been the lucky recipient of her torn panties.

Joe sat next to her and watched, completely unperturbed, while she flirted with Derek and Craig. He knew that later it would be him screwing her in her enormous four-poster bed, or on the carved oak chest, or possibly over the back of the overstuffed armchair.

After dinner they all repaired to the bar, except Fiona who left in disgust having come to the conclusion that no business was going to get discussed tonight. She tried to take Craig with her, but he barely glanced up from his enraptured contemplation of Sue's cleavage.

Someone began organising games. When 'hide and seek' was announced, Sue decided she wanted to play. The boundaries were set and the self-appointed master of ceremonies decreed that the first time, the women should hide and the men find them. A glance around the bar told her that she didn't want to be found by any of the men except Joe.

She'd had the advantage of a complete tour of the hotel and managed to whisper, 'I'll be in the third floor linen cupboard.' He nodded and at the signal from the master of ceremonies, she set off.

The linen cupboard was actually a small room lined by racks holding the clean sheets and towels for that floor. Sue crept in and flicked the lights on briefly to get her bearings, then crawled onto the bottom shelf of the rack on the far wall and stretched out on her back.

The pile of fluffy towels made a comfortable bed and she waited with a titillating sense of carnal anticipation for Joe to find her. He was certainly taking his time and at least ten minutes must have passed before she heard the door creak open.

He didn't put the light on and she heard him feeling his way along the racks nearest to the door. She suppressed a giggle when there was a bang followed by a muffled curse and knew he'd walked into something in the dark.

At long last he reached her and she felt him touch her hair. He didn't say a word, just ran his hand down over her shoulder and then over her silk-covered breasts.

She sensed he was kneeling beside her on the floor as he continued with his silent exploration of her body. It was almost unbearably erotic there in the dense darkness. Sue

117

felt the prickling of her female juices as they gathered in her velvet interior and eventually overflowed into her ivory silk camiknickers.

He drew her breasts from her dress and caressed them fervently, rolling her jutting nipples between his fingers in a way which made her catch her breath. He squeezed and fondled them as if they were new toys he'd just been given for his birthday.

One hand continued to caress them as the other roamed over her belly until it found her hidden delta. He probed it over her dress, then slipped underneath the fine fabric to stroke her mound over her camiknickers.

The dampness of the material made him groan and he delved beneath it with his fingers, plunging into the welcoming stickiness he found there. Sue sighed and drew up her legs, opening them wide to facilitate his amorous exploration.

At that moment the light clicked on and Sue's eyes flew open to see Fiona looming in the doorway, almost foaming at the mouth with fury.

'You *slut!*' she shrieked. 'You dirty little slut!'

Sue glanced at Joe half amused, half annoyed, then froze in shock.

It wasn't Joe with one hand buried in her crotch, the other massaging her breasts – it was Craig.

'*Craig!*' she gasped in dismay.

'*Sue!*' exclaimed Joe from the doorway where he'd suddenly appeared behind Fiona.

Craig snatched his hands away from her as if she was red-hot. Sue's wantonly spread legs snapped together and she hastily pulled her dress up and her skirt down.

'I thought you were Joe!' she accused him. Fiona marched across the room, grabbed Craig by the collar and hit him across the face. She looked as if she'd like to do the same to Sue, but obviously thought better of it. She let go of the hapless security man and stalked out of the room. He lurched to his feet, clutching his stinging cheek and staggered after her.

'Fiona! It was a mistake!' he called desperately.

'Was it?' asked Joe, still lounging in the doorway.

'Joe – where have you been? Why didn't you find me? I thought that was you.'

'There are two linen cupboards on this floor,' he told her. 'I've been sitting in the other one. I thought you'd gone to the loo or something.

'I was only shown this one when I was given the tour. How did Craig know I'd be here? Or did he think I was Fiona?'

'He heard you telling me. I saw him behind me as I went into the wrong cupboard – he must have thought it was his lucky day when he found you in here. Of course he didn't think you were Fiona – she wasn't even playing.'

Sue started to laugh. 'Did you see her face? She was livid – oh, Joe, you're not annoyed with me are you? I really didn't know.'

'All men are alike to you in the dark, are they?'

'I'd have known as soon as he got close enough for me to smell him, or if he'd kissed me, but I was expecting you and when someone came in and started caressing me I assumed it *was* you.'

Joe grinned and she saw that he wasn't really annoyed. In fact, he realised suddenly that coming across them like that had unexpectedly turned him on. The sight of Sue with her breasts exposed and her knees bent and wide apart, being touched intimately by another man, made him want to drag her knickers down and plunge the heavy length of his aching cock straight into her pussy.

He strolled over to her and without a word pushed his hand up her skirt. He felt immediately how wet she was and took up where Craig had so abruptly left off, sliding his fingers along the slippery groove of her female channel, then pushing two inside her.

She gasped and bore down against his hand, opening her legs wide.

'I see he got your engine running,' he muttered softly. 'Now it's time for a thrill-packed ride.'

He jerked his hand out and dragged her camiknickers down, before grabbing her by the hips and swinging her to bend over the second shelf of the linen rack, her skirt around her waist.

He wrenched his zip down, freeing his cock from the constraints of his briefs which were stretched to the limit in their struggle to contain him.

The full moons of her curvaceous bottom were thrust provocatively out to him. As he stepped towards her she opened her legs wide so he could see the soft, glistening folds of her private parts, surrounded by downy wisps of hair.

Cock in hand, he paused to admire the alluring sight then positioned himself behind her.

She turned to look over her shoulder and murmured, 'You'd better be right about the thrills.'

It had been a gloomy day in England but way up above

the clouds, the evening sunshine was bright and strong as it shone in through the small perspex windows of the plane.

Gemma adjusted the blind and gestured imperiously to the stewardess. The girl refilled her empty glass with complimentary champagne and Gemma took a gulp and tried to suppress her simmering anger. It was her fourth glass in less than an hour and she was starting to feel the effects.

It was Friday evening and she was on her way to Majorca to spend the weekend with Rob. He'd called the night before to tell her he'd borrowed a friend's villa there and to suggest that she join him.

Except it had been more like an order.

He'd arrogantly expected that she'd drop everything for a couple of days with him. She'd planned to spend most of the weekend working, so it wasn't at all convenient, but when she'd tried to refuse he'd lowered his voice and told her in explicit detail just how they'd pass the time.

A wave of heat had washed over her and her pussy had begun to throb at his lewd description. She'd found herself weakly acquiescing and, as soon as she'd put the phone down, she'd pulled open her silk robe and masturbated for over an hour, bringing herself to climax after climax. But it hadn't stopped the hot pulse of erotic anticipation from beating ferociously and unremittingly between her legs ever since.

All day she'd been working at a breakneck pace, trying to do at least some of the work she'd intended to deal with at the weekend; but images of dirty, depraved sex kept imprinting themselves remorselessly on her consciousness.

She was furious with herself.

She should have told him coolly that she was too busy to make it at such short notice. Instead she'd thrown her

sexiest lingerie and beachwear into a case and had Tish
spend the morning on the phone trying to find her a seat
on an evening flight to Majorca – no easy matter in mid-
August and she'd ended up having to travel first class.

She had the window seat, the middle one was empty and
the aisle seat was occupied by a youngish man in jeans
and a tee-shirt, his fair hair pulled back in a ponytail.

He'd looked at her admiringly when she'd stepped past
him to get to her seat, but she'd ignored him – she was in
no mood for making polite conversation.

She was wearing a buttercup-yellow linen suit over a
black silk tee-shirt. It felt warm on the plane and she began
to remove the jacket, but to her annoyance her elbow
caught in the folds of the sleeve. She jerked at it impatiently
and was rewarded by a ripping sound.

'Allow me,' said a deep voice and the man took hold of
the jacket by the collar and drew it down her arms. She
felt his hand graze over the back of her neck and a shiver
of sensual response passed unsettlingly over her.

Then his hands smoothed over her bare arms, pushing
the jacket down them until he reached her elbows. He
deftly extricated the one which had caught and removed
the garment. His hands caressed her forearms as he did so
and all the tiny golden hairs there stood to attention as her
body recognised his male sexuality.

He handed her the jacket with a smile, turned to sit down
and knocked her glass of champagne into her lap.

She gasped as the icy liquid soaked through her linen
skirt, then her silk panties to reach her fevered private
parts.

She should have been annoyed – but it felt wonderful.

Her pupils dilated and her mouth formed an 'ooh' as, for the first time since Rob's call, the heat which consumed her pussy was briefly quenched.

Too briefly.

Her fellow traveller grabbed a handful of paper napkins and began to dab at the swiftly spreading wet patch. One large, tanned hand rested on her stocking-clad knee while the other rubbed a wad of paper against her mound.

The results were electrifying.

She could feel a completely unexpected climax begin to build at the impromptu stimulation.

If she'd been hot before, now she was molten.

She could smell the clean scents of his body, a heady mix of soap, shampoo and some light cologne she didn't recognise. The hand on her knee was well cared for with a sprinkling of dark hairs on the back, vanishing beneath the plain black strap of his platinum watch.

She could feel the deep-pink flush of arousal on her high cheekbones, lending colour to her pale oval face. She swallowed and tried to block out the tide of sensation surging outwards from where he was still working on the stain.

It was no good – she was nearly there.

Just as she thought she'd reached the point of no return, he stopped.

'I think that's got it,' he told her, looking up. 'Champagne doesn't usually stain.'

Her usual cool poise abandoned like a laddered stocking, Gemma clutched his wrist.

'Don't stop,' she begged him.

He took in her flushed face, feverishly glittering eyes and

parted lips and understanding dawned like a new moon rising.

'You want me to . . .?'

'Yes.'

He dropped the wad of damp napkins and placed his hand over her mound, then rubbed her delicately between the legs with his fingers. His broad back was blocking the view of anyone walking past, but even so she didn't dare pull her skirt up to make it easier for him.

She opened her legs slightly so he was able to reach her most sensitive spot through the two layers of material. He massaged her there while she struggled not to gasp and moan. It didn't take long, the direct stimulation was more than she could take.

Her head fell back against the seat, her eyes closed and she let out a long, deep breath as she shuddered into orgasm.

She was dimly aware that he'd got up from his knees and had sunk into the seat next to hers.

'You're my dream woman,' he murmured in her ear.

'Mmm. Why?' she asked with an effort.

'A woman so hot that she can come like that. I usually lose the feeling in either my fingers or tongue from stimulation prolonged way beyond my pain barrier as I try to get some woman to come. If you want to do it again – just say the word.'

Gemma did want to do it again – and more.

He gestured for the stewardess and had her glass refilled. 'Sorry about the accident – I'm not usually so clumsy,' he said as he passed it to her.

She looked at him sideways from under her lashes. 'It

was my pleasure – as I'm sure you noticed.'

'Do you mind if I ask you something?'

'What?'

'Are you always so . . . ready?'

Gemma smiled and took a sip of champagne.

'No. But I'm on my way to spend a couple of days with a lover and I've been like a cat on heat since he phoned me last night.'

She glanced sideways at his groin where a huge erection was patently testing the strength of his zip. 'I'm going to freshen up – why don't you join me in a couple of minutes? My pussy feels like it's on fire again.'

In the tiny cubicle, Gemma removed her damp panties and stuffed them in her bag before emptying her bladder and washing her hands. There was a tap at the door and she opened it so he could squeeze in next to her.

A moment later they were in each other's arms and he dragged her skirt up around her waist and pulled her roughly against him so she could feel the granite hardness of his cock against her bare stomach.

His hand delved between her legs and she let out a muffled exclamation as she felt how cold it was – he must have been holding an iced drink.

But it felt wonderful as he ran his fingers over the painfully distended lips guarding the entrance to her honeypot. It felt even better when he squeezed her clit between his thumb and forefinger, making her shudder with pleasure. He explored her swollen vulva with his hand, spreading the hot moisture over the silken triangle of her bush and along the creases at the top of her thighs.

She was running with it, it cascaded out of her like an

overflowing fountain, soaking into her stocking tops. He swiftly brought her to another climax, then lifted her by the waist so she was perched on the rim of the hand basin.

He fell to his knees, then spread her legs. She felt his warm breath on her thighs, then he ran his tongue delicately along the rim of her outer lips. She gasped in shock – his tongue was as cold as his hand had been – he must have been sucking an ice cube.

His tongue glided backwards, leaving an icy trail in its wake, then flicked wickedly against the hood of her clit. She shuddered, then reached down and pressed his face hard into the steam heat of her pussy. She felt his tongue spearing into her, pushing in as far as it would go, then he began to lap thirstily.

He drank like a dehydrated man at a desert oasis, finding every drop of moisture with his questing mouth, making her moan and gasp in her precarious position on the edge of the basin. She locked her legs around his neck, holding him trapped against her aching, melting honeypot.

After another climax she uncrossed her legs and opened them wide.

'Fuck me,' she invited him.

He unzipped his jeans and a thick red cock, heavily marbled with throbbing blue veins, sprang out. He held it positioned at the entrance to her dripping cavern, just inside her outer lips, while he eased her black silk T-shirt out of the waistband of her skirt. He pulled it over her head revealing her small perfect breasts, the toffee-coloured nipples swollen to two painful points.

She could feel his organ poised there, tormentingly nudging against her clit, then his hands closed over her breasts and he slid it slowly, oh so slowly, inside her an inch at a time.

Gemma wriggled as far forward on the edge of the basin as she dared, trying to get him completely inside her, but he wasn't to be rushed.

He bent his head to take one jutting nipple into his mouth and sucked hard. She seized him by the buttocks and dragged him against her, at last feeling him slide in up to the hilt. He commenced a slow withdrawal, teasingly pausing at the last moment so the head of his cock was still nestling like a sun-warmed plum just inside her.

She peeled his jeans and briefs down over his hips and stroked his balls from behind, feathering over them with her fingertips, cradling them in the palm of her hand, then running her nail along the cleft leading to his anus.

It had the intended effect because he groaned and began to thrust in and out of her, long satisfying strokes which made her dig her nails into his buttocks and gasp at each one.

It was over too soon for Gemma, but she knew he'd held back as long as he could.

He came in a flood of molten lava, which she felt surging up inside her, prompting another climax as she gripped him tightly with her internal muscles.

He pulled out and sank onto the toilet seat. Gemma felt his come dripping slowly out of her and wondered how she was going to clean herself up enough to meet Rob – her entire lower body seemed to be covered in their mingled juices.

From her seat on the edge of the hand basin, she filled it with cold water and then cautiously lowered herself into it. It wasn't ideal – she really needed a shower, but at least she was able to rinse her private parts, wetting her suspender belt, stockings and quite a lot of her skirt, still bunched up around her waist, in the process.

When she'd finished she slid gracefully down and dried herself off with a handful of tissues. She pulled her T-shirt back on and tidied her hair while he took her place and washed her copious secretions off his face.

'Let's hope there isn't a queue,' he remarked, tucking his cock back into his jeans. 'Ready?'

Chapter Nine

Descending from the plane at Palma airport, already slightly hung-over, Gemma felt her silk T-shirt sticking to her back.

It was in the eighties and the warm night air closed over her like dark, scented velvet as she walked towards baggage reclaim.

More than anything she wanted a shower – it seemed a lifetime since she'd taken one that morning. After a full day working in central London, and then the urgent sex with her unknown travelling companion, she felt hot and sticky.

Rob was waiting in the arrivals hall looking tanned and fit, his hair sun-bleached to an even lighter blond, but for once her stomach didn't lurch with lust at the sight of him. He led the way to his hire car, an expensive-looking Cabriolet with the roof down, and threw her case in the back.

As soon as she slid into the passenger seat he put his hand up her skirt and grunted with satisfaction as he felt the soft stickiness of the silken floss curled around the entrance to her honeypot. Gemma had forgotten to put her panties back on after her session in the toilet, but Rob obviously took it as a sign of her eagerness to have him touch her.

He thumbed her still-swollen clit.

'Have you been bringing yourself off?' he asked. 'You feel like a ripe fruit – I can't wait to eat you.'

She thought for a moment that he was going to do so there and then and recoiled from him – he'd be bound to taste another man on her, even after her hasty wash.

An airport security guard paused by the car and glanced inside, then kept on looking when he saw Rob's hand up her skirt.

'Can we go please?' she asked, trying to pretend that he wasn't massaging her vulva in full view of a total stranger. 'Right now I need a shower more than anything in the world. How far away is the villa?'

He grinned at her and gave her clit a regretful squeeze. The security guard watched impassively as Rob withdrew his hand and put the car into gear.

'About thirty miles.'

They drove in silence for a while until the road they were following narrowed and began to wind up among pine-covered hills. Gemma could smell the evocative scent of the trees mingling with that of herbs and wild flowers. Below to the right she could see the moonlit Mediterranean and the lights of a fishing port strung out along the bay.

Without slowing down, Rob unzipped his khaki trousers and pulled out his cock.

'Suck me off,' he ordered without preamble.

'Rob – I'm hot and tired and until I've had a shower and something to eat, you can forget it.'

'Suck me off or I'll strip you and drive though the nearest resort at ten miles an hour.'

He would too – the bastard!

And, even though she was furious with him, a squirming little flicker of heat licked at her groin, making her shift edgily on the seat.

Reluctantly she unfastened her seat belt, then bent uncomfortably sideways and took his member in her hand. He wasn't quite hard, but she knew he would be soon. She didn't bother with any subtle preliminaries, just slid the full length into her mouth and sucked hard.

The taste and smell of him filled her head and she felt her own sex organs begin to heat up as his heavily knobbed cock throbbed in her mouth.

She lost track of time as she worked him to a climax. It could have been three minutes she spent with her head in his lap – it could have been thirty.

His body jerked and one hand buried itself in her glossy dark hair as he came, filling her mouth with a hot flood of creamy liquid.

Gemma knew he liked her to swallow, but for once she didn't feel like it. Instead, she sat up and spat into a tissue. He didn't comment but, glancing at the hard set of his jaw, she knew she'd pay for her action later.

She shivered in the warm night air.

As he drove south through London, Joe was dreading the return to his apartment.

The morning he'd awoken to find Mandy bouncing around astride him was the morning he'd been summoned to Scotland. He'd been unsure what to do about his wayward cousin and had ended up doing nothing, telling himself he'd deal with the problem when he got back.

As he lifted his case out of the car he decided that the

best course of action was to find her another flat, pay the first month's rent, then leave her to it.

But deep inside he knew it wasn't going to be that simple.

His first thought when he stepped inside the door was that he'd been burgled. The second was that Mandy must have given a party and he was going to kill her.

She was stretched out on the sofa watching a soap and wearing a pink Snoopy T-shirt, her baby-blonde hair tied up in two bunches with matching pink ribbons.

She looked sublimely unaware of the chaos of her surroundings. Every glass he owned was strewn around the room, many of them on their sides having disgorged their sticky contents into the pale carpet. Empty cans and bottles covered every available surface, as did ashtrays and saucers overflowing with cigarette ends.

His videos, CDs, cassettes and records were all out of their cases and a quick glance was enough to show that they were liberally spattered with drink and ash. From where he was standing he could see several burn marks on the furniture and even one on the cream sofa.

He was so angry that he couldn't move or speak. All he could hear was the blood pounding deafeningly through his veins. Mandy waved a casual hand in his direction.

'Hi, Joe. Good trip?' she greeted him, then her eyes flickered back to the TV.

He half expected a blood vessel to burst as he managed to say though gritted teeth, 'What the fuck has been going on here?'

'What? Oh, I just had a few people from the other flats round last night.'

She obviously thought the subject didn't merit any further

discussion because she yawned and stretched out even further on the sofa.

Fighting for self-control, Joe picked up the remote and zapped the TV.

'I was watching—' she began, but he cut across her.

'*A few people!*' he roared. '*A few people!*' Words failed him as his jaw moved but no further sound came out.

'What's the matter with you?' she demanded petulantly. She glanced around at the chaos as if seeing it for the first time. 'Don't get in a rage because we used a few glasses,' she said sullenly. 'Deirdre will soon clean it up, if you ask her nicely.'

Her tone indicated that the subject was now closed and she reached for the remote control again. He grabbed her by the arm and jerked her to her feet.

'And will she be able to clean that up?' he yelled, pointing at the burn on the sofa. 'Or that?' He indicated another on the table. When she didn't reply he shook her fiercely and noticed for the first time that she was naked beneath the T-shirt, which had now ridden up to expose the triangle of golden hair covering her mound.

She tried to pull away but he had her in a vice-like grip by the upper arm.

'Don't make such a fuss!' she retorted, and to Joe's astonishment stuck her tongue out at him.

In a blood-red mist of fury, Joe somehow found himself dragging her across his knee on the sofa. Like a thunder clap echoing around the room, he heard the sound of the flat of his hand making contact with the smooth pink and white skin of her bare bottom.

She howled and struggled to free herself, but to no avail

as his hand rose and fell, smacking down sharply each time and making her buttocks quiver and bounce.

Joe had never hit a woman in his life and would have been appalled by the idea that he ever might, but the sight of Mandy's little rump turning bright pink as he spanked her was one of the most satisfying he'd ever seen.

He didn't hit her with anything like the force he was capable of but, from the way she was howling, anyone listening would have thought he was beating her with a baseball bat. He could feel his fury abating slightly as he warmed to the task, adding a few slaps across the backs of her thighs for good measure.

What he didn't expect was to feel his cock hardening rapidly.

As it reared up beneath her wriggling, squirming stomach, he paused in confusion. She immediately took advantage of the fact that he'd relaxed his hold and scrambled off his lap. She retreated to a safe distance clutching her abused bottom, now a mass of pink splodges.

Her face was flushed, her eyes brimmed with unshed tears and her lower lip trembled as she stared at him reproachfully. As his anger receded it was replaced by a strong desire to throw her on the bed, spread her legs and give her the seeing-to of a lifetime.

He swallowed and fought for self-control.

He wasn't really the sort of scum who liked hurting women before fucking them – was he?

His dick seemed to be telling him that he was and it confused him.

He took refuge in anger.

'Now clear this mess up!' he ordered, turning on his heel

and heading for his bedroom. 'And put some clothes on!' he added, not wanting to have to look at her glowing backside knowing he'd caused it.

He slammed his bedroom door and sat on the bed. His dick was throbbing so urgently that he took it out and tossed himself off, trying to conjure up a vision of Sue lying wantonly under him on a bed of wet bracken and not his infuriating cousin's plump little rear bouncing under his hand as he spanked her.

He took a long cool shower then forced himself to go and see how she was doing. She'd pulled on a tiny pair of black lace panties, but they covered so little of her bum that most of his recent handiwork was still on view.

She'd picked up all the glasses and loaded them inexpertly into the dishwasher and was now on all fours on the carpet rubbing at a stain. Joe tried hard to shut out a titillating picture of going up behind her, pulling her panties down and thrusting into her, his balls slapping into her buttocks, reminding her what a bad girl she'd been, his cock buried up to the hilt in her juicy . . .

Shit!

She'd turned him into a sicko.

The sooner he got her out of his life the better.

She cleared up the worst of the mess, then retreated to her room. He'd never known her to be so subdued and suppressed a pang of remorse. He told himself that she'd had it coming – she'd done nothing but cause trouble since she'd arrived.

Maybe now she wouldn't be so keen to stay with him, not after she'd seen for herself what a brute he could be.

He drank a considerable amount of whisky, but sleep was

still a long time coming and when he did eventually drift off his dreams were full of dark and disturbing images.

He woke up to find a soft, warm body fitting itself against him under the quilt like a spoon. Before he knew what was happening, his cock was being guided into the slippery haven of a female honeypot from behind. He groaned and his hand slipped up her thigh and found her silken bottom which felt burning hot to the touch.

A wave of molten, shameful excitement swept over him, leaving him sweaty and trembling as he remembered spanking her and watching her rear turn bright pink under his punishing hand.

He caressed it while he humped her hard and fast, his other hand fumbling for her breasts in the enveloping confines of the quilt.

As soon as he'd grunted into a sticky, shuddering and very satisfying climax, she disentangled herself and slipped silently away into the darkness.

Gemma slept late and woke up to find Rob tying her hands to the bed-head before jamming his cock into her and screwing her vigorously.

The previous night he'd joined her in the shower and had soaped her thoroughly before spraying the needles of water from the shower onto her clit. He'd held her outer lips open with his other hand so the arousing jets could stimulate the swollen sliver of flesh from all directions.

She'd come quickly, her tiredness forgotten as he'd washed the day's stickiness from her. Afterwards, they'd gone to bed and fucked until the early hours when she'd fallen into a deep, sated sleep.

Her pussy must still be overflowing with their juices, he slipped into her so easily without even a preliminary caress. As she arched her back and writhed lasciviously under him, Gemma remembered her amorous encounter with her ponytailed companion in the plane toilet. She hadn't even asked his name, just used his mouth, hands and cock to pleasure herself shamelessly.

When they'd finished Rob pulled out of her and lay beside her, his head on her breasts, his hand toying lazily with her bush.

'Aren't you going to untie me?' she asked him, stretching languorously.

'Maybe. Maybe not. Perhaps I'll keep you lashed to the bed all weekend and invite all the local waiters to take it in turn with you while I watch.'

'Will you charge them?'

'I'll have to think about that one.'

There was a tap at the door and to Gemma's horror he called, 'Come in.'

The sheet was around her waist and she couldn't pull it up because her hands were still tied. She had to lie there half naked while a young Spanish girl entered the room carrying a tray.

To Gemma's astonishment the girl was also naked to the waist and her bush was only just covered by a tiny yellow triangle of material, held in place by two thongs, one in the cleft between her pert buttocks and the other around her hips.

She didn't seem remotely fazed to see Gemma tied to the headboard.

She smiled at them and put the tray down on the bedside table.

'This is Luisa,' he explained. 'She's the resident house-keeper. Luisa – Gemma.'

He seemed to think that took care of the introductions because he picked up a glass of orange juice and downed it in one go.

'*Buenas dias*,' the girl greeted her. 'I hope you enjoy your weekend. Please, just ask if there is anything you want.'

She looked about twenty and had a lovely sensual face, full red lips and a lush figure. Firm, heavy breasts with large olive nipples tapered down to a luscious backside.

'Thank you,' managed Gemma faintly. Luisa smiled again and padded out of the room on bare, tanned feet.

'Rob? Untie me this minute!' she snapped. 'How could you let her see me like this?'

'She's seen much worse – I've borrowed this villa from a Spanish film director notorious in the area for his wild parties. She didn't bat an eyelid.'

He untied her and she rubbed her wrists before slipping into a silk robe and helping herself to some coffee. Still fuming, she went over to the curtains and pulled them back to reveal a small tiled terrace. She opened the door and stepped out to be greeted by one of the most stunning views she'd ever seen.

The villa was on a hillside overlooking the Mediter-ranean, which gleamed a dazzling cerulean blue in the late-morning sunshine. The terrace seemed to be suspended above it among the tree tops because the surrounding area was wooded with tall pine trees.

Down below she could see the terracotta tiled roofs of several other villas and at the foot of the hill there was a small resort comprising a couple of hotels and a handful of bars and restaurants.

The narrow crescent beach was of white sand and tiny white-edged waves lapped at it. There were a few swimmers, but most people were stretched out either in the sun, or in the shade of brightly coloured umbrellas dotted at intervals along the sand.

Gemma stood and drank it all in, glad now that she'd allowed Rob to coerce her into coming. A couple of days' rest and relaxation was just what she needed – she'd worked nonstop for the last few months, rarely taking a day off as she put all her energies into making the agency a success.

She rested her coffee cup on the wooden rail around the terrace and looked directly down. Even better – there was a pool set on two levels linked by a waterfall.

A swim would be wonderful.

She went back into the bedroom, where Rob was just finishing a croissant, and delved into her case, pulling out a scarlet bikini.

'I'm going for a swim,' she told him.

'You won't need that – there's no one here but us.'

She ignored him and stepped into the briefs, then fastened the top into position. Rob swung his legs off the bed and came up behind her, cupping her small, uptilted breasts in his hands.

He stroked them and her nipples hardened instantly.

'It's a house rule,' he muttered persuasively into her ear. 'You can wear either the top or the bottom, but not both. You must always have something on display so I can touch you whenever I feel like it – now which is it to be?'

She hesitated.

139

'Unless, of course, you'd rather I took a knife to everything you've brought, then you'll have to go naked.'

He stopped caressing her and his hands closed on her bikini top. One yank and the thin strap holding the two triangles of scarlet fabric together broke and it fluttered to the floor.

Gemma went barefoot downstairs, the grey marble floor cool beneath the soles of her feet. The villa was sumptuously furnished in muted shades of grey and peach. She caught a glimpse of Luisa plumping cushions, but didn't stop.

She was uneasy about being bare-breasted. Topless sunbathing had been in vogue in Europe for decades now, but it wasn't something she'd ever done, as she didn't usually holiday in beach resorts. But as long as there was no one else around . . .

She dived into the pool and swam several lengths, her slender body cutting through the water like a seal. She had to admit that it felt wonderful on her naked breasts – her heavy nipples jutted out like acorns, the aureolas puckered and pitted by the cool water.

The small waterfall cascading from one pool to the next gushed over several rocks and she perched on one, letting the spray play over her. There was a splash and Rob dived into the lower pool. She idly admired his lean, tanned body as he swam stark-naked from one end to the other.

After a few lengths he climbed out and joined her on the rock. Without speaking he bent his head and took one succulent nipple in his warm mouth, which to Gemma felt red-hot in contrast to the drift of cooling spray falling on her. He sucked and tugged with his lips until she sensed the familiar heat building in her groin.

The sun beat down on her upturned face and a direct line connecting her nipples to her pussy twanged and tautened as he suckled at her breasts.

Suddenly he scooped her up and flipped her over so she was face down on her stomach on the sloping rock, legs dangling in the water. He dragged her scarlet bikini bottoms down around her thighs, parted her buttocks roughly with his hands and stabbed at the puckered bud of her anus with his tongue.

He probed and licked at it until she was squirming with a renewed surge of lust, then worked his way downwards until he reached the swollen entrance to her honeypot.

Instead of plunging his tongue into her as she expected, he forced her buttocks even further apart, then his heavily knobbed cock butted up against her dripping cunt.

She gasped as he drove into her and proceeded to piston in and out like a man possessed. It was a short and vigorous coupling but, even so, she came in a strong, body-racking series of shudders.

When she opened her eyes it was a shock to meet those of Luisa, who was setting the table on the terrace. The girl smiled enigmatically, then turned her back and continued with her task.

Joe woke up late on Saturday morning feeling like shit. Today was definitely the day Mandy moved out before he did anything else he regretted.

A soon as he'd got rid of her he'd phone Sue and see if she wanted to do something this evening. A night spent screwing another woman would soon wipe the unsettling memory of Mandy from his brain.

There was no sign of her and the door to her room was closed. With a faint feeling of relief Joe made himself coffee and poured some cereal into a bowl. He was seated at the table reading the paper when she emerged fifteen minutes later.

He looked up cautiously as she came into the room. She was wearing a short, pink, frilly nightie which plunged breathtakingly between her voluptuous breasts. He could see the tiny points of her nipples under the semi-transparent material and hastily averted his gaze.

'Do you want more coffee?' she asked, disappearing into the kitchen.

'No,' he said shortly.

When she came back into the room carrying a cup of tea and a packet of biscuits, she sat down opposite him.

'I thought you might take me out somewhere today,' she said, dipping a biscuit into her tea. 'After all, you haven't taken me anywhere yet, have you? I thought we could go to a posh restaurant for lunch. You know, somewhere the film people go. Then afterwards you can take me shopping – I need some new things.'

She munched her biscuit serenely while Joe stared at her aghast.

What the fuck was she talking about?

What went on in that candyfloss mind of hers? Why wasn't she repentant and subdued? Hadn't he got the message across last night?

'The only place we're going is flat hunting. I'm going to pay a month's rent on the first one we find vacant and leave you there,' he snapped. 'So as soon as you've finished breakfast I want you to pack your case.'

He braced himself for her reaction – he wouldn't let her tears or pleas sway him this time. She smiled at him and took another bite from a soggy biscuit.

'You know you don't mean that – you want me to stay here so you can have me any time you feel like it. Do you feel like it now?'

The terrible thing was that he did. However hard he tried not to look, his eyes kept being drawn to her thinly veiled breasts.

He felt perspiration gathering on his forehead and rose hastily to his feet and retreated towards his bedroom saying, 'Get dressed and packed – we're leaving in half an hour.'

No sooner had he closed the door behind him than she pushed it open again and stood provocatively in the doorway, one hand on her hip, the other on the doorframe. Her nipples seemed to be sending a mute but irresistible message that they wanted him to fondle them.

'Do you feel like it now?' she repeated, her voice a husky purr. He tried to speak but no sound came out. Slowly and seductively, Mandy slipped the thin straps of her nightie from her shoulders. It fell to her waist leaving an unfettered view of her luscious peaks.

Hips swaying, she strolled over to him and wound her bare arms around his neck. Her breasts, the nipples as hard as bullets, pressed into his chest and, in immediate urgent response, his dick leapt from semi-recumbent to bolt upright. Her hand slipped between them and rubbed it seductively.

'See – you do want me,' she said triumphantly. 'So what are you waiting for? Do you want to spank me first – is that it?' She moved away and, to add to his torment, bent over the bed and flipped her nightie up over her waist.

The full moons of her curvaceous buttocks taunted him, reminding him of just how satisfying he'd found slapping them the night before. In his few, still-functioning brain cells, he registered with relief that the pink splodges had faded, leaving her smooth skin unmarked.

To dampen down the white-hot excitement which consumed him, he tried to conjure up a memory of her as an annoying toddler or a precocious thirteen-year-old, but failed miserably.

She looked at him over her shoulder and wiggled her bottom.

'Come on – spank me again. I know you got off on it. I could feel how hard you were,' she murmured slyly. 'If that's what you like, I don't mind. Come on, Joe – remember how much you enjoyed it last night.'

Like a man in a dream – or was it a nightmare – he stepped forward and ran his hand over her backside, squeezing it like a piece of fruit he was testing for ripeness. She butted back against him, like a cat demanding attention, and he was unable to stop himself moving his hand down to feel between her legs.

Her silken bush was a moist tangle and, with a strangled groan he pushed his fingers roughly between her labia, unzipping himself with his other hand.

Satisfied that she was slick with anticipatory juices, he dropped his briefs and trousers to his knees and grabbed her by the hips. As he jammed his cock furiously into her she laughed softly. He gave it to her with barely restrained savagery, kneading her gorgeous breasts while he drove in and out as if his cock were engine-driven.

She pushed her well-rounded rump backwards against him, fuelling the fire of his angry lust as, with an alarming degree of pleasure, he remembered smacking it. When he came, he pumped his hot fluid into her until he was empty, then pulled out abruptly.

She turned around and sank down onto the bed, her pink frilly nightie bunched up around the waist, her legs apart showing him her deep-pink, well-fucked pussy, already leaking his juices onto the quilt cover.

'Well then,' she said gloatingly, 'now I think it's time for you to take me shopping. Oh and I'm short of cash – you can get me some while we're out.'

Without a word, Joe adjusted his clothing, picked up his jacket and left the apartment.

Chapter Ten

Gemma and Rob ate lunch on the terrace in the shade of a red-striped parasol with Gemma wearing only her damp bikini bottoms and a pair of sunglasses. Much to her discomfort, Luisa served them and Gemma was convinced the other girl kept looking at her breasts – she'd tried to cover up but Rob wouldn't let her, though *he'd* pulled on a pair of denim shorts.

When the housekeeper went back inside she said, 'Do we really need her here? After lunch, why don't you give her the rest of the day off?'

She knew she'd be much happier if it were just the two of them, then she'd gladly spend the afternoon naked.

'She comes with the villa,' said Rob, draining half his glass of ice-cold beer in a couple of gulps. 'Anyway, I like having her around.'

'Well I don't – she's making me very uncomfortable. She was watching us screwing by the pool earlier and I've never considered sex to be a spectator sport.'

'*She* probably does since she works for Carlos. She'll be used to remaking the bed around humping couples and even joining in sometimes.'

'And she keeps looking at my boobs.'

'Yeah?' smirked Rob. 'Carlos said she goes both ways.'

Oh great, thought Gemma irritably, just what I need. She recognised that Luisa had a gorgeous figure, but she didn't particularly want her lunch served by a topless waitress.

Luisa emerged at that moment with more food. As she unloaded her tray, Rob reached up and carelessly stroked her breasts. Gemma went pink and glared at them both, while Luisa smiled tolerantly and finished her task.

'Don't touch her like that in front of me – it's embarrassing,' snapped Gemma as soon as Luisa was out of earshot.

'She's got great tits – don't you think so?' he replied unperturbed, forking a slice of ham onto his plate.

'That doesn't mean you have to grope them.'

'They feel fantastic. Have you ever fondled another woman's tits, Gemma?'

'Hardly. Unlike our more cosmopolitan friend, *I* don't go both ways.'

'Wouldn't you like to try it?'

'Not particularly. What shall we do this afternoon?' she added, uneasy about the way the conversation was going.

'Siesta. Fuck. Beach.'

That sounded okay to Gemma – as long as the fuck was in the privacy of their bedroom.

It was after three when they emerged and set off for the beach. To Gemma's annoyance Luisa accompanied them and perched behind them on the hood of the Cabriolet, still naked from the waist up but now wearing more substantial bikini briefs and a pair of sandals. Gemma had pulled a T-shirt on over her bare breasts, saying she'd burn if she didn't cover up.

They hired three wooden sunbeds with blue-striped cushions and had them placed in the shade of a large straw umbrella. Luisa stretched out on her stomach, her head on her folded arms and smiled beatifically as Rob oiled her back.

Pretending to read a book, Gemma saw he was making a meal of it, skimming his fingers under the edges of her bikini bottoms and rubbing copious amounts of oil into her upper thighs.

No fool, Gemma was almost certain that he'd screwed Luisa at some stage before she'd arrived. Not that she really cared – they'd never had an exclusive relationship – but she didn't particularly want her nose rubbed in it.

When there wasn't a square inch of the housekeeper's olive skin not gleaming, she turned over. Rob held out the bottle to Gemma.

'You can do her front.'

'No thanks,' she retorted, without looking up from her book. He moved to sit on the bottom of her sunbed and lifted her dark glasses from the end of her small, straight nose.

'Do it for me,' he said softly. 'Oil her front, then let her do you.'

'I put some sunscreen on before we left the villa.'

'That's not the point. Do it because I want to watch.' His eyes, very blue in his deeply tanned face, caught and held hers and she felt herself being drawn into his sexual thrall.

Gemma could see where this was leading and she didn't like it one bit. It was a new one as far as she was concerned, although she was certain Rob had tried every permutation in the book. Up until now their sex life had only directly involved the two of them and she didn't want it to become three.

She'd come to Majorca for a weekend of sun, sea and screwing – but only with Rob. Now, as he turned the full force of his will onto her, she felt herself weakening.

Damn him.

He was the only man she'd ever met who could do this to her.

She snatched the bottle from him and went to sit on the edge of Luisa's sunbed.

'Is this okay with you?' she asked.

The other girl opened her thickly lashed dark eyes.

'Certainly it is. I find you *very* attractive.' The perfect oval of Gemma's pale face flooded with hot colour and she bent her head and let her dark hair swing forward to hide it, as she tipped some oil into the palm of her hand.

She started with the other girl's feet and worked her way up her legs, keeping her movements as brisk and business-like as possible. Luisa was built on sturdier lines than she was and her calf muscles felt strong and well exercised under Gemma's hands.

Her thighs were satin-smooth and tendrils of wiry dark hair sprang out from the edges of her bikini briefs. Sweat had gathered in the creases of her upper thighs and she shifted her bottom on the blue-striped cushion as Gemma applied the sunscreen.

Methodically, Gemma coated all the front of her body except her breasts, then paused. She didn't want to touch them – it seemed such an *intimate* thing to do. Large and heavily nippled, they were the same olive hue as the rest of her body. Luisa obviously didn't have any reservations about displaying them publicly so the sun's rays could reach them.

Gemma swallowed, then poured a lavish pool of oil into the palm of her hand. She circled the outer slopes at first, dipping into the girl's deep and perspiration-dotted cleavage. She could smell the musky scent of her body and kept circling, getting nearer and nearer to the jutting nipples which seemed to be taunting her to touch them.

Steeling herself, Gemma stroked oil into the puckered points and felt them harden instantly. It was a strange experience, knowing her touch was arousing the Spanish girl. She heard her make a faint purring noise deep in her throat, and with a slight shock she felt a surge of moisture soaking into her own briefs.

She found herself making a thorough tactile exploration, massaging, squeezing and kneading the full, firm breasts; flattening the nipples with the palms of her hands then letting them spring erotically upwards again. When both large orbs were gleaming with a thick coating, she stopped and handed the bottle back to Rob.

He didn't say a word, just gestured at her T-shirt.

Slowly, reluctantly, she pulled it over her head and lay swiftly on the sunbed on her belly.

He took a long time over her back and she was in a state of stomach-churning lust by the time he'd finished, particularly when the tips of his fingers brushed over the damp material between her legs. She was still in the shade of the umbrella, but even so she could feel the heat of the sun bouncing back at her from the sea and sand.

When he said, 'Turn over,' she kept her eyes closed behind her dark glasses and rolled onto her back. She felt

Rob's weight leave the end of the sunbed, then Luisa took his place.

Her hands felt small and somehow alien as she worked her way up Gemma's slender thighs. Her movements were slow and sensuous, as if she were giving a massage rather than applying a sunscreen. She smoothed over her stomach, then her shoulders, then there was a pause which had Gemma holding her breath in anticipation.

A few seconds later she felt a tiny dribble of oil around one nipple, then the other. Luisa's warm hand glided over her breasts, spreading the liquid and coating her pale skin. Even if she hadn't actually known, Gemma would have sensed it was a woman and not a man, something in the delicacy of the touch would have told her.

Even though she was uncomfortable with it, she felt the insidious eroticism of the situation – a woman she'd only met that morning handling her intimately on a public beach for the voyeuristic pleasure of her lover.

Or should it be *their* lover?

She felt her nipples harden and press against the hands moving over them so sensuously. A renewed surge of moisture between her legs told her she was enjoying it far more than she'd anticipated. The hands left her breasts, then she felt a feather-light kiss on her shoulder and it was over.

She rolled onto her stomach and opened her eyes to become acutely aware that their party was the main focus of attention on the small beach. Several men were staring at them unashamedly and had obviously been enjoying the show.

But not as much as Rob.

He was smirking triumphantly that yet again he'd got her

to do something she didn't want to and she'd ended up
enjoying it.

After leaving his apartment, Joe drove to his offices and
spent the day there. There was no one in except the duty
controller who greeted him without surprise – he often
called in at odd hours.

He sat at his desk trying to deal with some paperwork
and cursed himself for his stupidity in letting Mandy pro-
voke him into screwing her again.

Last night, the spanking he'd given her appeared to have
had the desired effect and she'd seemed chastened, but it
hadn't lasted long.

This morning she'd been right back on form.

Despite what he would have considered to be the over-
whelming evidence to the contrary, his infuriating cousin
obviously thought she had some claim on him – or rather
on what he could give her.

As if it wasn't bad enough that she'd moved in when
he'd made it plain she wasn't welcome, running up bills
with take-away food places and wrecking his apartment,
she now seemed to think that he should buy her clothes
and keep her as well.

What she needed was a rich lover who would set her up
as his mistress. As far as he knew she'd made no attempt
to get an Equity card, enrol for acting lessons or even get
the part-time job she'd vaguely mentioned. She occasionally
donned a pink leotard and practiced dance steps, but that
was as far as it went.

No, little Mandy had clearly come to the conclusion that
he could keep her in luxury in return for letting him fuck

her. But Joe had never paid for it in his life and wasn't about to start now.

That didn't mean he was tight – far from it, he was always extremely generous with his girlfriends. But taking them out for meals and buying them presents was a long way from Mandy's bare-faced demand that he refurbish her wardrobe and supply her with cash.

As he sat and brooded in the late afternoon, the fax machine clicked into life and began to disgorge sheets of paper onto the floor. He picked them up and started to read.

That was strange – another masked gunman had terrorised the staff and guests of the Paris hotel belonging to the group he advised, in an incident which sounded very similar to the one he'd witnessed himself.

Coincidence?

Joe didn't think so.

When the gunman who'd run amok in the London hotel had left after causing half an hour of havoc, he'd been put down as a psycho. He hadn't demanded any cash, so robbery wasn't his motive. After conducting an inquiry the police had filed the case away unsolved, particularly as no one was seriously hurt.

But a copycat crime in a sister hotel?

What was going on?

He didn't know, but he was going to find out.

His mind temporarily distracted from Mandy, Joe reached for the phone.

Sue was working on the hotel brochure when her doorbell went. She lived in a sunny, but untidy flat full of dying plants in Muswell Hill. She loved plants, but had difficulty in remembering to water them and was always having to throw them away and buy new ones. She'd have liked a cat but suspected she'd forget to feed that too, so resisted the temptation to get one.

She opened the door and started with surprise.

'Quentin!'

'Hello, Susan. I've been put to the trouble of coming to see you because you haven't returned my phone calls,' he greeted her coldly.

After the last time she'd spoken to him, Sue had been amazed when he'd left a couple of messages on her machine and then at work asking her to call him. She couldn't imagine he had anything to say that she wanted to hear.

'Aren't you going to ask me in?' he asked.

'I suppose so,' she returned ungraciously, stepping back from the door.

When she'd been seeing Quentin she'd been careful never to have him back to her flat. She knew from having seen his own immaculate apartment that he'd be appalled by the chaotic squalor she lived in.

She was right.

He looked around him, his patrician nose quivering with distaste.

'Have you been burgled?' he asked at last. Sue shook her head.

'Nope. It's always like this,' she told him cheerfully. He took a handkerchief out of his pocket and dusted one of the upright chairs before sitting on it.

'I assume you've thought over what I said to you when last we spoke?'

Sue couldn't actually remember what it had been – something about helping her rise above her unfortunate background or some other crap.

'No.'

Quentin looked taken aback, but obviously decided to continue anyway.

'I think we should start seeing each other again. I've said I'm prepared to overlook your behaviour in the hotel that night and I believe that to be a more than generous offer.'

Sue sank onto the sofa, wondering why she'd let him in.

'Are you referring to the fact I took my panties off in the ladies?' she asked, wondering what she'd ever seen in this pompous prick.

He flushed and looked down his nose at her.

'There's really no need to embarrass yourself by referring to it directly.'

'Quentin – have you at any stage asked yourself why I did that?'

He pursed his lips and looked annoyed that she wouldn't drop the subject. 'As I think I said at the time – you've been subjected to some extremely unfortunate influences.'

'I took my knickers off and then told you what I'd done because I was hoping you'd find the idea exciting. I was wrong and that made me certain we weren't in any way sexually compatible. Just out of interest – when would you have got round to making a pass at me, if ever?'

Quentin directed the sort of look at her which Sue could imagine quelling an entire courtroom.

'When after due consideration *I* decided it was propitious to take the next step in our relationship. This entire distasteful conversation only serves to convince me that you need my guidance. I'm prepared to resume seeing you on the understanding that you put yourself in my hands and let me direct your behaviour.'

Sue stared at him blankly. He sounded as if he was talking about a dog.

'But I don't want you to direct my behaviour,' she protested.

Quentin rose to his feet and towered over her as she sat on the sofa.

'No, but you *need* my direction, Susan. You need help to get yourself in order. Just look at this place – it's as disgracefully chaotic as the rest of your life.'

Sue couldn't think of a single thing to say. What had she ever seen in him?

She was spared the necessity of replying when he said sternly, 'Phone me when you've thought it over and realised I'm right.'

She showed him out, then sank back down on the sofa. What a good job she'd chucked him when she had – the idea of having him tell her what to do, as if she didn't have a mind of her own, was too awful to contemplate.

The phone rang at that moment, making her jump. she picked it up and said, 'Hello?'

It was Joe.

'Safely back from the wilds of Scotland?' he asked.

'I certainly am. Being in London seems like heaven after a sojourn in the back of beyond. Not that it didn't have its moments.'

They chatted for a while before Joe asked, 'Want to do something tonight?'

'I can't, I'm afraid. I'm going to the cinema with a friend

157

of mine, then we're going for something to eat.'

'How about tomorrow? I could pick you up around twelve and we could make a day of it.'

'That sounds like a good idea. See you then.'

After he'd hung up, Joe swung round on his chair, ran his hands through his sleek, dark hair and stared moodily out of his office window. Now he was going to have to go back to his apartment tonight, unless he checked into a hotel.

If he never saw Mandy again it would still be too soon. But he knew she'd be there waiting for him, her pouting mouth pink and inviting, her round blue eyes challenging, her curvaceous figure taunting him.

He dreaded to think what she might have been up to in his absence. But it was too late to take her flat hunting today, so he was stuck with her until Monday.

Chapter Eleven

Gemma, Rob and Luisa ate their evening meal on the terrace of a restaurant overlooking the sea. They were close enough to hear the hissing of the small, lace-crested waves as they broke on the gently sloping beach below, providing a pleasant background noise to the muted conversations taking place around them.

The warm night air felt good on Gemma's bare shoulders as she sipped her wine and absently nibbled at the plate of tapas on the table in front of her.

She was wearing a wisp of a short, ivy-green sleeveless silk dress which clung to her slender body like a second skin.

Underneath, she was completely naked.

She was well aware that her total lack of lingerie was obvious to anyone who looked closely enough. It had been bad enough examining her reflection in the bedroom mirror and seeing her nipples jutting eye-catchingly through the fine fabric, but her mound and the taut contours of her backside were also clearly outlined.

As they'd walked into the restaurant she could feel the silk slithering sexily over her pussy, catching for a moment between her pert buttocks and then freeing itself to whisper around her thighs.

She would have self-consciously imagined that every eye in the place was upon her, if it hadn't been for Luisa.

The Spanish girl was resplendent in a full-skirted, halter-necked, canary-yellow frock which dipped virtually to her naval at the front. Her magnificent olive-skinned breasts were barely contained by the narrow strips of material covering them and the outer circles of her aureolas kept popping into view every time she reached for her glass.

Gemma could see several nearby diners who were mesmerised by the sight and who were obviously waiting eagerly to see if a nipple would emerge. She almost choked on her tapas when she saw one man miss his mouth and accidentally stick his fork in his cheek instead.

She knew that Luisa, too, was naked under her dress. Before they'd left the house Rob had pulled up her skirt, revealing a thick thatch of wiry dark hair at the top of her strong thighs. He'd fondled her luscious buttocks, watching Gemma's face all the while, until she looked away embarrassed.

They ate in a desultory manner, none of them very interested in the food. Gemma was aware of a build-up of sexual heat between them which owed nothing to the actual temperature of the balmy Mediterranean night.

She suspected that if she had any sense at all, she'd already be on a plane back to London, but she was aroused despite herself. She didn't know exactly what Rob had planned and she knew she probably wouldn't like it, but nevertheless she was as horny as hell.

He kept touching them both; a hand on a satin-skinned

thigh, then a touch on a smooth shoulder, followed by a brush against a soft breast. It was a game he was playing, keeping them both like cats on heat. She could see it in the hungry gleam in Luisa's dark eyes – the other woman was obviously no stranger to sex games.

After the meal they left the restaurant with Rob in the middle, an arm around each of their waists. Gemma could tell that there wasn't a man in the room who wouldn't have paid a substantial sum to swap places with him.

He was looking ruggedly handsome, tanned to a deep brown after a location shoot in Madrid. Gemma would have put money on it that most of the women present wouldn't have kicked him out of bed, though how many of them would have been interested in a threesome involving another woman, she couldn't begin to guess.

They went to the resort's one nightclub, already smoky and packed, although it was only around eleven. Rob ordered a round of drinks and they sat in a dark corner and watched the floor show. Gemma went to find the ladies and when she returned Luisa had left her own seat and was sitting on Rob's knee.

Her chair was slightly turned away from them, so Gemma sensed rather than saw that Luisa was gently rotating her pelvis in an erotic circular movement.

It came to her in a sudden flash of awareness that somehow, under the cover of Luisa's full skirt, Rob had his cock inside her.

He was fucking her in full view of everyone, in a crowded nightclub.

She turned to look properly and her eyes met his. He grinned lasciviously and she felt her internal muscles clench.

Suddenly she realised that she wished he had his cock deep inside *her* pussy, that it was *her* on his knee, impaled on his throbbing member.

At that moment a voice to her right said, 'Hi there – we meet again.'

Turning her head, she saw her ponytailed travelling companion from the day before. She immediately saw a way to play Rob at his own game.

'Hello,' she greeted him huskily, 'how nice to run into you like this.'

'Do you mind if I join you?' he asked, indicating Luisa's empty chair.

'I'd rather dance,' she told him. Then, without a glance at Rob, she led the way to the dance floor. They edged their way between the closely packed bodies and he took her in his arms.

'Is it my imagination, or are you naked under this dress?' he enquired, after running his hands lightly over her back.

'It's not your imagination.'

She felt his dick harden and pressed herself against him.

'So, where's the lover boy you flew out to spend the weekend with?'

'He's the one with the girl in yellow on his lap.'

'What went wrong?'

'Nothing. Rob just likes to play games.' He digested this for a few moments while they continued to dance pressed closely together. 'In case you hadn't noticed, she's actually giving his cock a work-out while she sits there.'

He stared over into the corner and whistled silently.

'You want to do that too? With me, I mean.' She could feel by the way his member was rearing up against her stomach, that he was getting more excited by the minute.

'I'm wearing the wrong type of dress,' she pointed out. 'It needs one with a full skirt.'

'Pity. Want to find somewhere quiet down the beach?'

'Perhaps later.'

After a while she saw Luisa leave Rob's lap and walk towards the ladies, voluptuous hips swaying.

'Let's go over and I'll introduce you,' she suggested. 'What *is* your name by the way?'

'Nick.'

They went back to the table just as Luisa returned. Gemma performed the introductions, telling them she'd met Nick on the plane yesterday. Luisa licked her glossy red lips and seemed quite happy that he'd joined them, but Rob looked put out.

'Let's dance,' he said to Gemma.

'I need another drink,' she told him, beckoning for the waiter.

'What do you do?' Luisa asked Nick, leaning forward to give him the full benefit of her stunning cleavage. He looked suitably impressed and swallowed hard before replying.

'I own a recording studio in London.'

'Do you meet many famous people?' she was avid to know.

'Some. What about you? What do you do?'

'I'm a student for the most part of the year, but in the summer I work as a housekeeper in a villa here.'

'And I'm a TV producer.'

Rob was swift to jump in and attempt to dominate the conversation. He immediately launched into an account of his recent shoot in Madrid while Gemma drank another glass of wine. She was starting to feel the effects of the several glasses she'd consumed, but didn't care. One way or another she was going to need something to get through the night.

Luisa placed her hand on Gemma's arm, 'Why don't we dance while the men try to establish who is the . . . dominating male – is that the correct expression?'

'Dominant male,' Gemma said automatically. She looked at the two men. Yes, they were both jostling for conversational supremacy and taking no notice of the women. 'Good idea,' she agreed, rising to her feet.

They joined the swaying couples on the dance floor and fell into the rhythm of the soft music.

'He is handsome, your friend,' Luisa murmured. 'Will he join us later do you think?'

'I imagine there's nothing he'd like better.'

'Good. It will make it even more . . . interesting.'

'Do you do this sort of thing often?' Gemma was curious to know. Luisa smiled and moved her hips voluptuously to the music.

'If I find the people attractive – yes. Carlos, the villa owner, has many glamorous friends who come here. If I like to join in, I do. If I don't like to, I don't. Tell me – do you find me attractive?'

'You're beautiful,' Gemma admitted, 'but I've never been with a woman.'

'It's good. Who could know better than another woman what women like. Men, we need them, but they lack . . .'

'Subtlety?'

'Subtlety,' agreed Luisa, moving closer, then winding her

arms slowly and sinuously around Gemma's neck.

Gemma felt the soft cushiony pressure of the Spanish girl's breasts against her chest and smelt the musky scent of her perfume. She took a deep breath, then slid her own arms around Luisa's waist. They danced close together, hips swaying against hips, while other dancers regarded them with amusement and, in some cases, envy.

'Here comes Rob,' Luisa breathed into Gemma's hair. 'He's noticed us and he's ready for some more action. Shall we amuse ourselves and put on a show for him? And Nick too if you'd like that.'

Gemma nodded and when Rob put his arms around them and said, 'Shall we go, girls?' she smiled her agreement, but kept hold of Luisa's hand. Rob led the way off the dance floor on the opposite side from Nick and steered them towards the door.

Oh no you don't, thought Gemma and broke away.

'I'll just get Nick,' she told them.

'I don't want him there,' protested Rob.

'We do – don't we, Luisa?'

'Certainly we do,' affirmed the other girl. 'Don't be greedy, Rob.'

'Do you want to come back with us?' Gemma asked Nick when she reached him. 'I should warn you – it looks like being a wild time.'

'Count me in – as long as I don't have to make it with the guy – I only like women.'

They returned to the villa where Luisa took control and imperiously ordered Rob to pour drinks, then touched Gemma's hand and led the way up to a room she hadn't seen. It was obviously the master bedroom, large and luxuriously appointed, with a mirror on the ceiling over a huge bed, facing a deep squashy couch.

There was a wide verandah overlooking the pool and Luisa threw open the double doors which led to it, then arranged herself against a pile of soft pillows on the bed, beckoning Gemma to join her.

Through the open doors, Gemma could see a sprinkling of stars shimmering against the black velvet of the night. Some appeared to be perched on the outstretched branches of the surrounding pines, like lights on a Christmas tree.

The exotic sound of the cicadas drifted in and hung around the room, where the air was thick and heavy with sexual promise.

Nick lounged on the sofa and Rob handed out the drinks, then made to join the women on the bed.

'You sit there,' Luisa commanded him, waving at an easy chair a short distance away. He looked disgruntled that control of the evening was rapidly slipping away.

Luisa stroked Gemma's glossy sable hair, then kissed her, gently and sweetly. Her lips felt soft – much softer than any man's – and Gemma felt a stirring of sheer, erotic sensation deep in the pit of her stomach.

She relaxed and stretched out on the bed while Luisa kissed her neck, then her collarbone, then her breast through the flimsy material. Her nipple tautened in response to the heat of the other girl's mouth and she stirred languidly.

Luisa slipped the left side of the ivy-green dress down over Gemma's slender shoulder, baring one small, uptitilted breast, and the silence was broken by the sound of two aroused men swallowing hard in quick succession.

When Luisa began to stroke her silken orbs, one bare,

one silk covered, Gemma felt a direct response deep in her pussy. The other girl stroked her way down her belly, then ran the tips of her fingers over her mound.

Gemma felt her thighs pull apart as if they were attached to invisible strings, and knew from their barely suppressed grunts of excitement that both men could now see up her skirt to the soft, swollen outer folds of her honeypot.

Luisa began a gentle, insidious massage of her mound, still over her dress, then gradually began to dip lower until she was circling the swollen bud of Gemma's clit.

Unable to stop herself, Gemma drew her skirt up over her hips, exposing all her pussy to the hungry gaze of their audience.

She gasped when Luisa dipped her head and pressed her own warm lips to the outer lips of Gemma's private parts. It was like nothing she'd ever experienced before. The housekeeper had a sureness of touch which she'd never known from a man – however skilful a lover.

Her excitement mounted as Luisa rolled her tongue over the hot sliver of flesh which was her clit, then proceeded to lick her way sensually over her vulva, evoking tremors of uncontrollable excitement.

With delicate flicks of her wickedly knowing tongue, Luisa soon brought Gemma to the brink of orgasm. One last, swirling lick sent her over the edge and she cried out, her head thrown back and her spine arching.

She half opened her eyes to see Rob approaching, one hand on his zip, obviously all ready to plunge straight into her inviting, dripping pussy.

'Back!' ordered Luisa. 'We haven't finished here, so you must wait like a good boy.'

'I'm ready to come in my trousers,' he protested.

'What are you – fourteen years old?' Luisa derided him. 'Show some self-control please.'

Rob returned reluctantly to his seat while Luisa knelt on the bed in front of Gemma, her back to her, facing the men.

Gemma took her cue and knelt behind her, then reached up to undo the halter at the nape of her neck. The yellow material fell apart and Luisa's gorgeous, olive-hued breasts sprang out in all their gravity-defying magnificence.

Reverently, Gemma reached around her and covered them both with her small hands – or as much of them as she could, given their size. It felt wonderfully erotic to roll those large stiffened nipples between her fingers, then rub the palms of her hands over them. She tested their weight, enjoying their heaviness, so unlike her own delicate ones.

While the men watched, Gemma did all the things she liked having done to her and found she enjoyed it almost as much. While one hand continued to fondle Luisa's breasts she slipped the other up the full skirt of the yellow dress and found the thick thatch of damp hair which guarded the entrance to Luisa's hidden delta.

'We can't see,' Rob pointed out.

Gemma conceded he had a point, and anyway the dress was in the way, so she swiftly peeled it from the other girl's body, leaving her kneeling there completely naked.

'Rob – open the wardrobe door,' Luisa instructed him. The door was mirrored and when he'd opened it at an angle, Gemma realised that she could see their reflection.

It was the most visually erotic sight she'd ever seen.

Luisa was kneeling facing the mirror with her legs apart and her strong, supple thighs arrowing up to her nest of thick, dark pubic hair. Her satin-skinned breasts gleamed in the lamplight, one of them half covered by Gemma's paler hand, the nipple protruding between her parted fingers.

Without taking her eyes off their reflection, Gemma slid her other hand up Luisa's thigh until she reached her damp, wiry bush. She covered it and massaged it softly, the tips of her fingers separating the fronds of hair, until the deep-red nub of her clit was visible.

Holding her breath, she touched it, then inhaled sharply as a thrill of pleasure shot up her arm. Luisa moaned and leant back against her and she intensified the pressure, fascinated by the way the small point of flesh quivered under her touch.

Gemma couldn't take her eyes off their reflection in the mirror. Everything she was feeling was heightened by being able to watch.

She explored Luisa's wet, swollen pussy, aware for the first time how complex all those female folds must seem to a man. She stroked, pressed and rubbed the way she did when she was pleasuring herself, and was rewarded when she saw a clear snail's trail of lubrication creep slowly down the other woman's thigh.

Her knowledge of her own body made her acutely sensitive to the stages of Luisa's arousal. She knew when her climax was imminent and deliberately delayed it, moving her fingers away just as she felt the first muscle contractions begin, then die down again as the stimulus stopped.

In the mirror she could see that Luisa's eyes were glazed with lust.

'Please . . .' she murmured.

Gemma's fingers returned to her clit, stroking insidiously until the pressure built up again. She felt a swift surge of power knowing that all the attention in the room was directed at what she was doing between Luisa's legs.

Luisa's back was arched, pushing her luscious breasts towards their male audience, as if they were begging to be handled. Her thighs were wide apart, displaying her outer lips which were a dark engorged red.

Gemma felt Luisa's excitement as if it were her own and rubbed harder. When she felt the other woman was on the verge of climaxing she moved her hand away, but Luisa wasn't about to be baulked a second time.

Her own tanned hand dropped between her thighs and she finished what Gemma had started. Her full mouth opened to form a circle as she let out a low cry of ecstasy.

'*Ooooooooh!*' she moaned, pressing back against Gemma, who fondled her breasts gently as the spasms racked the voluptuous body.

Rob stood up and stripped off his trousers, revealing his massive, throbbing erection, then advanced towards them. Gemma could see the sheen of sweat on his brow and knew he'd been aroused beyond endurance by watching them.

Luisa turned her head and kissed Gemma on the mouth. 'Why don't you watch *us* now?' she suggested.

Like a woman in a trance Gemma crossed the room, one breast still bare, and joined Nick on the sofa. He reached for her hungrily, but his eyes were fixed on the couple on the bed.

Gemma had never seen anyone actually screwing before – unless she counted one time at Detroit's when she was working late.

She'd pushed open the door to the studio and found the senior art director vigorously humping the new account handler over the work surface. She'd caught a brief glimpse of his dome-like buttocks pumping energetically away and backed out again.

She'd found it curiously arousing and described it later to her lover of the time. He'd wanted them to creep into the building and do the same, but Gemma was too nervous about being seen – she had her position to think about after all – so he'd settled for taking her back to his flat and shafting her over the dining-room table.

Now, Gemma sat close to Nick, his arm around her shoulders and his hand on her bared breast, while they watched the tableau unfolding on the bed.

She knew that he wanted to screw her urgently, but the desire to play voyeur was stronger still.

Luisa sank back so she was half reclining against the pile of pillows and Rob thrust another under her hips and spread her legs, bent at the knee. For a few moments they could all see her vulva, wet and partially unfurled like the petals of crimson peony after a shower of rain.

Then he knelt between her thighs, pulled her legs up over his shoulders and plunged into her. From where they sat it almost looked more like fighting than fucking. What had taken place between the two women had been languid and sensual – this was hungry and animal.

Luisa writhed around beneath him as he thrust in and out of her, bucking as if she was trying to throw him off. Her nails raked his back leaving red weals until he grabbed her wrists and held them over her head, fastening his mouth over one distended nipple and sucking hard.

In a flurry of heaving limbs, she suddenly rolled on top of him and bore triumphantly down, riding him wildly as his hips reared rhythmically upwards, giving her a hard, fast ride.

They were both gasping and panting as they continued to wrestle on the bed, only their pelvic movements keeping perfect time.

But Rob wanted to be on top again – that much was obvious – and he seized her by the hips and pulled her back down on the bed. In the ensuing struggle they separated and his cock slipped out, glistening with her copious juices.

He grabbed her and pushed her over the cushions on her stomach, briefly giving their audience of two an intoxicating view of the full, firm globes of her buttocks, before throwing himself on her and impaling her from behind.

It was all too much for Nick.

At some stage he'd unzipped himself, releasing his impatient dick from the constraints of his clothing and now he dragged his jeans, briefs, socks and shoes off in one clumsy movement.

Gemma swung her legs up onto the sofa and reached out for him. His cock slid between her legs; a huge, hungry, throbbing organ, and filled her up completely.

In the balmy Mediterranean night they began their own gasping, panting, perspiring ascent into the ecstasy of mutual release.

Chapter Twelve

It was with great reluctance that Joe returned to his flat that evening. To put off going back, he'd had a meal he wasn't hungry for and had then gone to the cinema to see a film he didn't want to see.

He felt vaguely ridiculous that he was letting the antics of an eighteen-year-old girl get to him so much that he felt he couldn't go home. With some difficulty, he resisted the temptation to book into a hotel.

On Monday he'd see to it that she left for good, then she'd be out of his hair once and for all.

When he arrived she was sitting cross-legged on the floor surrounded by empty take-away containers from the local burger bar, reading a magazine.

'Where have you been until this time?' she demanded petulantly as soon as he came into the room. 'I thought you were going to take me somewhere nice.'

'You thought wrong,' he retorted shortly, going into the kitchen to get himself a beer. He went out onto the terrace, hoping she wouldn't follow him, but it was a short-lived hope.

The river smelt of effluent and ozone on this warm, late

summer night. A passing boat tooted and the sound echoed mournfully off the apartment building, then bounced against the warehouse on the opposite bank.

Mandy was wearing a short, baby-blue T-shirt dress which clung to her curves and made it obvious, even at a cursory glance, that she wasn't wearing a bra.

He sat at the patio table and she immediately perched on it in front of him, allowing her dress to ride up and affording him a close-up view of her beige lace panties and matching suspender belt which was holding up a pair of tatty, snagged stockings.

'I've been here on my own all day,' she complained. 'Hurry up and drink that and then you can take me to a club.'

He tried not to look up her skirt but it was difficult because she was only inches away.

Was that a suspicion of a damp patch on her crotch?

He felt his treacherous, misguided dick stirring as if anxious to take a look for itself and shifted his position on the slatted wooden chair. She saw him looking and opened her legs a couple of inches, then stroked her own thigh suggestively.

'Come on, Joe. We didn't go anywhere together earlier – the least you can do is take me clubbing now. It *is* Saturday night after all.'

'Forget it. Go inside, Mandy – I don't want you hanging around me the minute I get home. In fact go and sit in your room.'

'You don't really mean that.'

She slid to her knees on the cold tiled floor, deftly unzipped his trousers and reached inside. He willed his dick to show no interest whatsoever in the proceedings, but it sprang disloyally out, not totally tumescent, but certainly not as limp as he would have liked it to be.

She leant forward and fanned it with her warm breath and it immediately hardened perceptibly.

'Nearly,' she said with satisfaction, 'it just needs a *little* more encouragement.'

She turned sideways, still kneeling up, dragged her dress up around her waist, then pulled her panties down to her knees. She bent forwards from the waist and thrust her bottom in the air so he could see it in all its luscious, smooth-skinned glory, each perfect buttock neatly divided by a beige satin suspender.

The effect was electric.

His throat thickened with lust and his cock sprang into eager, pulsating life, the veins standing out like cords on a badly tied parcel.

He groaned and tried to block out the tormenting images which crowded to the front of his brain and jostled for position there.

It was useless.

He remembered his hand rising and falling on her bare backside as she lay across his knee and itched to re-enact the scenario.

Only this time he'd bend her over the table in front of him, make her peachy little rump smart, then fuck her over it in the same position.

That would teach her.

Or would it?

He doubted it somehow.

She was smiling up at him tauntingly and he closed his

eyes and gripped his can of beer as if it were a lifeline, trying to summon up the self-control not to touch her.

At that moment he felt her warm, wet mouth sliding down his cock and knew that he was lost. He let his head fall back and gave it to her, letting her suck away as if his member were a stick of rock in her favourite flavour.

He wondered fleetingly how she'd learnt so much about sex at her tender age – he hated to think how soon she'd started. Then, as she drew him into the familiar spiral of arousal, he gave himself up to disturbing but deeply erotic fantasies.

He imagined her bent over and touching the toes of her spike-heeled shoes, wearing only a black basque with her breasts spilling out, the rounded cheeks of her bottom already quivering from the first satisfying smack from the palm of his hand. He'd pause, making her wait for the second one, then smack her sharply again.

And again.

And again.

Or he'd make her crouch on the dining table on all fours, spine curved and bum well up in the air, wearing a scarlet bra and a tiny pair of matching panties. First, he'd drag the panties right up into the cleft between her buttocks, leaving them without even the scantiest protection, then he'd slap her high up on the right one and stand back until a faint red mark appeared. Then he'd slap the left one, aiming for exactly the same place until he'd gradually worked his way down to the tops of her thighs.

Or he'd lie her on the bed on her stomach over a pile of pillows, wearing the frilly pink nightie. He'd peel it up to her waist then rain fast, stinging smacks onto her provocative rear until his hand smarted. Then he'd take his dick out and ...

A voice penetrated the thick fog of Joe's dark, shaming fantasies.

His eyes flew open and to his absolute horror he saw his neighbour Alicia, a commodities broker, sitting at her own table on the adjoining terrace, talking into her mobile phone.

Only her head was visible and, as long as she remained seated, that was all she'd be able to see of him too. But if she stood up she'd see instantly that he was having fellatio performed on him by his eighteen-year-old cousin.

His eyes flickered wildly from her to Mandy and he wondered how long she'd been there. He heard his unwelcome house-guest laugh softly and knew she'd realised he'd just noticed that they weren't alone.

Then he suddenly lost interest in Alicia's presence as he erupted like a geyser deep into Mandy's throat, emptying himself uncontrollably in a series of hot, savage spurts, his hand buried in her soft blonde hair.

She withdrew her mouth and swallowed, while he clumsily zipped himself up with shaking fingers.

'Pull your panties back up before she sees you,' he managed to hiss.

She sat back on her heels, her dress still around her waist, and licked lips shiny with his juices.

'I thought you liked my bottom.' she taunted him. 'You certainly get hard enough whenever I show it to you.'

'*Mandy*! For fuck's sake!'

He could tell that Alicia was winding things up on the phone, and was terrified she was going to stand up.

177

'Tell me you like my bottom,' Mandy goaded him, stroking it tormentingly. 'Tell me or I'll climb on the table so she can see me.'

'I like your bottom!' he said desperately. 'I adore your bottom! I can't get enough of it!'

A slow, triumphant smile spread over her angelic face and she drew her panties slowly over her hips then rose sinuously to her feet so her dress fell back down over her thighs.

Not a moment too soon.

The commodities broker rose to her feet, nodded to them and went back inside.

'Can we go to a club now?' Mandy asked him.

Joe drew his forearm over his sweating brow, lurched to his feet and went inside where he locked himself in his room with a six pack of beer, ignoring her when she banged petulantly on the door.

The following morning he rose early, showered and left without even having coffee, telling himself that this was the last day he'd be driven out of his own flat.

He found a café open near the Embankment and enjoyed a large fried breakfast while he read the Sunday papers. Afterwards he went to the office intending to do a couple of hours work before he went to pick up Sue.

Big Eddie was just going off duty and, while exchanging a few casual words, Joe was struck by an idea. Eddie was one of his oldest employees, a giant of a man with a shock of red hair and a pushed-in face, whose very appearance was usually guaranteed to strike terror into the hearts of potential miscreants.

Six foot five, arms like hams and a neck almost as wide as Joe's waist, Eddie could always be trusted to follow instructions to the letter. What he lacked in brain power he made up for in thoroughness.

'It's your day off tomorrow isn't it, Eddie?' Joe enquired.

'Sure is, boss.'

'Do you think you could do something for me? I'll pay you double time and you'd be doing me a big favour.'

'Yuh? What?'

'I need someone to take my cousin around a few flat agencies, find her somewhere to live then get her settled in. Could you do that?'

'No problem.'

Joe gave Eddie the list of flat agencies and authorised him to pay the first six months' rent on anywhere he thought suitable. He'd only planned to pay the first month's rent on Mandy's behalf, but unfortunately most agencies demanded six months' in advance.

And anyway, he had a shrewd suspicion that after a month Mandy would be still be unemployed and undoubtedly end up on his doorstep again as soon as she was thrown out for non-payment of rent. Although he didn't hold out any high hopes that she'd be any nearer to gainful employment after six months, she'd almost certainly have found herself another meal ticket by then.

Eddie agreed to pick her up at nine-thirty the following morning and Joe felt like an enormous burden had been lifted from his shoulders.

He did some paperwork, then went off to Muswell Hill to collect Sue.

She looked gorgeous.

179

Her streaky blonde hair hung like a golden cloud around her heart-shaped face and her large almond eyes were hidden behind a pair of dark glasses perched on the end of her small, uptilted nose.

She was wearing a navy and white striped fisherman's T-shirt with a wide neck, which kept slipping to expose one bare, tanned shoulder. Her jeans were skintight and moulded to the luscious contours of her backside.

He wanted to peel them off her as she stood there, but instead contented himself with pulling her into his arms and kissing her hard.

'You look fantastic,' he said, wondering whether a quickie might be on the cards before they went out.

She read his mind.

'Not a chance,' she said determinedly. 'I spent all day cooped up in here yesterday working and today I want to go out. I know what will happen if we go to bed – we'll stay there and I don't have any food in.'

Joe wondered briefly why he never seemed to meet women who wanted to cook for him – all his girlfriends expected to eat out. He slipped his arm around her as they went downstairs.

'Where do you want to go?' he asked her as they emerged into the brilliant sunshine.

'What about Windsor or somewhere on the Thames? We could have a pub lunch then hire a boat or something.'

'I thought you hated the country,' he teased her. 'You couldn't wait to get back from Scotland.'

'There was nothing there – just miles and miles of depressing moors. The countryside around London's different – you can't move for hotels, pubs and tea shops – which is just the way I like it.'

On the drive out, he told her about the copycat gunman holding up the Paris hotel.

'What do you think that's all about?' she asked.

'Hard to say – it could still be coincidence but I can't see it. I'm going to get hold of a copy of the French police reports and see if I can spot any leads.'

They had lunch at a pub on the Thames which was so packed that they had to sit on the grass outside to eat their sandwiches and chips.

Sue was enchanted when a duck, followed by half a dozen fluffy ducklings, swam up. She fed them her crusts and tried to entice them out of the water, but the duck flapped its wings and quacked warningly and the ducklings hastily retreated.

'Shall we find somewhere to hire a boat then?' she said when they'd finished.

'What sort of boat?'

'A rowing boat. I'll lounge on a pile of cushions with my hand trailing in the water while you show off your muscles by rowing us upstream.'

Joe had been afraid she was going to say that.

His only experience of rowing was on a boating lake in a municipal park in Cheshire when he was a teenager.

Rowing up the Thames seemed to be an enterprise fraught with difficulty. It would be hard work for one thing. As well as that, if he remembered correctly, he'd have his back to the direction he was going, so if he didn't get the boat tangled up in fisherman's lines, he would probably row it over a weir.

'Let's see what there is on offer,' he suggested evasively.

Luckily there were also dilapidated motor boats available, although Sue still wanted a rowing boat.

'I'll be shagged out before we've gone half a mile,' he protested. 'This way we'll both be able to sit back and enjoy the scenery.'

The boat's top speed must have been five miles an hour and, after leaving a deposit which Joe thought would have been more appropriate for hiring a yacht, they chugged slowly upstream belching blue smoke.

It was a still, lazy afternoon – a perfect summer's day. They passed a string of millionaires mansions with gardens leading down to the river.

'Doesn't it make you feel like you've never achieved anything?' asked Sue. 'I'll never be able to afford anything like that – however hard I work.'

'I thought the agency was doing well.'

'It is. But Gemma and I aren't taking much out and probably won't be able to for a long time – if ever. I'm still living in the same scruffy flat in Muswell Hill. What's your place like?'

'Okay – it's a wharfside apartment, but not on the same scale as this lot. You must come round and see it – how about one evening this week?'

'That would be good.'

They passed a house where a garden party was in full swing. The sight of all those people sipping drinks made Sue thirsty again.

'We should have brought a bottle of something,' she remarked.

'We can always stop at the next pub.'

'True enough.'

The houses came to an end and they slid past open fields, the grass yellow and parched after the dry summer. When they passed a weeping-willow tree dipping its branches into the murky waters of the river, Sue suggested they tie up for a bit.

The battered motor boat slipped between the branches and they found themselves under a green canopy of pale willow leaves with shafts of sunlight slanting through and hitting the water and the dark moss of the bank.

Sue scrambled to her feet and leapt ashore, making the boat rock so much that Joe was nearly thrown in. He tied it to an overhanging branch and joined her.

'Gosh it's hot,' commented Sue, fanning herself. 'I should have brought a bikini – there's no one around, I think I'll just cool off for a minute.'

She stripped off her T-shirt, revealing her full, delectable breasts in all their naked glory.

'That's better,' she said contentedly, laying the T-shirt out on the moss and collapsing onto it on her back.

Joe couldn't tear his eyes from her creamy orbs, the deep pink nipples pointing pertly skywards.

'Why don't you take your jeans off too?' he suggested in a thickened voice.

'They'll take too long to get back on if anyone comes along,' she pointed out.

He managed to tear his eyes from her for long enough to glance around. They were completely hidden from view. The river was in front of them and a copse of trees behind. To be seen, someone would have to actually duck under the branches of the tree – and they'd hear them coming.

'We'd hear them long before they saw us,' he pointed out and moved over to kneel beside her. He covered one luscious breast with his hand and bent to close his mouth over the other.

'Mmm,' murmured Sue, 'sunshine always makes me randy.'

Joe traced a slow path downwards over her warm skin, grazing over her navel until he reached the zip on her jeans. He pulled it slowly down, revealing a pair of plain white cotton panties.

'You'll have difficulty getting my jeans off,' she teased him, folding her arms behind her head. 'I've put weight on since I bought them.'

She obligingly raised her rump and he hooked his fingers in the waistband and tried to pull them off, but it was as if the denim was glued to her skin and they wouldn't budge.

'You'd never make a rapist,' she told him as he struggled with them.

'Some help wouldn't go amiss – kneel up.'

She scrambled to her knees.

'You take the back,' she suggested, grabbing the waistband at the front. Between them they managed to peel them down, taking the white cotton panties with them.

Joe's head swam and he had to cough to clear his suddenly clogged-up throat as her glorious backside came into view, turned a luminous gold by a sudden shaft of sunlight filtering down through the branches.

For a few brief moments her silken derrière looked as if it had been cast in bronze, before a breeze stirred the tree and the shaft of sunlight vanished as suddenly as it had appeared.

She was kneeling in exactly the position Mandy had assumed last night on the terrace when she'd been determined to coax an erection from him. The only difference was that he didn't want to slap Sue's gorgeous bottom, he wanted to worship it.

On his hands and knees, he bent down and laid his cheek against it. It felt warm and smooth against his skin, making him aware that it was several hours since he'd shaved and he already had a stubble.

He turned his head and kissed it hungrily, tasting and licking, plunging his tongue into the cleft between her firm buttocks and exploring that damp, intoxicating valley. He nuzzled, browsed and grazed there in the leafy shade of the willow tree, while Sue knelt motionless in front of him.

When his questing tongue worked its way so far forward that he encountered the first sticky fronds of her bush, he raised his head long enough to mutter, 'Stand up.'

She rose from her kneeling position and he turned her round so his face was against her mound. He parted her legs and buried his face in her pussy, pushing his tongue into her as far as it would go.

His cock felt like a great big, aching, throbbing thing rearing up from his loins. It had caught uncomfortably in the elastic of his briefs and he unzipped himself and released it.

Once out, it twitched impatiently like a conductor's baton and he stumbled to his feet, unable to ignore its demanding message any longer.

Sue backed up against the trunk of the willow tree, naked except for her sandals and a fine gold ankle chain. His hands fastened over the firm, blossoming, swelling points of her breasts and he kissed her, his cock pressing hard against her stomach.

She took it and guided it to the moist, expectant entrance to her honeypot and he slid it smoothly into her, making her gasp as it forged its way deep into her core.

He put one arm behind her to protect her naked back from the rough bark of the tree trunk and screwed her lengthily, until his knees, which were bent to compensate for the difference in their heights, felt as if they were going to give way beneath him.

One last thrust and he came inside her, discharging his load high up in her pussy.

'Got to sit down,' he gasped, as the strain on his leg muscles became unbearable.

Sue's own climax had left her weak and quivering and she nodded her agreement. They tried to sink down onto the moss still joined at the groin, but to no avail and they separated prematurely.

They lay side by side too sated to speak until suddenly Sue exclaimed, 'Bloody hell!'

'What's up?' Joe hastily fastened his trousers, half expecting someone to appear beside them.

'The boat – it's gone!'

They peered out through the branches of the tree, but there was no sign of it.

'Oh dear – now what are we going to do?' wailed Sue.

'Set off walking,' was the best Joe could come up with.

Sue dried herself off with some tissues and pulled her clothes back on. They pushed their way out from beneath the willow and set off through the copse of trees. The sun beat down mercilessly and the walking was rough enough to make Sue curse as she turned her ankle for the third time.

'Surely we should have come to a road by now?' she said, leaning against him to adjust her sandal.

'I would have thought so,' he agreed. At that moment they both heard the unmistakable sound of a car in the distance.

'Thank goodness for that,' she breathed. 'Now let there be a pub somewhere in sight and I'll consider the afternoon redeemed.'

The road was deserted, but at least it was a road. After a couple of minutes another car came along and Joe attempted to flag it down, but to no avail. They trekked another mile or so with their thumbs out and were eventually picked up by a van driven by a teenager wearing a T-shirt emblazoned with the words, 'If you're over twenty – you're dead.'

He told them that the front seat belt didn't work and they'd have to get in the back which was unbelievably hot, scattered with dirty straw and smelt disgustingly of dung and animals.

'Nice T-shirt,' commented Sue, trying to breathe through her mouth as they careered along the narrow, winding lane at around seventy-five miles an hour. 'Do you think he means it? Will our dismembered bodies be found in a shallow grave some months from now?'

'I don't know – but if they are, they won't smell any worse than we're going to by the time we get out of here. Or maybe he means that anyone over twenty is likely to die of fright doing this speed on a road like this.'

Thankfully their journey was brief and he dropped them at the boathouse a couple of minutes later.

Joe had geared himself up to a heated argument vis-à-vis

the missing boat and the huge deposit he'd left, but luckily the boat had floated back downstream and been
retrieved by the owner.

He seemed disinclined to refund all the deposit as a
punishment for their carelessness, but seeing the man
blanch when he caught a strong whiff of a sweat, sex and
animal dung, Joe moved closer to him and continued to
argue the toss. After a couple of minutes the man refunded
the money just to spare his olfactory nerves.

'Dare we go in a pub reeking like this?' he asked Sue. 'I
could murder a pint.'

'Only if I can wait outside – I couldn't face the embar-
rassment of people moving away.'

In the end they bought a couple of cans of lager from
the village shop and drank them heading back to London.

Chapter Thirteen

Joe spent the night at Sue's flat and returned to his own apartment early in the morning to find Mandy still asleep.

'Wakey wakey,' he said cheerfully, throwing open the curtains.

She opened her eyes and blinked at him like a small, furry animal awakened from several months' slumber.

'Where were you all day yesterday?' she demanded sleepily. 'Do you think it's any fun for me being left on my own all the time?'

'I think I can safely promise you that it won't happen again. Get up, get dressed and get packed. Eddie's coming to help you find a new flat in about an hour.'

'What? Who's Eddie?' she asked sharply, sitting up so that the quilt fell from her naked breasts.

Joe hastily left the room.

When he'd heard no sign of movement after twenty minutes and she hadn't emerged, he went back in, dragged her case out and began to empty the contents of the drawers into it.

She stirred beneath the quilt and then sat up.

'What are you doing? Stop it!'

'I'm packing for you as you aren't showing any inclination to pack for yourself. Now get up.'

She still didn't move, so with a sudden movement he jerked the quilt off her and carried it out of the room. In the kitchen he stripped the cover off and stuffed it in the washing machine.

'Fetch the sheet and pillowcases in when you've dressed,' he called.

She appeared behind him pink and naked; a sly, seductive smile on her lips.

At that moment the doorbell went and Deidre let herself in with her pass key. Mandy immediately bolted back into her room.

'Has the little madam not gone yet?' Deidre asked, sniffing. 'I only agreed to come because you told me she was moving out.'

Joe had taken the precaution of asking her to come round early to clean the flat, knowing that her presence would stop Mandy from trying her usual tricks.

'Not yet. I can't get her out of bed and one of my employees is coming to take her to find her a new flat in a few minutes. Can you help at all?'

Deidre sniffed again and marched into Mandy's room. Joe couldn't hear what she said, but a few minutes later Mandy came out in her dressing gown and stalked into the bathroom carrying her clothes. A few minutes later she was dressed.

'Eddie – this is Mandy,' he introduced them as soon as his employee arrived. 'Mandy – Eddie's going to move you into your new flat.'

He handed Eddie Mandy's case and then took out his

wallet. He peeled off a wad of notes for the deposit and handed them to his employee, then swiftly counted out a hundred pounds and handed them to his cousin.

'That's to keep you going until you find a job,' he told her. 'Goodbye.'

'Good weekend?' asked Sue when Gemma came into her office. Gemma's usually pale face had a light tan and a sprinkling of freckles had appeared over the bridge of her small, straight nose.

'Great thanks – except I had to get up at four this morning to get an early flight back.'

'How was Rob?'

'Full of himself as usual, but the sex was fantastic.' Gemma stretched voluptuously and Sue hid a smile. It had come as a surprise to her to discover that despite her cool façade, Gemma was as hooked on sex as she herself was – perhaps even more so.

They'd never been close but the subject cropped up fairly frequently in their conversation.

'I'm deeply envious that you got a weekend somewhere hot. All I've had this year have been a few lousy days in Scotland.'

'At least yours were free – my plane ticket cost the earth. I had to travel first class because all the cheaper seats were booked up. Still, I met a *very* attractive man on the plane and then ran into him again the following evening.'

Gemma smiled a cat-like smile which spoke volumes.

'Not the mile-high club?'

Gemma nodded.

'And the following evening?'

'It was quite a party. How was your weekend?'

Sue told her about her day with Joe. They were interrupted by the phone.

'It's for you.' Sue handed the phone to Gemma and returned to her work.

'That's interesting,' Gemma said when she'd put the receiver down.

'Uum? What is?' asked Sue, looking up.

'The hotel chain want to bring forward next month's big meeting to next week – I wonder why?'

'We'll know soon enough. What do you think about this as a headline?'

Sue didn't see Gemma again until late afternoon and when she did, she looked ill. Her face was bone-white and the sprinkling of freckles over her nose stood out in startling contrast.

'What's up?' asked Sue in alarm. Gemma sank into a chair.

'I think you'd better pour us both a drink. That was Alan from Detroit's on the phone – he's heard that they're going to sue us for loss of earnings because we brought the bread account with us when we left. He thought he'd warn us so it wouldn't be too much of a shock when we get the solicitor's letter.'

Alan was the production manager at their old agency and an ex-lover of Gemma's.

Sue rose shakily to her feet and poured two generous shots of whisky. They both gulped them down and looked at each other.

'We can't afford to fight an expensive court case – even

if we win, the legal fees alone would wipe us out, unless we were awarded costs,' groaned Gemma. 'And that's a very big if.'

'And if we settle out of court, any sum they'd agree to would also be more than we could afford,' said Sue gloomily. She poured them both another drink. 'Why are they doing this now?' she continued. 'It's six months since we left. Why not then?'

'They were probably waiting to see if we'd go out of business. They've obviously heard that we're doing well and decided to move in for the kill. Shit!'

The two women sat in silence for a while.

'We need an expert opinion on this,' Gemma decided. 'Do you still have your contract of employment from Detroit's?'

'I'm not sure,' replied Sue vaguely. 'Why?'

'It may have something relevant in it. I think mine's at home. Have a look for yours and I'll phone our solicitor. I think I'm going to go home – it's been a long day. See you tomorrow.'

When Joe got home that evening he found his flat clean, tidy and most important of all – *empty*.

The bed in the spare room had been remade and all traces of Mandy expunged, including the drifts of talcum powder she left all over the flat, particularly the bathroom, where it had been a constant irritation to him, settling like scurf on the pristine surface of the black carpet.

Deidre had gathered up various possessions that Mandy had left behind and put them in a box in the kitchen. Joe was tempted to dump them down the rubbish chute, but decided instead to have Eddie drop them off at her new flat.

He had a shower, then stretched out on the sofa in his black towelling dressing gown to enjoy an evening of solitude. There was beer cooling in the fridge, Deidre had restocked the freezer with TV dinners and there was a film he wanted to watch on the TV. His throat felt sore, so an evening in was probably a good idea.

Tomorrow or Wednesday, he decided, he'd have Sue over. They'd send out for something to eat and have it in bed between bouts of carnal enjoyment. He hadn't dared have anyone back while Mandy was in residence.

The buzzer connected to the downstairs door went.

'Hello?'

'Boss – it's Eddie.'

'Hi, Eddie, come on up.'

Joe left the front door slightly ajar and returned to the sofa. Good old Eddie. To show his appreciation he'd make sure he got any cushy jobs going for a while.

When there was a bang at the door a few minutes later, he called, 'Come in – it's open!' and turned round ready to ask his employee if he wanted a beer. The words died on his lips when he saw that Eddie wasn't alone.

Mandy was with him.

'What the fuck are you doing back here?' he demanded furiously. To his horror he saw that Eddie was carrying her suitcase. 'What the fuck's going on?'

Eddie looked at him reproachfully. 'There's no cause to use language like that, boss.'

Joe felt there was every cause.

'Why have you brought her back here? I told you to find her a new flat!' he said wildly. He felt the blood ringing in his ears as he looked huntedly from one to the other.

Mandy had perched on the edge of an armchair and was wearing an expression he'd never seen before. It combined hurt innocence with a particularly nauseating sweet saintliness, and in Joe's opinion it shouldn't have fooled a three year old.

But it obviously fooled Eddie.

Mandy raised her round, baby-blue eyes to Eddie's face for a moment before murmuring sweetly, 'It's alright, Eddie – Joe doesn't mean to be horrible, I'm sure.'

'Too fucking right I do. Now tell me what the hell's going on? Is there suddenly not a single flat to rent in the whole of fucking London?'

Joe could feel himself losing it and made a concentrated effort to get a grip, as Eddie replied, 'We looked at lots of flats, boss – honest. But they just weren't nice places – not for a young girl on 'er own.'

'What!' The word came out as a strangled croak.

'They was damp, or in a rough area, or the other people living there looked dodgy.'

'My mother wouldn't have liked me living in any of them,' said Mandy virtuously. 'One of them had a shared bathroom and the bath was absolutely filthy.'

Considering that while staying with him, Mandy had never once cleaned the bath and usually left a scummy slick around the rim after using lavish amounts of bath oil, Joe felt that was rich.

'You'd 'ave thought the same if you'd seen them,' continued Eddie earnestly. 'It's not right, boss, a girl living on 'er own in places like that. I wouldn't 'ave 'ad my sister renting one of them.'

'Well, I'm sorry that there weren't a couple of rooms

going at fucking Buckingham Palace,' snarled Joe. 'Or would you have come trailing back saying it was a bit shabby and you didn't like the corgis?'

'Nice places is expensive, boss,' pointed out Eddie. 'You'd only given me enough money to put a deposit on a shit'ole . . . sorry – on a dump,' he amended hastily after a sidelong glance at Mandy.

'Well, I'm sorry if the small fortune I gave you wasn't enough. It would have paid off the national debt of a fucking third-world country – but you're saying it isn't adequate to rent a flat sufficiently luxurious to satisfy my grasping little cousin. It doesn't seem to have occurred to either of you that if she got herself a job of some sort she might just be able to chuck in a few quid herself. Why the fuck I should be expected to contribute towards her maintenance at all is a mystery to me!'

At the end of this outburst Joe's throat felt considerably worse and he broke out coughing.

'You see,' Mandy said to Eddie in a frail voice, 'I told you.'

They both stared at him reproachfully.

'She's an actress, boss,' explained Eddie patiently. 'Actresses need to be available for work, so they can't get normal jobs.'

Joe didn't believe he was hearing this.

'So you're saying I should support her while she sits on her backside all day doing fuck all? Is that what you're saying?'

At that moment there was a small, stifled sob from Mandy's direction and a perfectly formed tear trickled slowly down her cheek. Eddie's ugly, pushed-in face wore a look of such consternation that Joe would have laughed out loud if he hadn't been so angry.

'She's crying boss,' Eddie whispered hoarsely, in case Joe hadn't noticed, jabbing a spade-like hand in Mandy's direction.

'He doesn't want me here,' wept Mandy. 'He hates me. He's all the family I've got but he doesn't want me here. I don't want to go and live somewhere on my own – I'd be frightened.'

'What do you mean – I'm all the family you've got?' spluttered Joe. 'Have my aunt and uncle popped their clogs and you've forgotten to mention it? I don't think so.'

'I meant down here,' retorted Mandy sullenly, mopping daintily at her eyes with a scrap of Kleenex.

'You've got to let her stay here,' Eddie urged him in a fierce undertone. 'She needs looking after.'

'You know – I think you're right, Eddie, she does need looking after. Why don't you take her to live at your place?'

Eddie went puce and looked down at the floor.

'Me mum wouldn't like it,' he mumbled.

'Too damn right she wouldn't,' snapped Joe, mentally consigning Eddie to the graveyard shift for the duration of his employment with him.

He'd have to take the conniving little bitch flat hunting himself tomorrow. And she was moving into the first empty place they found. He didn't care if it had damp, cockroaches and a serial killer next door – she was taking it.

He held out his hand to Eddie.

'Money.'

Eddie rummaged in his pockets and drew out a wad of cash, to which a well-masticated piece of chewing gum and

some fluff had adhered. A quick glance was enough to tell
Joe that it wasn't all there.

'Where's the rest?' he demanded shortly.

Eddie looked down at the carpet and then at Mandy.

'Well?'

'I spent it, boss.'

'What on?'

'He spent it on me,' Mandy told him defiantly. 'We went
out for a meal and then to see a film.'

'*You did what*?'

'We were tired and hungry and I didn't want to come
back here because I knew you'd be angry. Eddie was just
trying to cheer me up.'

A quick flick through the notes told him there was over
two hundred pounds missing.

'It must have been some meal,' he commented. 'Where
did you go – the fucking Savoy?'

'No, the Ritz.'

Joe's face darkened ominously. A mental picture of
Mandy's bare backside bounding and quivering as he
smacked it repeatedly, danced tantalisingly in front of his
eyes.

'Well *you* never take me anywhere!' she cried. 'You
haven't taken me out *once* since I arrived here! I've always
wanted to go to the Ritz since I saw it on a film and Eddie
was kind enough to take me.'

'I'm stopping it out of your wages,' Joe told Eddie
between gritted teeth. 'Now get out before I decide to fire
you as well.'

Eddie cast an anxious glance at Mandy.

'It's okay, Eddie,' she reassured him. 'I'm used to Joe

being horrible to me – I'll be okay. Thank you for a lovely day.'

Eddie's pushed-in features wore an unaccustomed expression of near-worship which made Joe want to puke.

'Out!' he repeated, ushering him towards the door and then slamming it behind him. While his back was turned, Mandy grabbed her case and shot quickly into the bedroom. He followed her in.

'I'll have my hundred pounds back too – or have you spent that?'

Ignoring him, Mandy opened the case and took out a carrier bag emblazoned with the logo of an expensive shop on South Moulton St.

'Look,' she said brightly, taking out a scarlet frock and holding it up against her, 'isn't it lovely?'

The blood pounded through Joe's head like surf crashing on a shingle beach.

'Just out of interest – did you actually look at any flats? Between shopping, wining and dining and going to the cinema you couldn't have had much time,' he said from between clenched teeth.

In one swift movement Mandy shimmied out of the dress she was wearing to reveal a pink lace bra and matching panties.

'There was another one I liked too, but I didn't have enough money so I left a deposit. You can go and pick it up for me tomorrow,' she said airily.

The roaring in Joe's ears became so loud he wondered if he was having a heart attack. He launched himself onto her with an inarticulate grunt of rage and bore her down on the bed.

She twisted lithely out from beneath him and tried to scramble off, but he grabbed her by the lacy back of her flimsy bra and jerked her towards him. The bra ripped away in his hand leaving her distractingly bare-breasted.

He made a lunge at her, but she managed to evade him and backed away across the room laughing tauntingly and doing a series of little dance steps which made her breasts jiggle tantalisingly.

Breathing hard, he followed her until he had her backed into a corner, then seized her by the waist and threw her face down on the bed.

He grasped the back of her panties, dragged them down to the tops of her thighs and raised his hand. She squealed, rolled over and kicked out at him, somehow catching him a hard blow under the chin which made his head snap painfully backwards. He collapsed onto the bed and waited for the room to stop spinning.

He was dimly aware of Mandy bending over him and stroking his hair, murmuring, 'Poor Joe – you shouldn't get so worked up about things.'

He felt a hand slipping inside his dressing gown and closing around his limp cock. She began to work on it, squeezing and fondling it into expectant tumescence while he lay dazed and disoriented, his heart still pounding as if he'd run a marathon.

When she was satisfied it was hard enough, she shed her lacy panties and climbed astride him. She rubbed the end against her labia, spreading the moisture which had gathered there, then in one deft movement got him inside her.

He was still too dazed to participate in any meaningful way and could only watch dumbly as she caressed her own breasts, twiddling the tiny, puckered nipples until they darkened and hardened.

She began to ride him, slowly at first, then gathering speed. She took his limp hands and placed them against her breasts and he held on throughout the ride.

As he eventually shuddered into orgasm she looked down at him, flipped her baby-blonde hair back from her face and smiled her sly smile.

'Don't keep fighting it, Joe. Just accept it – you need me.'

The following day, Gemma and Sue discussed the impending court case over coffee.

'I dug out my contract of employment,' said Gemma, taking a cautious sip from her steaming cup. 'Did you manage to locate yours?'

'No. I spent all evening searching for it. I found several other things that I didn't even know I'd lost, but not that.'

'That makes it a bit difficult,' commented Gemma thoughtfully. 'They've obviously got a copy over at Detroit's – I wonder if Alan could lay his hands on it? It might be worth a try. Another thing that occurred to me is that Quentin, your disapproving ex, might be the right person to consult. This was his field, wasn't it?'

'Yes it was,' agreed Sue dubiously, remembering her last conversation with him. 'But there must be lots of other barristers we could arrange to see to get an opinion.'

'Yes, and it would cost us a small fortune. We're talking four figures just to get someone to spend ten minutes on it. Remind me – what sort of terms did you part on?'

Sue filled Gemma in on Quentin's unexpected visit to her flat and his suggestion that she let him direct her life.

'That's wonderful,' was Gemma's enthusiastic response. 'You can call him, agree that you need his guidance and at some suitable moment tell him about Detroit's taking us to court and ask for his advice.'

Sue was less enthusiastic.

'Do I have to? It'll mean me pretending to take him seriously. After all, I can't just bring it up the first time I see him again or he'll twig. I'll have to go through the motions of resuming our relationship.'

'So?' said Gemma briskly. 'You were keen enough on him for a couple of weeks – if you could put up with him then, you can put up with him now.'

'But he'll want to tell me what to do,' wailed Sue. 'He wants me to get my life in order and I like it just the way it is.'

'You don't actually have to take any notice,' pointed out Gemma. 'Just nod, smile and agree with whatever he says.'

'Alright,' said Sue gloomily. 'Meanwhile, will you see if you can persuade Alan to get hold of a copy of my contract?'

When Gemma had gone she took a deep breath, picked up the phone and punched in his number.

'Quentin? It's Sue – how are you?'

In the brief conversation which followed she told him that after mulling it over, she'd realised that he was absolutely right and they should start seeing each other again. She arranged to meet him for a drink after work the following evening, then put the phone down and pulled a face.

Down the corridor in her office Gemma phoned her ex-colleague and ex-lover Alan and asked him out for lunch.

Three hours later she slid into the seat opposite him in a small French restaurant. Alan's high colour and fleshy features indicated his liking for good food and drink. He was already well into his second gin and tonic when she arrived.

'What's got into them at your place?' she asked, having briefly perused the menu and then laid it aside. 'Suing us for the loss of one account seems a bit petty.'

'It was a very lucrative account,' he reminded her, 'but I agree it is a bit petty. Terry's behind it – and you know what an arsehole he is.'

Gemma knew only too well. He'd been one of the reasons she'd wanted to leave. An unpleasant and vindictive man, in the past she'd had more run-ins with him than she cared to remember.

'How's business anyway? And how's the new account director working out?' she wanted to know. She'd steer the conversation round to Sue's lost contract later. First she'd better exert herself to get Alan on their side.

She encouraged him to eat and drink whatever he wanted, even though the bottle of claret he chose to accompany the food was ruinously expensive. At the end of the meal, as he nursed a cognac, she broached the subject.

'That's quite a favour,' he said thoughtfully. 'I've already stuck my neck out by warning you of what's coming.'

'I know and I'm really grateful, but we need a copy of that contract to show our solicitor. I wouldn't ask if it wasn't so important.'

He beckoned to the waiter to bring him another cognac.

'You're looking good,' he told her. 'I've never seen you with freckles before.' He reached across the table and covered her hand with his. 'I miss you sometimes.' Just the

203

suspicion of a slur to his speech indicated that the drink had affected him.

She smiled back at him. 'And I miss you, but I've never been a one-man woman and that's really what you wanted.' Gemma had felt compelled to end their affair because Alan was terminally possessive, particularly when he'd had a few – and he always had. It wasn't a situation she'd found able to tolerate. 'But we still see each other occasionally – like today,' she reminded him. He leant back in his chair and looked at her speculatively.

'Do you know what I miss most?' he said suddenly.

'Surprise me.'

'Fucking you.'

Gemma hesitated briefly before replying. She recognised the deal which had just been obliquely proposed. Alan wasn't the sort of man to come right out with it, but it was as clear to her as if he had.

He'd get her a copy of the contract if he could screw her again.

She made up her mind.

'That doesn't surprise me.' She smiled at him seductively. 'We should get together more often. How about dinner one night?'

'That sounds like a good idea – are you free tomorrow?'

She wasn't but she'd cancel. The problem with Detroit's needed resolving as soon as possible.

'Tomorrow's fine. Where would you like to go?'

Alan rose to his feet and she saw that he'd put weight on since she'd last seen him.

'You choose and let me know,' he told her. 'It's on me this time, by the way.'

Chapter Fourteen

Feeling sick, dizzy and disgruntled, Joe lay back in bed with Mandy propped up on the pillows next to him watching an Australian soap and eating ice cream straight from the tub.

He'd been unexpectedly laid low by a particularly virulent bout of summer flu, which had made him so weak that he could barely make it to the bathroom unaided.

So much for his intention of taking Mandy flat hunting.

She hadn't troubled to conceal her glee when she'd found him slumped on his bedroom floor yesterday morning after trying and failing to pull some clothes on. She'd helped him back into bed and told him with honeyed solicitousness that she'd look after him.

Her idea of looking after him was to spend most of the day watching TV in his bedroom. But at least when she was in the flat she wasn't spending his money.

Yesterday, she'd calmly picked up his wallet from the dressing table and emptied it of cash. When he'd asked her what the fuck she thought she was doing, she'd reminded him about the dress she'd left a deposit on.

'You're obviously too ill to go and pick it up for me,'

she'd said with a hint of reproach, as if he'd deliberately caught flu to avoid doing it, 'so I'll have to go myself, won't I?'

Joe had tried to get out of bed, berating her in a hoarse croak, but had fallen against the pillows exhausted.

She'd come back several hours later, carrying at least a dozen carrier bags from various expensive shops and a bunch of grapes which she'd magnanimously told him were a present.

While he lay gnashing his teeth in impotent rage, she'd paraded backwards and forwards across his room, modelling her new purchases for him.

To add to his fury, he'd found himself becoming hard as she changed in front of him, flaunting her voluptuous pink and white curves as she wriggled into the new clothes.

Sweat from enraged lust mingled on his brow with that from his fever. She'd further teased and tormented him by stroking her own breasts until the small nipples jutted challengingly towards him.

Half delirious, Joe could only plot his revenge, as intoxicating images of spanking her until she couldn't sit down for a week jostled with equally intoxicating ones of keeping her permanently tied to her bed and fucking her repeatedly.

He'd use her as an unwilling receptacle for his bestial lusts – for months if necessary – until she promised that if only he'd release her, she'd pack her bags and vanish from his life forever.

Even worse, as he lay there imagining having her completely at his mercy, she'd whipped back the quilt to reveal his burgeoning hard-on and administered a brisk hand-job in the manner of a nurse with a difficult patient.

He'd nearly burst a blood vessel trying to will his dick into flaccidity, mortified by his body's seeming ability to function on a sexual level when he couldn't even get out of bed unaided.

Now, as she sat beside him and placidly spooned ice cream into her pink rosebud mouth, Joe swore that as soon as he was better, he'd get even for all the misery she'd caused him.

'Hello, Susan.'

Quentin bent down and stiffly kissed her cheek, before joining her on the curved banquette in a bar near the Inns of Court.

Sue wasn't looking forward to this. Ever mercurial, from finding him devastatingly attractive and burning for him to screw her, she now found him a complete turn-off. She summoned up a smile.

'Hello, Quentin – how was your day?'

He launched into a recital of a triumph in court which had apparently left the opposing party vanquished and bankrupt, while she half listened and made furtive eye contact with a good-looking man on the other side of the room.

If she could keep the conversation well away from what Quentin perceived as her shortcomings, she would.

No such luck.

When he'd finished he cleared his throat and embarked on a lecture which left her inwardly reeling. She couldn't help but wonder why Quentin was remotely interested in seeing her when he appeared to find every aspect of her person and lifestyle wanting.

She tried to tune him out but after a while she began to seethe. In the end she couldn't stand it any more and interrupted him.

'Is there anything about me which *is* to your satisfaction?' she asked acidly. He paused mid-flow.

'I think you have unrealised potential,' he told her patronisingly after a few moments' deliberation.

Terrific, she thought.

It was only the prospect of Gemma's wrath which prevented her from leaving there and then. She wondered how much more of this she could stand. Would the next time she saw him be too soon to ask for some free legal advice?

'How did it go?' Gemma asked her the following day.

'Awful,' groaned Sue. 'He doesn't like my hairstyle, my clothes, my taste in music, or my pigsty of a flat. He disapproves of my flippancy, my casual attitude to life and the things I choose to spend my money on.'

'Goodness,' said Gemma faintly. 'Is there anything about you he does like?'

'That's what I asked him – he said he thought I had unrealised potential.'

They both considered this in silence for a few moments.

'Why on earth does he want to see you then?' Gemma was puzzled.

'That's what I wondered. I've come to the conclusion that in his own tepid way he fancies me and that he sees me as a challenge – how much can he get me to change? I think I'm a sort of project for him. How did you get on with Alan?'

Gemma pushed a sheaf of photocopied pages across the desk to her.

'In return for letting him enjoy the fragrant delights of my body, he procured this.'

Sue was startled – her partner hadn't mentioned the unspoken bargain.

'You slept with him in return for getting this? You didn't have to do that – there must have been some other way.'

'It wasn't exactly a hardship, particularly since he wined and dined me lavishly first. I only stopped seeing him because he was so possessive. He used to go berserk if he thought I'd as much as looked at another man and it got wearing, but the sex was always good.'

Sue studied her old contract for a few minutes, then put it down.

'If you'll give me yours too I'll try and get Quentin to look at them at the weekend – he's invited me round to his flat on Saturday evening to begin my introduction to classical music and I'm dreading it.'

'Are you sure he doesn't want to get you into bed?'

'I'd rather that than spend an evening listening to him drone on about music I'm not interested in, but I don't think so. He isn't even feeding me first because that would cost money,' she ended dispiritedly. 'He's very tight.'

Sue fortified herself with a couple of double vodkas before taking a cab to Quentin's on Saturday night and as an afterthought stuffed a quarter bottle in her bag – Quentin didn't approve of women drinking much, so she knew she was unlikely to be offered more than a couple of glasses of wine.

She pulled her luxuriant blonde hair back in a French pleat, because that was how he liked her to wear it, and rifled through her wardrobe for something suitable to put on.

In the end she decided on a plain black dress with a slightly scooped neckline she'd once bought for a funeral.

She hadn't got round to doing any laundry recently and was unable to locate any clean underwear except a particularly tarty underwired scarlet bra trimmed with black lace and a matching pair of split-crotch panties. She giggled as she pulled them on. If Quentin knew what was under her severe, ladylike dress he'd have a fit and would probably give her up as a lost cause.

He'd opened a bottle of Chablis but only poured her a small glass, so she was glad of the vodka – it meant she could take a swig whenever he left the room or she went to the bathroom. He kept his own glass topped up but was less assiduous in refilling hers.

The evening seemed to last forever as he lectured her about different composers and then played her various symphonies, or concertos, or whatever they were.

At around eleven she made murmurings about leaving, when to her surprise he produced a bottle of cognac and sloshed a generous measure in his own glass and a smaller one in hers. He came to join her on the sofa and seemed suddenly nervous and fidgety.

Sue was just wondering what was up, when he cleared his throat and said, 'I've been giving it some thought and I've decided that there's really no need for us to wait before embarking on a physical relationship.'

She stared at him in astonishment. Why hadn't he been like this when she was keen on him? But at least the evening had suddenly become interesting again.

She decided to have some fun.

'Surely this isn't something we should rush into?' she murmured with lowered eyes.

'I feel that the time is right,' he told her pompously. 'That night – in the restaurant – was a cry for help and I'm prepared to give it to you.'

His eyes roved over her body then dropped to her stocking-clad legs. In a flash of insight, Sue realised that although he'd been shocked and disgusted by the impulsive removal of her knickers at the time, in the end he'd found it a turn-on but would undoubtedly never admit it.

'I don't know – I'm not sure I'm ready.'

'You must let me make decisions like this,' he said authoritatively. 'Now, I'd like you to shower, undress and get into bed in the room next to the bathroom. Call me when you're ready.'

'But I had a bath earlier,' she protested mildly.

'I believe that everyone has a duty to ablute immediately prior to intercourse.'

She lurched unsteadily to her feet, feeling the effects of the vodka.

'Really, Susan – if two glasses of wine and a small cognac affect you so much, you should seriously think about giving up drinking altogether,' he said censoriously.

Amused, Sue went into the bathroom, turned the shower on and let it run while she sat on the side of the bath and glugged the rest of the vodka. She knew she should really leave, but she couldn't bring herself to – this was just too fascinating.

After a few minutes she turned the shower off and went into the bedroom next door. One thing was immediately

211

clear – this wasn't Quentin's bedroom. It was obviously the spare room and she could only assume he didn't want to sully the pristine sheets on the bed he slept in with messy bodily fluids.

She pulled her dress over her head and burst out laughing when she saw herself in the mirror.

What on earth was Quentin going to say when he saw her tarty underwear?

Her creamy breasts were pushed up so high that they formed an even deeper cleavage than usual. They spilled over the top of the scarlet satin and threatened to overflow completely – one nipple was already half exposed and she tugged the bra into position to cover it again.

But it was the split-crotch panties which were particularly whorish. As one of her lovers once observed, with her thighs together they just looked pleasingly vulgar and common. But when she opened her legs so that her vulva was on display, pink and glistening in its nest of downy hair, they looked unashamedly lewd.

Surprise, surprise Quentin, she thought, stifling a giggle.

Should she lie on top of the bed with her legs spread like a prostitute awaiting her client? Or should she get under the sheets and let him make the discovery in his own good time?

She opted for the latter.

She heard him in the bathroom and called, 'Quentin – I'm ready.'

He came in a few minutes later, his chest hair still damp, towelling himself vigorously, another towel around his waist. As he approached the bed, she could see that beneath it he was semi-erect.

Sue had to concede that he had a good body, kept in

shape by regular games of squash, and she wondered if his technique would live up to the promise of his patrician good looks.

He lifted the sheet to climb in, uncovering her to the waist and then stopped dead when he saw her bra.

He gulped and cleared his throat when he took in the silken magnificence of her creamy orbs, but still managed to say in a disapproving tone of voice, 'That bra is only fit for a street-walker. Whatever were you thinking of when you bought it?'

It had been a present from a lover who delighted in her dressing sluttishly, but she decided not to tell him that, instead lowering her eyes and saying, 'I don't know.'

'Take it off at once,' he ordered her. Then as she sat up and reached behind her he added, 'You're never to wear anything like that again – do you hear me?'

'Yes, Quentin,' she murmured, unclipping it and letting her heavy breasts tumble out. He gulped again and sank onto the bed groping for them eagerly.

She could hear his breath rasping hoarsely in his throat as he squeezed and fondled them, weighing them in his hands and pinching her nipples as if they were melons and he was trying to decide which was the better value.

If the situation hadn't been so titillating she wouldn't have enjoyed it very much, but she found it a turn-on to be in bed with one of the most strait-laced men she'd ever met, wearing only a pair of scarlet, split-crotch panties.

He ceased playing with her boobs long enough to strip the towel from around his waist and place it on the bed, revealing a burgeoning erection of more than respectable size.

'Lie on this,' he directed her, arranging the towel so it

was exactly parallel with the edge of the bed. 'I don't want any stains on the sheets.'

Sue obediently rolled onto it so that her garish panties came into view, then let her legs fall apart so he was looking straight at her vulva, wantonly framed by a frill of black lace.

An expression of shocked disgust crossed his face while simultaneously his three-quarters erect cock leapt into ramrod hardness so fast that it vibrated like a tuning fork.

'What . . . what are those?' he demanded hoarsely.

'Split-crotch panties,' she told him sunnily. 'Do you like them?' She struck a few exotic poses to give him the full effect and was gratified to see a drop of sweat roll down his face.

Quentin never sweated.

'They're . . . they're *obscene*,' he croaked. 'Take them off at once!'

But before she could comply he fell on her, burrowed his hand in the sticky folds of her crotch for a few seconds, then took hold of his cock and stuffed it clumsily into her.

He moved over her, grunting and groaning as he thrust jerkily in and out, his hands clamped tightly on her breasts. It was over very quickly and he immediately grabbed a handful of tissues and shoved them under her bottom.

'Go and clean up,' he gasped, obviously terrified some drop of fluid might escape.

'I haven't come yet,' she protested mildly.

'Go and clean up!' he repeated. 'Quickly! It's leaking out!'

Sue clutched the tissues to her and went into the bathroom where she had a cursory wash in the bidet before returning, still in the whorish panties which were now very damp around the edges. Quentin got up and she heard him showering again a few moments later. When he came back he was wearing a dressing gown.

'Are you still wearing those ... those things?' he asked rhetorically. 'Give them to me!' Sue stripped them off and handed them over. He tossed them into the wastepaper bin with her bra.

'They're only fit for the rubbish bin. Next time I see you, I expect you to be more decorously dressed. Put your clothes on – I'll phone a cab.'

Sue stared at him open-mouthed. Was that it? Talk about wham, bam, thank you ma'am. Quentin had screwed her and now he wanted her to leave immediately.

And she'd put money on it that he wouldn't actually throw her bra and split-crotch panties away. He'd keep them to wank off with.

She wasn't about to let him get off so easily.

She stretched out on the bed on her side, one leg bent in classic vampish pose, her clit glistening pinkly.

'Didn't you hear me before? I said I hadn't come yet.'

He blinked at her impatiently.

'I'm afraid there's nothing I can do about that now. It shouldn't take you so long.'

'There is something you can do about it,' she corrected him gently. 'Try using your mouth.'

'That's a disgusting and unhygienic practice which no lady would ever suggest.'

'In that case I'll have to do it myself.'

She slid her hand down between her legs and began to stroke her clit while he watched like a mesmerised rabbit.

'You can join in if you want to,' she encouraged him, but he made no move to do so. She skilfully increased the pressure and climaxed after a few minutes, while he watched her silently.

A tentative erection poked through the opening of his dressing gown and he took a step towards the bed. Sue scrambled off and began to dress.

'Did you say you were phoning a cab?' she asked cheerfully. 'I think I will keep my underwear,' she added, fishing it out of the bin. 'You never know – I might get asked to a fancy-dress party.'

'What did he say?' Gemma wanted to know when Sue regaled her with her account of the evening.

'Absolutely nothing – he was dumbstruck. I even had to phone my own cab.'

'Did you get him to take a look at the contracts?'

'Sorry – I got distracted. I promise I'll ask him next time.'

'Is there going to be a next time?' asked Gemma dubiously. 'It sounds to me as if you might have frightened him off.'

'I didn't actually – he phoned me the following day and I'm seeing him again tomorrow. The power of sex, eh?'

Joe took a long time to recover from his debilitating bout of summer flu.

He phoned Sue and told her he was ill. She offered to come round but he put her off – he didn't want her seeing Mandy and getting the wrong idea.

He wasn't used to feeling as weak as a kitten and it made him permanently bad-tempered, but there wasn't much he could do about it.

Mandy continued to torment him. It seemed to afford her great satisfaction to work him up to boiling point. Then, when he was practically foaming at the mouth, she would either climb astride him or administer manual or oral relief.

It galled him that she only had to flaunt her voluptuous body at him and his dick responded like a particularly well-trained animal. It reached the stage that whenever she came into the room, it would sit up and beg like a dog which wanted petting.

He wondered how much it would cost him to have the South American in the penthouse flat ship her overseas and establish her in some third-world whore house.

It would be worth the price of a flight just to see her there, at the mercy of whoever could afford her. It would give him enormous satisfaction to see her forced to service an endless string of men, none of whom would tolerate her tricks for a minute.

He kept himself sane with fantasies like that and when at last after a week in bed he began to recover, he pretended to be weaker than he actually was – he wanted to surprise her.

And what a surprise it was going to be.

The surprise of her young life.

She was going to rue the day she'd come to London.

The first day he felt almost recovered, he showered and dressed while she was still asleep. He heard her taking her own shower, then she came wandering into the room just after he'd finished a hearty breakfast.

'You're up,' she exclaimed in surprise, looking anything but pleased.

'That's right – the fun's over,' he said amiably. She pouted at him winsomely and her hand fell to the buttons of her blouse. She undid them very slowly, allowing the material to fall open a little at a time, giving first a glimpse, then a full view of her firm, high breasts.

He smiled at her wolfishly, showing most of his even white teeth.

Then he pounced.

She shrieked as he grabbed her by the waist and carried her kicking and squealing into the bedroom where everything was in readiness. There was a pile of pillows in the middle of the bed and he threw her over them, face down.

He pinned her there with the weight of his body, giving her no chance to kick him again, while he efficiently lashed her wrists to the headboard with one of his ties.

It was the work of only moments to spread her legs and tie each ankle to a corner of the bed. He stepped back to admire his handiwork, then methodically checked each of the restraints.

He wanted her secure – she was going to be there a long time.

She pulled futilely at her bonds.

'Let me go! This isn't funny, Joe! Untie me!'

She was bent over the pile of pillows with her bottom well up in the air, in the perfect position for what he had in mind.

'You've enjoyed yourself this week, haven't you, Mandy?' he said gloatingly. 'Well now it's my turn, but I don't think you're going to enjoy this very much.'

She was wearing a tight-fitting emerald-green skirt and he tucked it carefully up around her waist revealing a skimpy pair of pale-pink cotton panties. They were so tiny they didn't cover very much of her.

He stroked her provocatively jutting bottom softly, running his hands over it, feeling the silken texture of her smooth skin. He slid his fingers down the cleft between her buttocks over the soft fabric and then round to savour the ripe swell of her hips.

'You've got a beautiful bottom, Mandy,' he said idly. She'd stopped struggling as he caressed her, but as he removed his hand she tensed and started to pull at the ties again.

'Don't you dare!' she warned him.

He went over to a drawer and took out several things which he arranged in a row on the bed. She twisted her head to look over her shoulder and let out a shriek.

There was a black leather belt with a heavy gunmetal buckle, a canvas deck shoe, a kitchen spatula and a cane relieved from its previous task of propping up a failing cheese plant. He only wished he had a riding crop lying around the flat.

He was delighted to see that she'd gone white. When she spoke again it was in a whisper. 'You wouldn't.'

In answer, he dragged her panties up into the cleft between her buttocks. He took a long time arranging the thin strip of fabric between her legs, pulling out her outer labia so that the material was wedged tightly into her pussy, then stood back to admire the effect.

'That looks good,' he informed her.

He stepped forward again and pulled the panties down this time, rolling them around the tops of her thighs so her pert little rear was completely exposed.

'So does that – which do you prefer?' Without waiting for her to reply he continued, 'We can try them both –

there'll be plenty of opportunity. Now then – what first?'

He picked up the cane and swished it through the air. She flinched and made a little whimpering noise but he ignored her.

'Let's see. For moving in here when I'd made it very clear you weren't welcome – a dozen strokes. Or should we make it two dozen? A dozen to start with I think.'

He laid the cane back down on the bed and picked up the belt, cracking it several times so it made an unpleasant whistling sound.

'For spending my money, or should I say stealing my money, six lashes with this – which end do you think I should use? The buckle would hurt most I should imagine.'

Mandy began to whimper in earnest.

When he put it down and gripped the spatula, she said pleadingly, 'Joe, please don't.' He hit the headboard with it, making a loud noise and she shrieked and jumped.

'And for generally making my life a living hell, about twenty with this.'

He took the deck shoe and flexed it in his hands, bending it almost in half then letting go so it sprang flat again.

'And last of all there's this. When I say last, I mean before I start all over again tomorrow, or even later today. In fact maybe I'm doing this in the wrong order. Perhaps I ought to start with either this or the spatula – get your bum glowing nicely before the real punishment starts.'

He fondled her backside again, caressing it intimately as he said, 'I don't think your bottom's going to be quite as beautiful by the time I've finished with it – do you?'

He moved back to the head of the bed so she could see him and rolled up his sleeves in a business-like way.

'Did I say that between punishments I'm going to fuck your brains out – just to give my arm a rest. Luckily for you I'm still a bit shaky from the flu, so for the first few days I won't be able to hit you anything like as hard as I want to.'

Mandy began to weep in earnest, tears flowing down her pale cheeks. He moved to stand behind her, rubbing his hands together and savouring the moment.

He didn't actually intend to use any of the implements on her, he just wanted her to think he was going to.

But he was going to spank her – he'd been looking forward to it all week.

He was going to spank her, then fuck her, then spank her again. He was going to keep her prisoner and use her any way he wanted. He was going to pay her back for all the misery she'd inflicted on him. He was going to keep her off balance and awaiting his pleasure, never knowing what was coming next – a slap or a caress.

He raised his arm and took careful aim.

The doorbell rang.

Who the fuck could that be? It must be Deidre come to see if he wanted any shopping, she'd been keeping the fridge stocked up during his illness, at twice the usual price because Mandy was still there.

Shit – he'd have to answer it or she might let herself in with her key. He grabbed a handful of tissues and stuffed them in Mandy's mouth – he didn't know whether she'd scream for help or not, but he wasn't taking any risks.

He opened the front door, and his mouth fell open when he saw who was standing there.

Mandy's parents.

'Aunty Elizabeth, Uncle Harold – what are you doing here?' he croaked, aghast.

Chapter Fifteen

Joe felt the room whirling round and had to hang onto the door knob or he would have slipped to his knees.

'Hello, Joe love,' beamed his aunt. 'We've come to see how our Mandy's getting on. Is she in?'

They both stepped past him into the sitting room. He was horrified to see that his uncle was carrying a suitcase.

'Are you alright, love?' his aunt continued, looking anxiously at his white face.

'I'm . . . I'm just recovering from flu,' he managed to croak.

'That's nasty,' she said sympathetically, beginning to remove her jacket. 'What a good job Mandy was here to look after you. Is she in?'

Joe had a mental image of Mandy bent obscenely over a pile of pillows, her bottom in the air and her mouth stuffed with tissues, an arsenal of weaponry lined up by her side. He let out a low moan and turned it into a cough.

He mustn't let them find her like that – they'd think his mother had spawned a psycho.

Maybe she had.

'She's in her room – I'll tell her you're here.'

He shot out of the sitting room and closed the door behind him, then dashed into his bedroom and locked the door. Many was lying exactly as he'd left her, but she was now red in the face from trying to breathe through her nose while crying.

He snatched the soggy tissues out of her mouth and whispered hoarsely. 'Your parents are here. They're sitting in my frigging living room on the other side of that wall.'

He fumbled desperately with the knot of the tie binding her wrists to the headboard, then swiftly undid her ankles while she rubbed her wrists.

As soon as she was free she grabbed the deck shoe and hit him in the groin with it, so that he let out a muffled scream, doubled up and sank to the floor clutching his privates.

'*You beast!*' she hissed, spitting out fragments of tissue, 'You great, big, bullying beast! I'll never forgive you – *never*!' She adjusted her panties to a more conventional position and pulled her skirt down, before flouncing out of the room.

As soon as he could walk again, Joe stuffed the weaponry into a drawer, threw the pillows to the top of the bed and returned to the sitting room where he found the three of them placidly drinking tea and eating biscuits.

Mandy had made a swift recovery and had obviously darted into the bathroom and splashed some water on her face, because she certainly didn't look as if she'd been crying.

'I was just telling Mandy we were going to book into a hotel for a few days, but she said you wouldn't hear of it and there was plenty of room here,' said his aunt. They all looked at him expectantly.

He sank into a chair and automatically accepted the cup of tea she passed him.

Mandy was making sure he didn't get the opportunity to carry out his threats – at least in the immediate future.

'Maybe the lad doesn't want his relatives descending on him with no warning,' suggested his uncle.

'No, it's okay – stay here,' Joe managed to say. 'I'm sure Mandy won't mind sleeping on the sofa – you can have her room.'

He could tell from his cousin's expression that she minded very much having to sleep on the sofa and had intended him to give up his room. 'It's great to see you, but I'm afraid I'll have to go into the office. I haven't been in for over a week and something urgent's just come up. Mandy will show you where everything is.'

He grabbed his jacket and escaped while he could.

Once at work he dashed into his office and sat behind his desk with his head in his hands. There was an immediate knock on the door and the Barry, the duty controller, came in.

'Are you better?' he asked. 'Your girlfriend said you were too ill to come to the phone whenever I called, so we've coped as best we could without you.'

'Yeah thanks – I'm a lot better. Why don't you fill me in on what's been going on?'

Damn Mandy – she hadn't even told him there'd been any calls. Whenever he heard the phone she'd said it was a wrong number.

Barry dropped a sheaf of faxes on his desk and pulled up a chair. It was all routine stuff except for one thing.

Another gunman had terrorised guests and staff at the

Marbella branch of the hotel group. Joe grabbed the fax and scanned it quickly for details. It sounded just like the ones in Paris and London. There was also an urgent message from the group asking him to contact the head of security as soon as possible.

He picked up the phone and when he put it back down again a few minutes later, he felt a lot better. Tomorrow they wanted him to fly to the hotel in southern Italy to attend a top-level conference being held there, ready to advise on how best to deal with the situation.

That took care of the Mandy problem – at least for a while.

By the time he got back, her parents should have gone home and he could then return to his original plan of moving her into her own flat.

It had taken the unexpected arrival of his aunt and uncle to bring it home to him exactly how crazy she'd driven him.

It already seemed unreal that he'd seriously intended to keep her tied to the bed for a few weeks, or at least until he felt she'd been adequately punished.

He couldn't believe he'd let her drive him to such extremes and could only blame it on the feverishness brought on by his flu. He didn't like to speculate what might have happened if her parents hadn't turned up so unexpectedly.

How long would he have kept her there?

It didn't bear thinking about.

Sue arranged to meet Quentin in a bar in Convent Garden. She'd been able to tell from his thickened voice on the phone that he was a man in the grip of sexual fever. He'd obviously never before come across a woman with her casually lascivious attitude to sex and, although apparently disapproving, he just couldn't wait to screw her again.

But once had been enough for Sue.

It had been enormously titillating at the time, particularly as she'd been half-cut, but the only physical pleasure she'd got out of it had been what she'd given herself.

She suspected that if she went straight to Quentin's flat as he'd suggested, he'd be so eager to get into her knickers again that he wouldn't give the contracts the attention they deserved.

As it was he kept casting furtive looks at her breasts and legs. She wondered if he was speculating what sort of underwear she had on today – if any.

She worked the conversation around to the contracts, indicating that she was so worried about the possibility of a lawsuit, that she couldn't think about anything else that evening.

He took them from her impatiently and studied them for a while, before saying, 'They'd be fools to take this to litigation – there isn't much chance they'd win. In my opinion they're trying to frighten you into an out-of-court settlement. I suggest you call their bluff. I'd be very surprised if they took it any further.'

That was good enough for Sue.

'Thank you, Quentin,' she said gratefully. 'Now I can relax again.'

'Good. Shall we go?'

'I just need to go to the loo.' She saw him wince at her choice of words. Goodness he was prissy – how would he have reacted if she'd said, 'I'm just going for a piss.'?

She went off and when she came back a few minutes later she asked, 'Do you have any change – I need some for the tampax machine.'

He blanched and then reluctantly fumbled in his pocket. When she returned from her second trip, she couldn't resist teasing him.

'Are you ready to leave? I can't wait to be alone with you.'

He wouldn't meet her eyes.

'Are you . . .? That is – is it your . . .?'

Sue feigned incomprehension.

'What?' she enquired ingenuously. He coughed and cleared his throat.

'Are you . . . menstruating?' he said at last.

'Yes. But I don't mind if you don't.'

He shuddered and she could tell that not only did he mind very much, but that he couldn't wait to get away from her.

'I've just remembered – I have to go back to my chambers – there's something I need to do. I'll call you.' He hurried off into the evening, leaving Sue certain that it would be at least five days before she heard from him again.

When she got home there was a message on her answering machine from Joe, asking her to phone him at work. She returned his call, pleased that he'd obviously recovered at last – he was just what she needed as an antidote to Quentin. She invited him round and he accepted with alacrity.

He'd decided against returning to his flat for the night if he could possibly help it. He wouldn't put it past Mandy to come creeping into his bed in the middle of the night. The idea of screwing her with his aunt and uncle asleep on the other side of the wall brought him out in a cold sweat. If he could stay with Sue it would solve a lot of problems.

She was quite agreeable to the idea and when he eventually left around eight the following morning he was sorry to say goodbye to her. In a way it was bad timing that he had to fly to Italy – they never seemed able to spend any length of time together.

As soon as he got back and rid of Mandy, he'd make her a priority.

His flight was at one. He went into the office first then phoned his flat around mid-morning. When there was no reply he decided it was safe to go round there and pack his case.

For once the apartment was immaculate. Aunt Elizabeth was very houseproud and had already cleaned it thoroughly – Mandy had turned it into a pigsty again while he was ill and Deidre had declined to do more than hand over bags of shopping at the door.

At least while his aunt and uncle were staying there he needn't dread coming home to find out what his cousin had been up to.

He packed a case and left a note telling them where he was going. Then, with a light heart, he set off for Heathrow.

'*Italy*!' squealed Sue with delight. She would have hugged Gemma, but her partner wasn't the sort of woman given to spontaneous displays of affection.

They'd just come back from their meeting with the hotel group where they'd been asked to attend a conference being held in Italy, dealing with all aspects of repositioning the group in the world's luxury-hotel market.

'I can't wait,' she continued, dancing around her office. 'The weather should be perfect too – September's a great month to visit southern Europe. And Joe's there,' she added. 'Won't he get a surprise when hc sees me?'

Gemma was pleased too, just less demonstratively so that Sue. She was a bit apprehensive about both of them being away from the agency at the same time, but she intended to keep in daily contact by phone and fax.

'Calm down,' she said. 'We're going to work, not on holiday.'

'It's easy for you to say – I haven't been away this year because I don't count Scotland. I wonder how many bikinis I should take? Don't you just love Italian men?'

'You just said Joe was going to be there,' pointed out Gemma.

'I know. But one doesn't necessarily rule out the other,' was Sue's airy response.

The hotel, built into the cliff face just off the coast road between Sorrento and Positano and overlooking the bay of Naples, was luxurious in the extreme. Sue and Gemma had been given a suite with a bedroom and bathroom each and a shared sitting room with a large balcony which ran the length of the suite.

'Wow!' was Sue's response.

Her bedroom was a sumptuous boudoir of muted blues, white and beige. Gauzy white draperies wafted in the gentle breeze from the windows between a pair of heavier peri-winkle-blue curtains, held back by matching satin loops. A huge bed, also draped in gauzy white, dominated the room.

There was cane furniture throughout the suite and vases of fresh flowers scented the balmy air. After examining the rooms and exclaiming over the complimentary bottle of Prosecco and basket of exotic fruit, Sue stepped outside.

The tiled balcony was edged with weathered terracotta pots overflowing with bougainvillaea, hibiscus and pink geraniums. She sank into one of the two cane chairs and drank in the view.

'Gemma,' she called, 'come and look at this!' When Gemma didn't reply she turned her head to see her partner already on the phone, speaking to Tish at the agency.

'I've ordered coffee,' Gemma told her a few minutes later when she joined her on the balcony.

'I thought we might split the bottle of Prosecco,' said Sue, disappointed.

'Open it if you want to. It's a bit early for me.'

'I suppose you're right,' said Sue, glancing at her watch. 'The holiday atmosphere just got to me. Look – there's an island over there. Which one do you think it is?'

'Capri,' replied Gemma, whose grasp of geography was stronger than Sue's.

'Can we visit it?'

'I should imagine so – if there's time.'

The coffee arrived, brought by a handsome dark youth with unbelievably tight trousers and an expression of unfeigned admiration for the beautiful signorinas. Conversation was suspended while they both watched him pouring coffee with an incongruously macho flourish.

'Mmm,' was Sue's comment, watching his retreating back while she took her first sip of steaming coffee. Gemma, who hadn't had sex since her evening with Alan, felt the familiar demanding itch high up in her pussy.

Better do something about that soon.

'Who are we seeing this afternoon?' asked Sue, thinking much the same thing. She must ask at reception which room Joe was in and surprise him.

They spent the afternoon at various meetings, discussing the ways in which the hotel group could be promoted to gain a larger market share and returned to their suite in the late afternoon ready for some relaxation.

'I'm off to the pool for a couple of hours,' Gemma announced, throwing her briefcase onto the table, then going into her room and beginning to undress. 'Coming?'

'I'm going to see if I can locate Joe – if I can't I'll join you.'

Gemma left the suite with a towelling robe over her bikini, carrying a bag containing her sunscreen and some faxes sent through from the agency while they were in the meeting.

Sue obtained Joe's room number from the reception then showered and changed into a champagne-coloured silk teddy and a pair of high-heeled cream suede shoes. She threw on a robe and carrying the chilled bottle of Prosecco, set off to find him. His room was three floors above theirs and when she tapped on the door, it opened slightly.

She pushed it cautiously, calling, 'Joe! Are you in?' There was no reply, but she could hear the shower running and, smiling to herself, locked the door behind her and opened the wine.

She considered going to join him in the shower, but

decided instead to embark on an erotic game.

She drew the curtains, casting the sunlit room into shadow, then stretched out on the bed against a pile of pillows, the wine and two glasses on the bedside table next to her.

She slipped her left shoulder strap down to expose one creamy breast, then undid the two small buttons which fastened the teddy between her legs and folded back the flimsy material so the golden triangle covering her mound was on view.

As a final touch she blindfolded herself with the wide belt of her robe. She hoped Joe would be pleased to see her – the hot Italian sunshine had already upped her libido several degrees.

As she lay there she could feel warm moisture gathering in her throbbing pussy, poised ready to trickle out and damp the curling fronds of her silken bush.

When she heard the shower stop and a few minutes later the bathroom door opening, she murmured throatily, 'Surprise, surprise. Don't say a word – just fuck me.'

There was silence then she heard the sound of his bare feet on the tiled floor as he walked towards her. It was unbelievably erotic not to be able to see him, not to know how he'd reacted to her presence.

She felt the bed dip to her left, then a large hand closed over her exposed breast, flattening it against her ribcage, before pinching the nipple, then running slowly over her hip to cover her mound and press possessively down.

She moaned as his lips closed over her distended nipple and he sucked so hard she hovered on the border where pleasure approaches pain. His fingers slid into the slippery groove between her labia, stimulating the side of her clitoris and making her gathering juices overflow and seep stickily out.

His lips left one breast and turned their attention to the other, flickering and circling her swollen nipple, then nipping at the underside of her satin-skinned orb until she groaned and her head fell back against the pillows.

He stopped stimulating her pussy and explored the rest of her body, tracing every curve and pushing his hand under her bottom to squeeze her curvaceous buttocks. He moved away from her and left the bed for a few moments.

When he returned she felt something wrapped around her wrist, then it was pulled back against the headboard and tied firmly to it. He did the same with her other wrist while she wriggled her backside against the cotton bedspread with carnal anticipation.

Her thighs were roughly parted, then an icy cascade of wine hit her squarely on her hot, aching pussy. She shrieked, then gasped as a hard mouth descended and proceeded to lick up every drop before embarking on an oral exploration of her honeypot which made her come in a hot, shuddering spasm.

Sue could rarely remember having been so excited, she was trembling with lust, more than ready for every lewd, depraved cul-de-sac of amorous foreplay, before he thrust into her and fucked her into mindless ecstasy. She was literally running with the hot moisture her private parts were producing, as if someone had left an internal tap turned on.

She came again before his mouth left her pussy and she could feel the perspiration covering her overheated body in a fine, slick film.

She felt him shifting position, then something hot, smooth and very, very hard butted up against her lips. She opened her mouth and sucked the end of his cock, swirling her tongue over the glans, flickering against the underside in a demanding rhythm, for what seemed an eternity.

His cock felt enormous, even bigger than she remembered, and her jaw began to ache from the effort of keeping her mouth so wide open. He began to slide it in and out of her, pushing it in until it butted up against the back of her throat, then withdrawing it.

When he stopped she closed her mouth gratefully as he shifted position. She waited in unbearable suspense for what was to come next.

Her head shifted on the pillow and her blindfold slipped off her eyes, making her blink. Even in the dim, shadowy light of the curtained room she realised immediately that there was something wrong.

The man crouching between her parted thighs wasn't Joe.

He was a total stranger.

She let out a scream and he looked up at her, grinning lasciviously.

He looked about thirty with a broad-shouldered, muscular body and a flick of damp, dark hair falling forward on his brow. There was something undeniably sinister about him. He looked like the popular idea of the mafiosa, right down to the gold chains around his neck and what looked like a jagged knife scar across his wrist next to his flashy gold watch.

Sue had noticed the strong, unfamiliar scent clinging to him when he'd joined her on the bed, but she'd assumed he'd been using some highly scented soap supplied by the hotel – the one in her own bathroom was fairly overpowering.

Now she realised belatedly that he didn't smell like Joe, because he wasn't Joe.

She also recognised too late that she was tied to his bed and he was just about to thrust the biggest, thickest cock she'd ever seen into her honeypot.

'This is a terrible mistake!' she gasped. 'I thought you were somebody else – I've got the wrong room.'

He didn't react and her heart sank as she realised he probably didn't speak English. She opened her mouth to try Italian – she spoke a little, but he deftly pulled the blindfold down and effectively gagged her.

She tugged fruitlessly at her bonds and tried to roll away from him, but he forced her thighs apart, then pushed her legs up over her head to expose the whole of her vulva, open and ready for him.

The sheer size of his cock was half frightening, half arousing. It was bad enough that she'd just invited a total stranger to fuck her, but she had to choose one with the biggest dick in southern Italy.

He positioned it over the entrance to her honeypot, then pushed. She felt the first few inches slide in and tensed her muscles in panic. He paused and muttered something, while she struggled again. He pushed harder and smacked her a couple of times, but was unable to make any progress.

She breathed a sigh of relief when he withdrew and she tried to work the gag free so she could explain to him that when she'd invited him to fuck her, she hadn't actually meant it.

A difficult message to get across to any aroused male, but even more so in foreign language.

He kept her legs back over her head, then pushed his

fingers high up into her cavern, massaging her internally, spreading her copious female secretions around until every fold was thickly coated. He ignored the way she was squirming and struggling, just concentrated on the task in hand.

When he'd finished, he began to rub her clit, squeezing and stroking it, muttered what sounded like encouraging obscenities in Italian.

Sue tried to fight the renewed waves of heat washing over her tense body but it was no good. He worked her to the point of orgasm, then as she hovered on the brink, plunged his huge cock deep inside her.

Her scream was muffled by the gag as she came in a series of ferocious, racking waves. She was burningly, painfully distended as his massive organ plunged in and out of her.

Somehow her aroused body managed to accommodate him and she couldn't help but move under him as he worked towards his own climax. He let out a primaeval cry as he shot his juices into her, then collapsed on top of her.

After a few moments she distinctly heard him snoring. Annoyed and uncomfortable with her legs still bent back over her head, she bucked her hips to wake him up. She wanted him to untie her, but he jerked rudely out, patted his cock appreciatively and went into the bathroom.

She heard him showering again, then he emerged and proceeded to dry himself vigorously, while she made muffled noises from behind her gag.

He dressed and spent a long time combing his hair in front of the mirror. When he was satisfied with his appearance he pulled a wad of notes out of his pocket and peeled several off. He bent over her, squeezed her breast and dropped the money beside her. He undid one wrist, pinched her thigh painfully and left before she could rip her gag off. With trembling fingers Sue freed herself and hurriedly pulled her robe back on.

He'd obviously thought she was a prostitute.

She didn't know whether to be amused or insulted.

She staggered back to the suite, her legs trembling and poured herself a glass of wine from the bottle of Prosecco she'd had the presence of mind to bring back with her.

This was the second time she'd found herself with another man when she'd thought it was Joe. The occasion in the linen cupboard in the hotel in Scotland was still fairly fresh in her mind – she should have learnt her lesson then.

Never again.

When Gemma came in half an hour later she found Sue inspecting her private parts with a mirror.

'What are you doing?' asked Gemma faintly. Sue put the mirror down and pulled her robe closed.

'What would you say if I told you I'd just been tied up and well and truly fucked by a total stranger with the biggest cock in southern Italy?'

Gemma perched on a chair opposite her.

'I'd try and ascertain whether you wanted me to phone the police or be deeply envious. Care to give me a clue?'

'I'm not quite sure myself. I was just inspecting my privates to make sure there was no damage.'

'And is there?' asked Gemma alarmed. 'Should I call a doctor?'

'There doesn't seem to be.'

'What happened? Didn't you find Joe?'

Sue gave her partner a succinct account of her coupling with the mafiosa type.

'And he actually left me some money,' she wailed at the end of recounting the story.

'How much?' enquired Gemma.

'I didn't stop to count it, but I'd say about fifty pounds in lira.'

'I wonder if that's the going rate?'

Sue suddenly burst into giggles. 'Let's hope I don't bump into him again – it would be too embarrassing for words.'

'Would you recognise him again?'

'It would depend on what he was wearing – naked or in swimming trunks definitely.'

They both burst out laughing.

'Are you sure you're okay?' Gemma asked.

'Nothing that a warm bath won't cure. Remind me – who are we having dinner with?'

Chapter Sixteen

Blackmail

Joe had suspected as much when he'd heard about the gunman holding up the hotel in Paris. When the third incident took place at the Marbella hotel, he was certain.

The letter had been delivered the morning after he arrived in Italy. Whoever was behind it obviously knew the Italian hotel was hosting a top-level conference and that all the directors, managers and consultants were assembled under one roof for a series of discussions.

The letter demanded an astronomical sum of money, or threatened that within a week around a dozen guests and staff in one of the hotels would be killed. It stated that the international press would be informed that the hotel group had known about the danger, but had failed to cancel all bookings.

'We'll be ruined!' was the immediate reaction of the company chairman. 'An incident like that, resulting in the deaths of several guests with all the attendant publicity, would mean a mass cancelling of reservations. No one would book into any of our hotels and we'd be forced to close the lot.'

A silence fell around the table. The only people to be told so far were the board members, the group head of security and Joe as security consultant.

Joe mentally reviewed the options.

There weren't many.

However heavy a security presence they placed in each of the hotels, it would be impossible to have everyone entering searched to see if they were carrying a gun. Any security would have to be unobtrusive if guests weren't to be alarmed.

In countries where guards were allowed to be armed, with a bit of luck one of them might take an attacker out with a well-placed bullet, but the resultant publicity would be disastrous and the terrorist group would undoubtedly have more than one assassin on its payroll.

And, if they paid the money, it wouldn't stop there. The hotel group would be bled dry until bankruptcy became inevitable.

'Have the police been informed?' Joe wanted to know.

'Not yet,' was the chairman's terse reply. 'It'll be difficult to keep it quiet once they're told.

'Who the hell can they be?' demanded the head of security.

'Take your pick,' said the chairman. 'The world's full of nutters. Gentlemen – your suggestions please.'

Sue and Gemma had a dinner meeting with the group advertising manager and head of PR. Both women were tired after the flight and a full day – particularly in Sue's case – and went to bed early.

Gemma woke up the next morning feeling as horny as

hell after a night disturbed by a series of erotic dreams which left her craving sex like an addict needing the next fix.

It was a beautiful day.

On the horizon, Capri was hung in gold and azure mist as the sun rose behind the hotel and cast its strong, clear light over the bay.

She stood on the bougainvillaea-strewn balcony, drinking in the unfamiliar scents and sounds, trying to ignore the fact that her loins were on fire. She decided to go for a swim in the hope of working off her inconvenient state of arousal. There didn't seem to be anyone in the pool yet – she'd have it all to herself.

After swimming twenty lengths, she climbed out and sat on the edge with her legs dangling in the water. There was no one about except a couple of gardeners and the pool attendant, laying cushions on the sun loungers ready for the first guests to come down.

She watched him from behind her dark glasses. Only young, he had slim hips and a firm boyish backside under his tight-fitting white trousers. He kept casting burning glances in her direction and his movements became more overtly macho until he was practically strutting around the pool.

Gemma had never had an Italian. Were they all as enormous as Sue's partner of yesterday had been?

She itched to find out.

Even swimming in the cool water hadn't been able to quench the heat burning in her pussy.

She sauntered into the women's changing room, sending him a coolly inviting glance over her shoulder as she went through the door, then stood under the shower in her bikini to wash the chlorine out of her hair.

She wasn't at all surprised to hear a sound behind her and to see the boy had followed her in. He stood silently at the other end of the room and watched her until she stepped out from under the water, then he moved forward, his expression one of unmistakable carnal intent.

She hesitated for a moment, then slowly and seductively undid the tie of her black bikini top. The sodden scrap of material fell to the floor, exposing her small, high breasts, then she pulled him into her arms, her heavy nipples flattening against his white T-shirt.

She fondled his firm buttocks, gripping them in her hands and squeezing them hungrily. His cock reared up under his white trousers and pressed against her stomach, making her tremble with anticipation.

Deftly, she unzipped him and drew it out. A deep engorged crimson, it throbbed in her hand like a large vibrator, the veins standing out tautly. It wasn't the biggest organ she'd ever handled, but it came close.

Gemma sat on the low bench behind her and opened her mouth. He buried his hands in her wet hair and thrust his hips forward to push the proof of his virility between her parted lips. She sucked softly, feeling her private parts lubricate, the hot moisture an erotic contrast to the cool water drying on her skin. She bore down on the hard bench as she felt it soak into her already wet bikini bottoms.

He groaned and exclaimed in Italian as she took his eager shaft deep into her throat, sucking hard, then let it slip out again. She twirled her tongue in circles, then slid it along the full length, tasting and licking until he was in a fever of arousal.

Unable to wait any longer, she released him and lay on her back on the narrow bench, her legs apart and her feet flat on the tiled floor. Two sharp tugs were all that it took to untie the bows holding her bikini bottoms together, so that it fell apart revealing the neat sable triangle of her bush and the moist pink haven of her honeypot.

He ripped off his trousers and straddled her athletically, his cock in his hand, then jabbed it against her in the wrong place, making her wince. She guided it a couple of inches upwards, then gasped as he plunged it into her right up to the hilt. She wound her legs around his waist as he proceeded to screw her fast and rhythmically, his loins piston-driven by his urgent lust.

The bench was hard against her bare back as he slammed into her again and again, but she didn't notice as her hips rose to meet each determined thrust, her climax building fast.

He came in a copious stream of hot fluid which she milked from him with her internal muscles until every last drop was inside her. It had only taken a couple of minutes and she wasn't quite ready to climax, so when he tried to pull out she tightened her legs around his waist and continued to move under him, determined on her own satisfaction.

He made a couple of half-hearted movements with his hips and it was enough. With a low moan Gemma came, her back arching and her eyes closing as waves of hot, shameless pleasure washed over her body.

He pulled out of her and zipped himself up, a huge grin on his face. At that moment a fat German woman came in, her salmon-pink flesh overflowing from her swimming costume. She took in the scene and exclaimed something, then stood there with her podgy hands on her hips as Gemma rose unconcernedly to her feet and pulled her bikini back on.

The pool attendant slid hastily from the room and Gemma couldn't help but notice that there was a lascivious gleam in the woman's eyes as she took in his athletic frame and taut buttocks. She wondered if she'd try her luck with him at any stage.

She'd like to be a fly on the wall for that encounter.

She smiled blandly at the woman and sauntered out of the changing room, suddenly ravenously hungry.

She found Sue on their shared balcony, drying her hair in the sun and tucking into a large breakfast.

'Coffee?' she asked with her mouth full.

'Yes please,' replied Gemma, sitting opposite her.

'Try one of these sugared pastries – they're out of this world,' Sue urged her. They devoured everything on the tray, then Sue rang for some more.

'Good swim?' she enquired, fanning her wavy blonde hair back over her shoulders.

'Yes thanks. But not so good as the swift but satisfying encounter with the pool attendant which followed.'

'Really? Where exactly did this encounter take place?' asked Sue, fascinated.

'On a bench in the women's changing room.'

'Weren't you afraid someone would come in?'

'Not enough to let it stop me. Actually an overweight German woman did appear – luckily he'd just pulled out and rearranged his clothing. I, unfortunately was still flat on my back on the bench with my legs apart. I could see she was torn between disapproval and outright envy.'

'It was taking a bit of a risk though, wasn't it?'

'Not to someone used to being screwed by Rob – as far as he's concerned the more public the venue, the better he likes it. How are you today after your hour of dalliance with the Italian stallion?'

'Fine and ready for more if I manage to find Joe today. I think this time I'll leave a message at reception – I must have misheard the room number yesterday.'

Joe was waiting for her when she came out of her morning meeting.

'Joe!' she greeted him, a hot little tongue of lust flickering in her groin. He swung her into his arms and kissed her hungrily.

'When did you arrive?' he asked when at last he released her.

'Yesterday morning. I tried to find you in the afternoon but I got the wrong room.'

Sue didn't feel it politic to tell him about how she'd tried to surprise him but ended up being surprised herself. Gemma was standing to one side and Sue introduced them before Joe suggested they all go for a drink.

'I can't thanks,' Gemma said, glancing at her watch, 'I need to go and phone the agency. I'll see you in an hour, Sue. Good to have met you, Joe – bye.'

Sue and Joe went to have a drink on one of the terraces cut into the steep cliff face. They sat in the shade – the midday sun was scorchingly hot – and chatted while they drank Camparis. Just behind them a mass of wild roses in pale, delicate pink rioted down the cliff, blooming luxuriantly and filling the air with their heady scent.

A long way below them a toy-town boat left a creamy frill of a wake across the deep blue water of the bay as it bore another group of tourists to Capri.

'Isn't this heaven?' said Sue. 'I want to move here – London suddenly seems totally lacking in appeal.'

She crossed her bare, honey-coloured legs and her beige skirt rode up her thighs. Her full breasts were thrusting against her tight-fitting black top, threatening to burst the buttons. Joe forgot what he'd been about to say as he felt the familiar shifting of flesh beneath his zip.

'Shall we go up to my room?' he asked hoarsely. She raised her dark-glasses from her almond-shaped eyes and smiled at him provocatively. The toe of her high-heeled shoe traced a path from his knee to his ankle.

'There's nothing I'd like more, but Gemma and I have another meeting in about fifteen minutes. What time will you be free this evening?'

'About eight I think – how about you?'

'Difficult to say – probably about then. Shall we go into Positano for something to eat if we can?'

'Great idea – I haven't left the hotel yet and I'm dying to see something of the place.'

Sue parted from him, regretting that there hadn't been time for a carnal interlude.

Still, it would give her something to look forward to that evening.

She stepped into the lift along with several holidaymakers and they all stood staring forwards and upwards, the way people in lifts tend to do. The doors opened at the third floor and two men in dark suits and dark glasses got in.

She immediately recognised one of them as the well-endowed Italian from the day before and backed into the corner keeping her head down, praying he wouldn't recognise her.

She was out of luck.

The lift stopped at the next floor and everyone else got out. The man's eyes flickered over her briefly, then he smiled knowingly in a way which made Sue go hot and cold.

It wasn't just that she'd urged a total stranger to fuck her by mistake – she could have lived with that – it was the fact that he'd patently taken her for a prostitute.

What must he have thought when he discovered she hadn't wanted his money?

She heard him muttering something to his companion, then he smirked at her and said something in Italian. She was so flustered that she didn't catch what he'd said. He switched to English.

'*Buon giorno*, beautiful juicy cunt.' She was uncertain whether this was supposed to be a compliment or an insult, but decided to ignore it anyway – they were almost at the floor she wanted.

She was taken aback when he pushed his hand up her skirt and squeezed her mound over her silk panties, his fingers probing her damp cleft while his friend grinned lecherously. Outraged and shamefully a little aroused, Sue hit him with her briefcase, then thankfully the lift shuddered to a halt and she hastily stepped out to find Gemma waiting for her.

'Hey, juicy cunt!' called the man. 'Come up to my room again tonight and we party, huh? We both fuck you this time.' He indicated his companion who flicked his tongue at her lasciviously. 'Your friend too.'

The lift doors slid closed leaving Sue scarlet with mortification and Gemma mildly taken aback.

'Another conquest?' she enquired interestedly. Sue looked hastily around and was relieved to see that no one else was within earshot.

'My mystery fuck from yesterday. I was rather hoping he'd checked out.'

'Are we going to go? They seemed like nice boys.'

Sue shuddered and tried to block out a half-titillating, half-repellent image of lying tied to the bed while both of them screwed her in turn, the other watching and maybe . . .

She pulled herself together and said, 'If work doesn't call I'm going into Positano with Joe. Want to come?'

'Maybe. Let's see how it goes.'

In the end Gemma did join them, along with Paulo, the hotel's deputy manager who obviously had a bad case of the hots for her. That would have been fine except he was about fifty, overweight and sweated copiously.

She'd decided that he was less likely to become amorous if they were with other people.

'Do you mind?' she'd asked Sue as they'd dressed for the evening. 'If you want to be alone with Joe I'll try and rope in someone else from the hotel.'

'No – it's fine,' Sue had reassured her. 'Joe and I will have plenty of time to be alone later.'

All three of them were in a holiday mood and enjoyed walking around the steep, picturesque streets of Positano, trying to decide where to eat. Sue declared that the pasta in the small restaurant they eventually chose was the best she'd ever eaten.

The evening was slightly marred for Gemma by Paulo constantly pawing her. Sue took pity on her and, when Gemma excused herself to go to the ladies, slid into the chair next to him on the pretext of asking him something about the hotel, leaving a relieved Gemma to sit next to Joe when she returned.

From her seat opposite Joe, Sue was able to put her foot in his lap and rub his cock, making him hard and horny so that he quickly lost track of the conversation.

At around midnight they returned to the hotel. They had some difficulty shaking off Paulo who insisted on escorting them to their suite and hovered on the threshold obviously hoping to be invited in. Joe had already gone up to his room on the floor above where Sue had arranged to meet him a few minutes later.

'I thought he'd never go,' said Gemma, sinking into a chair and kicking off her shoes. 'Thanks, Sue – I'd still be fighting him off if you'd left me alone with him.'

After Sue had vanished to join Joe, Gemma felt restless. She envied her partner having an attractive man to share her bed.

She also felt irritated with Paulo.

Why wasn't he young and fit?

She slipped off her dress and, wearing only an eau de nil silk slip and a pair of matching panties, poured herself a drink and wandered out onto the balcony to enjoy the sight of the night-dark sea glittering in the clear moonlight.

The pool was directly below her, still and silent. She mentally re-ran her swift coupling in the changing room that morning and wished the boy was here right now, on his knees with his tongue doing delicious things to her pussy.

She remembered the German woman looking at him hungrily and wondered if she'd made a move.

Good luck to her – women should take the initiative more often.

With that thought in mind she slipped a gauzy silk robe over her slip, went into the sitting room and rang room service for some more ice.

The good-looking young waiter who'd gazed at them admiringly arrived with it a few minutes later.

'Put it there,' she directed him, indicating the coffee table. He obeyed her.

'Will there be anything else, signorina?' he asked, his hot gaze roving over her body, concealed by only two thin layers of silk.

'That depends,' she said softly, letting the robe slip from her shoulders. His eyes were riveted on the dark circles of her heavy nipples thrusting demandingly against the semi-transparent silk, then moved slowly and heatedly over her slim hips and down her long, slender legs.

His large dark eyes returned questioningly to her face. She walked towards him, every step an essay in wanton, carnal desire.

'That depends,' she murmured softly, 'on whether you'd like to screw me or not.' She didn't know whether his English was good enough to understand that, but he certainly understood her body language.

He seized her and pressed a series of hard kisses on the smooth skin above her breasts, one hand stroking her silk-clad backside.

Her hands on his shoulders, Gemma pushed him to his knees until his face was level with her crotch. He laid his cheek against her mound and rubbed it backwards and forwards, his slight stubble rasping against the fine fabric.

He slid his hands up her thighs beneath her slip and slowly, reverently, drew her panties down her hips. They fluttered to the ground and she stepped out of them and opened her legs.

With his hand covering her buttocks he flicked his tongue into her bush and browsed, grazed and nuzzled there, inhaling her female scent. His mouth was a warm, teasing, arousing instrument of pleasure; transforming her private parts into a steamy, dripping jungle.

His hair was thick and glossy and Gemma twined her hands in it as he pleasured her. He lapped his way along the rim of her outer lips before sliding between them to reach her clit, probing it with the tip of his tongue until it hardened into a small triangular peak. He strummed it for long exquisite minutes until Gemma felt the wave of nerve-tingling, hazy heat which preceded her climax.

'*Oooooooh!*' she gasped, holding his face hard against her pussy as a prolonged spasm of pleasure suffused her slender body.

He looked up at her, his face glistening with her juices, then his hand fumbled for his zip.

There was a noise at the door and Gemma heard a key turning in the lock. She looked round to see her partner standing there, her blonde hair dishevelled, a surprised expression on her face.

Their eyes met. 'Sorry,' said Sue, grinning, and withdrew again, closing the door behind her.

Gemma drew the room-service waiter to his feet and led

him into the bedroom. Once on the bed she unzipped his tight trousers and took out his hot, twitching cock. In his eagerness to undress he struggled to get his trousers, shoes and socks off at the same time and became entangled in them, tugging fruitlessly and cursing under his breath.

She left the room for a minute and when she returned she was sucking a large cube of ice. He was just discarding his shirt to reveal a muscular, tanned torso with dense chest hair. Then he lay back on the bed naked, his thick magenta cock rearing ceilingwards.

Gemma smiled at him and ran her hand lightly over his chest. She bent over and kissed him softly, tasting herself on him, and felt her nipples harden in response.

She reached for his cock and bent her head to slide it in between her parted lips. He let out a yelp and tried to pull away as it made contact with the icy interior of her mouth. She held it firmly in position, then sat astride his thighs to hold him down as she drew the full length of him in.

His erection subsided slightly as the whole of his thick, throbbing cock was enveloped, but as she sucked away, warmth gradually returned until eventually he was as thick and hard as before.

She raised her head and looked down at him, a surge of power flooding through her body at the sight of him lying prone below her. She adjusted her position so she was riding one of his hairy thighs and began to rub her clit backwards and forwards.

He watched her through eyes glazed with lust as she slid the shoulder straps of her slip down her arms to expose her small, perfect breasts. Her eyes holding his, she began to caress them, tugging gently on the already distended nipples, then pressing them flat against the lighter skin of her aureolas with the palms of her hands.

He wanted her to sit on his cock, she knew. He grabbed her hips and spoke to her in Italian, his voice imploring, but she ignored him. When she was good and ready she squatted above his iron-hard pole, her pale green slip bunched around her waist, and slowly, oh so slowly, lowered herself.

It really was exceptionally thick, though only of average length and she felt her internal muscles being stretched to capacity to accommodate him. When he was deep inside her she began to ride him in earnest, rising and falling as if astride a hobby horse.

Sweat began to gather in his chest hair as he lifted his hips to meet her on each of her downward movements, his hands clasping her breasts. It felt good and she increased the pace, leaving him with no choice but to follow.

His face contorted as if he were in agony, then he let out a loud, hoarse groan and ejaculated high up into her honeypot.

Gemma's sleek, dark hair fell forward over her face as she jerked into her own climax. Beneath her the boy's body was slick with perspiration as he lay with his head to one side and his eyes closed.

She climbed off him so that his limp member fell back against his groin with a soft slapping sound, then stretched out beside him. He put his arms around her and buried his face in her neck and they lay peacefully together for a while.

She considered keeping him there all night, waking him at intervals to pleasure her again. But presumably at some stage he'd be missed by other members of staff and she didn't want to get him into trouble.

Reluctantly, she shook him gently.

He sat up, glanced at the bedside clock, then took his dick in his hand and examined it tenderly. Satisfied that it had sustained no damage, he left the bed and padded into the bathroom to relieve himself.

When he came back Gemma was brushing her hair prior to taking a shower and going to bed.

He had other ideas.

He came up behind her and caressed her breasts, nuzzling her neck and digging the promising beginnings of another hard-on into her bottom. She leant back against him, assessing its rigidity. He pressed it into the cleft between her buttocks, sliding it up and down while fondling her between the legs so that a renewed surge of clear moisture trickled down her thigh.

He was obviously determined to be in control this time because he led her forward, then bent her over the back of an armchair, legs spread.

He plunged joyfully into her again, almost sending her toppling headlong over the chair, and began to screw her with short, vigorous thrusts.

She could feel his hirsute chest scraping over the smooth unblemished skin of her back and his hairy balls smacking into her buttocks as he serviced her enthusiastically. By the time he came again Gemma was moaning and panting wildly, driven into mindless ecstasy by his virile young body.

When he'd finished and left, she was too exhausted to take a shower, so she just collapsed upon the bed and immediately fell into a deep, dreamless sleep.

Her last waking thought was to wonder whether she should have tipped him.

Chapter Seventeen

Sue was in heaven.

She loved it all. The luxurious hotel, the beautiful setting, the warm climate, the mouthwatering food, the wonderful wine and the gorgeous flowers.

Most of all, she loved having frequent and inventive sex as the icing on the cake to all the other pleasures.

Although their work load was fairly heavy, all three of them found time to swim and sunbathe in breaks between meetings. And if as a result none of them were getting enough sleep, who cared – there would be plenty of time to catch up once back in London.

Joe's room turned out to be directly above their suite and late one afternoon, just after Sue had returned from giving a presentation, the phone rang.

It was Joe.

'What are you doing?' he asked.

'I've just got in. I'm about to oil myself and then stretch out on the balcony in a bikini. Why – have you got a better idea?' she asked.

'Maybe. Where's Gemma?'

'Talking budgets with the financial director. She never

wants me around when money's being discussed.'

'I want you to to do something for me. I want you to undress slowly, oil yourself all over in the most lubricious way possible, then bring yourself off.'

Sue felt a thrill of wanton anticipation pass over her body.

'Okay,' she agreed and put the phone down.

She guessed what he was up to.

He was going to climb down from his own balcony to theirs, then watch her secretly, hidden from view, while she pleasured herself abandonedly.

She half drew the gauzy white curtains, adjusted the full-length mirror so she could watch herself, then brought a bottle of suntan oil from the bathroom.

Dreamily, she unbuttoned her wedgwood-blue and cream striped linen jacket and threw it over a chair, then drew down the zip of her tight cream skirt, before letting it fall to the floor and stepping out of it.

Underneath she was wearing a pair of pale blue cami-knickers with a matching camisole and suspender belt. The camiknickers were cut high on the hip, making her shapely legs look almost as long as Gemma's and she posed in front of the mirror, one hand on her hip, one knee slightly bent, to admire the effect.

Her wavy blonde hair cascaded around her shoulders, its colour a pleasing contrast to her smooth skin, tanned now to a light honey-gold. The contours of her full breasts were accentuated by the thin, clinging silk, her deep-pink nipples making two darker points in the centre.

With one foot on a chair, she undid the suspenders holding up one pale stocking and rolled it slowly down her leg.

She paused when it reached her ankle, then turned to sit on the bed to remove her shoe and then her stocking. She rolled the other one down with her leg in the air, bent at the knee, tossing it carelessly to one side when she'd removed it.

She undid her suspender belt and pulled it out from inside her camiknickers, then moved to stand in front of the mirror again.

She caressed her own breasts, holding them from underneath for a few moments and trying to imagine what it would be like to be a man touching them. They felt warm and heavy through the cool silk as she held them. Facing the window, she pulled the camisole over her head revealing them in all their luscious beauty.

Was Joe crouched out there now, watching her like some Peeping Tom? Would he come and join her once he'd seen what he wanted to see? Or would he climb silently back up to his room and masturbate too?

Sue sighed pleasurably and toyed with her nipples, watching the crinkled, pink nubs swell and harden under her fingers.

She knelt on the bed and poured a generous amount of oil into the palm of her hand and began to smooth it along her arm, massaging it into her skin. She covered her shoulders and back, then returned her attention to her breasts. She could feel an answering tugging in her groin as she delicately anointed them, making swirling patterns with the tips of her fingers, coating them liberally so they gleamed in the shafts of sunlight filtering into the room.

When the whole of her upper body was oiled she climbed off the bed, turned her back to the window and bent forward from the waist. Slowly, very slowly, she slipped her camiknickers over her backside, revealing the paler skin of her buttocks an inch at a time.

Maybe in a few seconds Joe would come in, his cock ramrod-ready, about to plunge into her well-lubricated pussy from behind.

Her camiknickers slithered to the ground in a whisper of silk and she turned towards the window in her nude glory.

She oiled up to her knees and then her belly, circling around the golden fleece between her thighs. She turned her back and smoothed it into her buttocks, then sank onto the bed against the pillows.

With her knees bent and apart she coated her labia and clitoris, then began to stroke herself with her forefinger, watching herself in the mirror.

The whole of her body was tingling with arousal. Her cheeks were flushed and her nipples distended as she worked herself to her first climax. She became so absorbed that she forgot where she was, forgot that Joe was secretly watching her, forgot everything except her own wanton pleasure.

Out on the balcony, crouching among the terracotta pots of lemon-scented geraniums, Joe was breathing so hard that he began to feel dizzy.

His cock rose up club-like from between his thighs, twitching and throbbing as he watched what was happening in the bedroom.

Except that it wasn't Sue's bedroom.

It was Gemma's.

He'd glanced inside as he slipped past, then sank down out of sight, heart drumming wildly in his chest at what he was seeing.

Cool, poised Gemma was on her hands and knees with her skirt rucked up around her waist, her panties around her thighs and her naked breasts hanging out of her unbuttoned blouse.

Shafting her energetically from behind was a young Italian waiter. He had her by the hips and jammed her back to meet each lusty thrust. She was moaning and gasping deliriously, a far cry from the aloof, touch-me-not woman he'd sat next to in a restaurant in Positano.

As always, with any attractive female, he'd imagined screwing her. He'd seen her lying beneath him as still as a statue while he moved above her, her only indication of enjoyment a slight flush on her high cheekbones. Perhaps when she came she'd sigh softly through parted lips, her eyelids fluttering, remote and keeping him at a distance even in the throes of orgasm.

What he'd imagined was a far cry from the lewd animal coupling he was witnessing.

He was frozen to the spot, unaware of the painful cramp in his calves, or the hot sun beating down on his back.

He daren't even blink in case he missed anything.

The youth suddenly withdrew and flipped Gemma onto her back, tearing her panties from around her thighs before pulling her legs up over his shoulders and driving into her again.

Her moans became louder, reaching a crescendo as he fucked her so hard and fast that Joe half expected to see smoke and sparks from the friction.

She let out a cry and he could tell she'd climaxed as her body jerked three times then went rigid, a hot flush flooding her face, neck and breasts. She had beautiful breasts, small and perfectly shaped. Not as lusciously full-blown as Sue's, but beautiful nevertheless.

He itched to cover them with his hands, the intoxicatingly heavy toffee-hued nipples protruding between his parted fingers for him to bend his head and lick.

At that moment the waiter convulsed into orgasm, his buttocks clenching as he emptied himself into her. He rolled off and lay on his back, his cock limp and drained while Gemma sat up and stretched like a cat. Her face had resumed its usually cool expression, incongruous with her rumpled clothing and wantonly parted thighs.

He could see the soft sable triangle of her bush, damp around the edges, and the swollen folds of her vulva, and swallowed hard at the arousing sight.

The cramp in his calves became unbearable and he sat down suddenly, rubbing them ferociously and trying not to moan out loud as his brain belatedly registered the searing pain. He hoped fervently that Gemma wouldn't take it into her head to step out onto the balcony before he could get the use of his legs back.

He rubbed harder and after a few minutes was able to crawl painfully along the hard tiled floor until he was outside Sue's bedroom window.

It wouldn't look as bad if he was discovered there.

At last, when the pain receded he peered cautiously into the room to be met by the sight of Sue, naked and gleaming with oil, her hand moving rhythmically between her thighs.

It was too much for Joe.

He stepped over the threshold, hands shaking with pure undiluted lust as he wrenched down his zip. He didn't wait to remove his clothes, just launched himself onto the bed, cock in hand, and plunged into her.

Later, as a hazy amethyst twilight fell outside the window they lay in a warm tangle of limbs, too exhausted to move.

'I've never known you so insatiable,' murmured Sue. 'You obviously enjoyed playing Peeping Tom.'

'It was one of the most exciting things I've ever done,' he assured her truthfully. He wondered how long Gemma and her youthful lover had continued to fuck each other's brains out.

Maybe they still were.

He reached out a hand and fondled Sue's breast, grazing the swollen nipple with his thumb and making her purr deep in her throat.

He'd been wrestling with his conscience ever since he'd been informed that the blackmailing terrorists had threatened to attack one of the hotels. He'd been told not to tell anyone, but he wanted to warn Sue to be on her guard without unnecessarily frightening her.

Now was as good a time as any.

He told her about the blackmail note and the threat it contained, then swore her to secrecy.

'I'll have to warn Gemma too,' was her reaction, 'although I suppose the chances of them choosing this hotel instead of one of the others are fairly slim.'

'I don't know about that – they know that the board of directors and all the managers are here – it makes it quite a target.'

'No point in worrying about it,' she decided. 'But maybe we should eat and drink elsewhere whenever possible. That's just reminded me – I'm parched.'

'I'll go and raid the mini-bar.'

Reluctantly, Joe left the crumpled, oil-smeared sheets and pulled his trousers on. He opened the door to the sitting room and stopped when he saw Gemma, cool and elegant in a pale primrose linen dress, studying a balance sheet, a calculator on the table in front of her.

His dick sprang instantly back into rampant mode, when only a few minutes previously he'd been certain he wouldn't be able to get it up again that evening, if ever, after the heavy-duty usage of the last few hours.

Had she really been on all fours with a young Italian waiter behind her, up to the plums in her luscious pussy?

Or had it just been the overheated imaginings of his diseased brain.

She smiled at him.

'Hello there.'

'We . . . we just wanted something to drink,' he stuttered, trying to get a grip on himself. 'Can I get you anything?'

'A glass of white wine would be welcome,' she said, glancing at her watch. 'Is Sue in there by any chance? I presume you've both forgotten the reception? It started about half an hour ago – I'd lost track of the time myself.'

'Shit. I had forgotten. I'll just tell Sue.'

The three of them arrived at the reception an hour later and separated to do some professional socialising. Resplendent in a tight, black off-the-shoulder dress, Sue drank copious amounts of dry white wine and thoroughly enjoyed herself, chatting and flirting. Although the windows leading to a terrace were flung wide open to the fragrant evening air, it was hot in the room with so many people present.

Feeling the effects of the wine, Sue staggered off to the ladies to splash some cool water on her face and take a breather from circulating.

There was no one else there and she sank onto a chair in front of one of the mirrors to rest for a few minutes.

In the wide corridor leading back to the reception room she was suddenly struck by the silence that had replaced the hum of voices from a few minutes ago.

Someone must be about to make a speech.

She hesitated, wondering whether to take a stroll outside – speeches bored her rigid – when the silence was suddenly rent by a scream.

She froze on the spot, her heart thumping a heavy tattoo in her chest, then crept forward to peer round the corner.

Through the open doors she could see three men in evening dress with their backs to her.

That in itself was in no way remarkable.

What was remarkable, was that they were all wearing masks and pointing large guns at the crowd. Two of them were in front and one behind, glancing from left to right, covering them.

Black, choking fear gripped Sue and she found herself unable to move. The scene swam in front of her eyes, then she heard more screams and great spurts of red seemed to spring from the chests of the guests at the front of the crowd. She heard no shots and could only assume they were using silencers.

She saw a couple of people fall to the ground, then the three men backed away out of the room and towards her, their guns still pointing at the panicking mob.

The man behind the other two drew level with her at

that moment and Sue felt her legs trembling as her eyes fell onto his gun.

He was going to shoot her – she knew he was.

She saw his finger curled round the trigger and inhaled sharply.

Then she saw something else.

The jagged scar on his wrist.

She could tell he knew immediately that she'd recognised him.

She closed her eyes and waited for the explosion which would end her life, but instead found herself seized by the arm and forced along the corridor at a breakneck pace, while the men shouted to each other in Italian. Her heels skidded on the highly polished tiles and her other arm was grabbed by another man.

Like some terrifying nightmare, they raced through the foyer dragging Sue with them to where a car was waiting just outside, the doors open and the engine running. She glimpsed a man in the driver's seat, then she was thrown into the back and the two men jumped in on either side of her.

They were all screaming at each other deafeningly. She looked wildly around and tried to see which direction they were heading in. Had they turned left or right when leaving the hotel?

Scar-wrist grabbed her and forced her head to his lap so she couldn't see out of the window. Bent uncomfortably double, she panicked and kicked out. The man on the other side of her hit her legs before pinioning them over his lap, so she was stretched out over them like a roll of carpet.

She could hardly breathe with her face pressed against

Scar-wrist's groin. She could smell his overpowering cologne and was afraid she was going to pass out.

She was even more frightened than she'd ever been in her life, but even so she felt strangely distanced from what was taking place – probably because she was woozy from drinking so much wine.

What if they stopped the car and pushed her over the cliff? They were hardly likely to let her live since she'd just witnessed them performing a massacre. Scar-wrist knew she could identify him and which room he'd been in. His fingerprints would be all over it.

How many people had they already killed and injured?

And why had they taken her with them?

Was she some sort of hostage?

She had to keep calm, but it was difficult. She tried to concentrate on breathing evenly and hoped that when the car eventually stopped, there'd be an opportunity to escape.

They were all silent now. The car was careering wildly along the coast road, but she didn't have the faintest hope that the police might stop it – everyone in Italy seemed to drive like homicidal psychotics on speed.

It suddenly seemed to strike the man grasping her legs that it wasn't in fact a roll of carpet over his knees, but a woman, because in the darkness she felt his hand slide up her skirt and he squeezed her thigh.

She tried to raise her head, but Scar-wrist jammed it back down again. The other man began to fondle her thighs and buttocks with the rough, intimate handling of a butcher assessing a joint of meat. She gritted her teeth and kept her legs tightly pressed together against his probing fingers.

She started to feel sick and wondered how Scar-wrist

would react if she vomited into his lap.

After what seemed an eternity the car turned off the coast road – at least she assumed it was the coast road – and began to climb a steep hill. When at last it stopped, she didn't know whether to be grateful or even more frightened.

She was bundled out of the car, got a brief impression of a dark cluster of buildings, then something was thrown over her head. she could barely breathe again in the enveloping folds. It was terrifying being dragged forward, unable to see where she was going.

She stumbled several times and thought irrelevantly that her shoes would be ruined. She got an impression of flagstones under her feet, then a flight of stairs, then she was thrown forward to land like a rag-doll on something soft.

She heard a key turning in the lock and wrenched the jacket off her head, blinking in the light to find herself on a double bed in a large, bare room.

Thankfully she was alone.

For a long time she could only lie there limply, her breath coming out in ragged gasps, while the room swirled around her.

When at last she felt able to, she sat up and took stock of her surroundings. The room had wooden beams, white-washed walls and only a bed, table, two upright chairs and a dusty-looking armchair in the way of furniture.

She slid cautiously off the bed and went over to the window, where a pair of heavy wooden shutters blocked out the night sky. She struggled with them but they were held in place by a rusty bolt and her fingers were trembling so much that she was unable to undo it.

There was a door leading to a spartan bathroom with a

stone sink, a cast-iron bath heavily stained with rust and a primitive-looking toilet. She drank some water and splashed some on her face. There was a tiny window above the bath and by standing on the edge she was able to peer out.

She couldn't make out much in the darkness: there seemed to be a cluster of outbuildings surrounding the one she was imprisoned in, making her think this must be a farmhouse – not that it did her any good to know that.

From below she could hear a lot of shouting and frequent bellows of laughter, making her shiver as she visualised the four men fired up by the murders they'd just committed. She hoped fervently that they'd forgotten she was there.

No such luck.

After about an hour she heard the key turn in the lock then Scar-wrist staggered in, a gun in one hand, a bottle of red wine in the other.

She recognised immediately that he was dangerously drunk and backed away until she reached the wall, white-faced and shaking with fear.

'*Buona sera*, juicy cunt,' he slurred, waving the gun at her. He stumbled after her holding out the bottle. 'Drink?' he mumbled. Sue shook her head.

With exaggerated care he placed the bottle on the rough surface of the table and went up to her, making her flinch as she caught the overpowering whiff of wine and cologne.

He squeezed her breasts, then dropped his hand to her mound and pushed his fingers rudely into the delta immediately below, scrabbling at her pussy through the material of her dress.

He was still holding the gun so she stayed absolutely

motionless, not daring to resist. If he wanted to fuck her she'd just have to let him – anything was better than dying.

She'd feel better if she could just get him to put the gun down – it was liable to go off if he kept waving it drunkenly around. She didn't know enough about firearms to know if the safety catch was on, or indeed if there was a safety catch.

She tried to force her lips into a smile but her face was rigid with terror. She made herself put her hand on his chest, although the thought of touching a cold-blooded murderer made her feel ill.

She nodded at the weapon and tried to look seductive.

'Why don't you put that down?' she murmured. 'You might shoot yourself in the foot.' He looked puzzled and staggered back from her. 'You might shoot yourself,' she repeated.

He pointed it at his chest and shouted, 'Bang! Bang!'

She half hoped it would fire and kill him, but it would make a terrible mess and she'd undoubtedly be traumatised. And then the other gang members would probably shoot her, thinking it must be her fault.

To her horror he whirled round, pointed it at the wall and pulled the trigger.

Sue fell to the floor and her hands flew to cover her ears. But instead of a hail of bullets richocheting around the room, suddenly, inexplicably, the opposite wall was covered with blood.

Scar-wrist was laughing uproariously and it took Sue several seconds to realise that it wasn't blood at all.

It was red paint.

Mentally, she replayed the scene at the reception and

realised that it hadn't, as she'd assumed, been blood spurting from wounds, but the guests being sprayed with red paint – presumably as a warning as to what would happen if the group didn't pay up.

The relief that she hadn't fallen into the hands of murderers – or at least not definitely – made her feel faint with relief.

Scar-wrist threw the gun down, picked up the bottle and took a swig, then held it out to Sue. This time she gulped down several mouthfuls – if he were about to fuck her and she was pretty sure he intended to – the drunker she was the better. She didn't think she was going to be able to get aroused and remembering the size of his cock she hoped desperately that the wine would help her get through it.

He took her wrist and pulled her over to the bed, pushing her down on it and wrenching clumsily at the zip of her dress. She didn't want him to tear the one garment she had with her, so she scrambled hastily out of it. Underneath she was wearing a strapless black bra with a matching suspender belt, panties and sheer black stockings.

His eyes glazed with lust at the stirring sight and he pawed her eagerly, snatching the bra off her breasts and kneading them roughly. Sue lay still and tried to resist the temptation to knee him in the groin.

He may not be a murderer but he was absolutely about to force himself upon her and the urge to defend herself was almost overpowering.

His mouth closed over one nipple and he sucked hard, his hand going to unzip his fly. His cock was only semi-erect, but huge even in that state. He held it as he continued to suckle, while Sue lay motionless, wondering if she could get him to use his mouth on her private parts in the hope of spreading some much-needed moisture around.

His mouth at her breast became less insistent, until he'd stopped sucking altogether. His head fell heavily against her and she was just wondering what was happening, when she heard the unmistakable sound of a snore.

He'd fallen asleep.

Unable to believe her luck she slid gently out from beneath him and considered her options. If she managed to creep downstairs and get outside, how likely was it she could make it to safety?

The thought of walking miles down a rough mountain road in the dark, either in her high heels or barefoot wasn't an appealing one. She might be lucky and find the keys still in the car, but she doubted it. And the danger that one of the other gang members would hear her was very real. Scar-wrist may have fallen asleep, but that still left three of them, any or all of whom might rape her.

She was probably safer where she was – hopefully no one else would come up while they assumed their chum was busy shagging her brains out. It was probably a better bet to wait until first light, then slip stealthily downstairs and try to make good her escape while they were still asleep. Even if the car wasn't an option she might hitch a lift from a milk lorry or whatever was on the road at that time.

Having decided on a course of action, Sue glugged down a couple more swallows of wine to help her sleep, then crawled under the bedcovers and closed her eyes.

Chapter Eighteen

Sue was awakened by the sound of prolonged and noisy urination and lay there blinking blearily as she tried to work out where she was. She was unpleasantly reminded when Scar-wrist staggered in from the bathroom, still stuffing his dick back into his trousers.

He must have a bladder with the capacity of a hot water bottle to piss for so long, she thought groggily, wondering what time it was.

Shit!

She'd obviously overslept because not only was Scar-wrist up, but sounds of activity from downstairs indicated that the others were too.

Happily he didn't seem to have an amorous interlude on his mind, because he clutched his head and groaned, then left the room without looking at her.

Feeling grubby, Sue went into the bathroom, closed the door and took a hasty bath in tepid water, hoping she'd be finished before he came back. She pulled her clothes back on, then went over to the window to struggle with the rusty bolt again.

This time she was successful and she managed to get one

of the shutters open. She leaned out of the window and gulped when she saw the sheer drop below. The farmhouse was on a steep hill and the bedroom she was in overlooked a gorge.

There was no escape that way.

In the bright sunlight streaming in through the window her situation seemed somewhat less desperate than it had last night. The men downstairs were obviously a gang of blackmailing crooks, but the fact that so far they hadn't hurt anyone – at least not to her knowledge – made her feel slightly better.

If they'd planned to kill her, surely they'd have done it last night. It was much more likely that they intended to hold onto her until they'd picked up the blackmail money.

She didn't dwell on what might happen if the hotel group declined to pay up.

She tried the bedroom door and to her surprise it opened. Maybe she'd be able to walk out before they even realised she was gone.

She took her shoes off and crept down the steep flight of stairs, only to discover it led straight into the living area where the gang were sprawled around drinking coffee and smoking.

Her appearance was greeted by a lewd cacophony of whistles and catcalls, with one of the men punching Scarwrist on the arm as if to congratulate him for having presumably spent the night fucking her.

He grinned and beckoned her. Warily, she put her shoes back on and went over to him. He pulled her onto his lap and fondled her breasts, while the others made various expressive and lascivious gestures of appreciation.

Sue tried to smile and look as if she found it perfectly okay to be sitting on the lap of a blackmailing mafioso, being mauled. If they thought she didn't mind being there it would be easier to escape if and when the opportunity arose. Crossing her legs seductively she wound her arm around his neck and took a drink from his coffee cup.

One of the men suggested in Italian that she might cook them breakfast and Scar-wrist pushed her to her feet saying, 'Hey, juicy cunt – you make us food now.'

He slapped her backside in a way which made her itch to drive her spike heel into his instep and suggest he make his own sodding breakfast, but instead she gritted her teeth and went over to the rickety cupboard standing next to an ancient fridge and a grease-encrusted cooker at one end of the room.

Unfortunately cooking wasn't one of Sue's strong points – she'd never learned and probably never would, so she was nonplussed to open the cupboard and discover it held only coffee, sugar, salt, butter and a couple of loaves of bread. She'd vaguely hoped there might be sugar puffs or something – her own preferred breakfast.

And more to the point, easy to prepare.

Gino, the youngest mafioso, followed her across the room and stood watching as she hesitated, uncertain what to do. He said something in Italian which she didn't catch.

'*Non capisco,*' she said, shrugging prettily. He opened the fridge and took out a carton of eggs and a polystyrene tray containing thick slices of raw meat and handed them to her.

He pointed to a large blackened frying pan on the cooker, then took out a cigarette lighter and lit one of the rings which exploded into noisy, uneven flames and singed the hairs on the back of his hand.

'*Grazie*,' she murmured, eyeing the ham – or was it steak? – with distaste. She threw a chunk of butter into the pan then nervously tried to crack an egg on the side of the fridge. It shattered and a thick stream of albumen and yolk slid down the side and settled in a concealed mess on the stone floor.

She tried again and this time managed to catch most of it in her hand. She dropped it in the spitting fat along with a lot of fragmented egg shell, feeling quite pleased with herself. When most of the eggs were sizzling ferociously – not a single one whole – she turned her attention to the meat.

She dropped the lot in the pan, then looked around for some plates. There were a stack in the cupboard and she took them out and put them on the fridge ready for the food. She turned the meat to discover that the underside was well blackened, pushed it around the pan for a minute or two then started to dish up.

Gino had been watching in stunned disbelief, which turned to total incredulity as she handed him two plates of burnt eggs, full of shrapnel-like shards of shell, and blackened slices of ham which, if the pink liquid seeping out of them was anything to go by, were still raw in the middle.

Scar-wrist and Gino abandoned their disgusting breakfast after a couple of mouthfuls, but the other two were made of stronger stuff and managed about half of it each before giving up.

One of them said something which she correctly interpreted to be, 'Let's hope she fucks better than she cooks,' to the accompaniment of ribald laughter.

Sue made herself some coffee and ate a chunk of bread. She wasn't hungry but she was working on the principal that she didn't know where her next meal was coming from.

She observed the men while she ate. She supposed they were all quite attractive in a Mediterranean low-life sort of way – if you liked that sort of thing. She noticed that they seemed restless and unable to sit still without a lot of the flexing, scratching and thrutching which signified an excess of testosterone.

She wondered idly which one would be best in bed.

She'd already tried Scar-wrist – she supposed he was okay if you liked your lovers coarse, dominant and hugely endowed.

Marco was the one who'd fondled her while she was thrown over his lap like a sack of potatoes. She considered him to be the most potentially dangerous; his muscular, thick-set frame was full of menace and she didn't like the expression on his face whenever he looked at her.

Ricardo seemed to be the crudest and usually led the lewd catcalling, making her suspect that he was a victim of arrested development. He played with a pair of dice a lot, presumably making mental bets with himself, cursing obscenely whenever he lost.

The last of the quartet, Gino, was younger than the others, perhaps in his early twenties, and the way he looked at her made it obvious that he fancied her. He was extremely good-looking and out of all the men, he'd been least offensive and most helpful – he might prove to be a useful ally.

There was sunlight streaming in through the open door so

she wandered over to stand in the doorway. No one seemed to be taking any notice of her so she went outside. There were two cars parked there and she glanced optimistically into both in the hope of finding the keys in the ignition.

Not surprisingly they weren't, so she perched on a rock, assessing her chances of getting away if she made a run for it.

But the terrain was rocky and fairly barren and, although there were some olive groves providing cover, she could only assume that four fit young men with two cars at their disposal wouldn't have too much difficulty in recapturing one lone woman in a tight-skirted evening dress and a pair of stiletto-heel shoes. There was no other habitation within sight and no traffic on the unmade road leading to the farmhouse.

Gino appeared in the doorway to see what she was up to. He smiled at her and offered her a cigarette.

She shook her head, saying pleasantly, 'No thanks – I don't smoke.'

His English was limited and she thought it might be a good policy to pretend she only knew a couple of words of Italian – that way she might hear something which would be of use to her – so conversation was difficult.

He seemed quite happy to sit on a nearby rock and watch her while he smoked. When she wandered around the disused outbuildings he followed her but didn't seem to mind her peering into the dim interiors.

Time passed slowly, making her long for a book or a TV. In the early afternoon Gino handed round some bread, cheese and red wine and Sue found herself drinking copious amounts to take the edge off her anxiety and help pass the time.

After they'd eaten, Scar-wrist took her arm and pulled her against him, then pinched her backside hard saying 'Upstairs now, Mees juicy cunt.' The obscene rutting gesture he made with his hips made it clear that it wasn't a siesta he had in mind.

The other men burst into the obligatory catcalls as he pulled her towards the stairs. Sue grabbed a half-drunk bottle of wine from the table and went reluctantly with him.

Damn.

She supposed she was going to have to go along with it – it was one way of passing the time after all and anyway if she refused him he'd probably just rape her. She'd always been casual about sex so it wasn't the problem to her it would have been to most women – but she resented not being given the choice.

She just hoped she could get aroused. If she couldn't it was going to be painful.

Once in the spartan bedroom he stripped off his clothes and stretched out on the bed with his hands behind his head. His shaft was a big, limp floppy thing, lying peacefully dormant against his stomach. He gestured to her to take off her clothes and she slowly slipped off her dress with her back to him.

The strapless bra followed and his cock twitched appreciatively. It grew hesitantly into semi-tumescence when she slid her silk panties down her legs. When she reached to undo her suspenders he stopped her with a gesture, so she was left clad in just her stockings and suspender belt.

Another gesture told her what he wanted her to do and, with an uncharacteristic lack of enthusiasm, she knelt beside him and took his cock in her mouth, where it grew to full rigidity with alarming speed.

It occurred to her that if she were lucky she might get him to come in her mouth – she didn't really feel like sex so it seemed like a more desirable option than trying to accommodate a massive cock in an unyielding vagina.

She worked on him with every bit of sexual expertise at her disposal and was gratified to soon have him moaning and groaning at each clever contortion of her mouth.

But just as she thought he might be about to erupt, he pulled out.

He drew her down beside him and fondled her breasts and buttocks greedily, sucking her nipples and licking his way down over her navel to her bush. She opened her legs for him, grateful for any moisture he might spread around with his tongue. She could tell she was still dry and tight internally as he probed and lapped at her labia.

When he licked her clit a tiny frisson ran over her body, but she was still a long way from being ready for penetration. At least he kept it up for quite a while so she was fairly damp around the entrance to her honeypot.

When at last he positioned himself to thrust into her, she tensed her muscles involuntarily. He shoved hard, but to no avail. He withdrew with a muttered obscenity and felt roughly at her vulva with hard fingers. He pushed one inside her and found how dry she was and looked puzzled.

'Hey, juicy cunt – not so juicy today, huh?' She shook her head wanly and made a gesture with her hand to indicate her willingness to bring him off that way.

He left the room, his cock slapping obscenely against his stomach. When he returned a couple of minutes later he was carrying a tube of suntan cream. He parted her thighs and squirted a huge dollop of goo into her pussy, then proceeded to rub it in until the whole of her outer folds were glistening slickly.

He held her open and squirted more cream high up into her, then used two fingers to spread it around, until the whole interior of her honeypot was thickly coated.

He seemed to like massaging her because he flipped her onto her stomach and greased her bottom, rubbing it thoroughly, until against her will she felt herself relax. Then he turned her over again and worked on her breasts.

Sue had a sudden vivid picture of oiling herself, then masturbating for Joe's salacious delectation as he hid outside the window. The memory made a warm coil of lust begin to unfurl in her groin and she knew to her relief that her body was at least making half-hearted preparations to accommodate a male member.

She held on tight to the memory of her various carnal interludes with Joe, and between that, the wine and the heat she became relaxed and languorous.

Scar-wrist massaged his way down her belly then located her clit and began to stroke it rhythmically. The warmth in her groin became a heat and she parted her legs, feeling her own lubrications mingling with the suntan cream. He slid his fingers inside her again and this time they slipped in easily. He gave a grunt of satisfaction, then shoved a pillow under her hips.

She kept her eyes closed so she couldn't see his massive shaft, but she could certainly feel it. Slowly but surely he edged it in, withdrawing an inch then gaining two.

When it was all the way in, he rested with his weight on

her for a few moments, breathing hard. Then, with a couple more grunts, he withdrew and plunged it back into her.

It wasn't quite pain and it wasn't quite pleasure, it was somewhere in between. After a few more thrusts, pleasure began to dominate, even though she felt stretched to capacity.

He kept muttering encouraging obscenities as he grasped her curvaceous buttocks tightly and screwed her with rough bestial enjoyment.

Sue had always been highly sexed so her body responded in its customary manner, and it wasn't long before she felt her climax approaching.

The strength of it took her by surprise, making her cry out and dig her nails in his hairy back. He came himself in a great surge of hot release, his eyes bulging and the veins standing out on his forehead, before collapsing on top of her, his body a dead weight.

Sue hastily wriggled out from under him before he could fall asleep. He squeezed her drowsily on the thigh, then his eyes closed and he began to snore.

She lay there for a while listening to the faint sound of the breeze stirring the olive groves, wondering what Joe and Gemma were doing, then drifted off into sleep herself.

When she woke up, dusk was gathering outside the window and the cicadas were well into their evening chorus. Scar-wrist had gone and Sue staggered into the bathroom for another bath in the rust-stained tub. Thankfully, the water was warm this time and she made a mental note to wash out her stockings and underwear before going to bed that night.

She wandered downstairs to find Gino stirring something in a large saucepan on the ancient stove and deduced correctly that her services as cook weren't going to be requested a second time.

Keeping out of reach of Scar-wrist, who was far too fond of either pinching or slapping her curvaceous rump, Sue helped herself to a glass of wine, ignoring what seemed to be a description of her performance in bed given for the edification of the others. Taking no notice of their lecherous looks and lewd comments, she strolled towards the door.

It was a warm night and she stood in the doorway inhaling the scent of herbs and sun-warmed earth, cooling now as a grapefruit moon ascended unhurriedly over the olive trees.

The smell of stew drew her back indoors and she ate a large plateful with some crusty bread, wondering why no one had thought to buy any salad to go with it.

Later the men decided to play cards and she was despatched to wash the greasy dishes as best she could with lukewarm water and a bar of rough green soap.

Scar-wrist came over to get another bottle of wine and lifted her skirt as she leant over the sink, displaying her bum – only half covered by a tiny pair of panties – for the others to see. She gritted her teeth as he fondled it with both hands, parting her buttocks and pushing his fingers between her legs to rub her cleft over the thin silk.

Hanging onto the edge of the sink, it took all Sue's self-control not to turn round, grab his balls and squeeze as hard as she could.

The other men made lascivious, noisy comments and she heard Marco suggest that they all get a go with her, but luckily Scar-wrist didn't seem too keen on the idea of sharing. His open display of carnal possessiveness culminated with the inevitable hearty slap across the buttocks.

Sue was starting to feel like the moll in a gangster movie – and she didn't like it one bit.

As soon as she'd finished the washing-up she took her glass and would have gone back upstairs, but Scar-wrist pulled her onto his knee as Ricardo dealt another hand. She had to suffer more of his fondling and squeezing between games of cards and felt his hard-on rearing up under her thigh as the evening wore interminably on.

When Scar-wrist went upstairs to empty his bladder, Marco pulled her onto his own lap and dragged the front of her dress and her strapless bra down to expose her full breasts. Gino looked uncomfortable and Ricardo whistled and made rude smacking noises with his lips as Marco buried his face in her generous cleavage and nuzzled noisily there.

When he eventually emerged he pulled her head down and kissed her wetly upon the lips, while pinching her nipple painfully. Pink with humiliation and unable to stand it a moment longer, Sue bit him hard on the lower lip. With a howl he pushed her off his knee clutching his mouth, just as Scar-wrist came back downstairs.

Marco looked murderous and she knew he would have hit her if Scar-wrist hadn't stepped in front of her and given his partner-in-crime a rough push on the chest. All the men began to shout at once and then the two of them jumped on each other and started to struggle.

Sue dragged her clothing back up and hastily scrambled to the top of the stairs where she could watch unobtrusively without the risk of being hurt. They bellowed at each other as they fell to the ground, Scar-wrist saying that she was his woman until he said differently and Marco insisting they should take turns with her.

As fights went it was fairly tame and Scar-wrist swiftly emerged the victor after managing to knee his opponent savagely in the balls. Flushed with triumph, he ordered Sue upstairs and then returned to his game with the two other men, while Marco dragged himself outside. A few moments later she heard one of the cars roar off down the rocky road.

Sue expected Scar-wrist to join her later to exercise his carnal rights over her, but when she woke up in the morning she was still alone. When she went downstairs both he and Ricardo were fast asleep at the table among the overflowing ashtrays and dirty glasses and there was no sign on Gino.

Silently, she began a swift, frantic search for the keys to the remaining car, but they were nowhere to be found. The sound of an engine made her dash to the door, hoping it wasn't Marco returning.

It was Gino, who'd obviously been shopping because, after nodding at her and saying, '*Buon giorno*,' he unloaded a couple of bags of groceries.

She noticed that he dropped the keys into his trouser pocket after he'd locked the car.

That was useful information.

If the slightest opportunity arose to get them off him she would.

She wondered what was happening back at the hotel and whether Gemma and Joe were frantic with worry.

Presumably the police were combing the area for her – or maybe not. It was impossible to tell.

One thing was certain, she needed to escape as soon as possible, and preferably before Marco got back. She'd gathered from the men's conversation that they were waiting for something, but had been unable to tell what.

Some response to their blackmail threat presumably.

She didn't want to be stuck up here much longer – she needed a change of clothes for one thing.

Both Scar-wrist and Ricardo seemed hungover and vanished upstairs after they'd woken up, leaving Sue alone with Gino. After breakfast she indicated that she wanted to go for a walk in the olive groves and he went with her.

Her mind was racing.

Suppose she seduced him?

If she was really lucky he might fall asleep immediately afterwards, then she could grab the keys, race back to the car and drive off before anyone even realised she'd gone.

It was worth a try.

If he had the good manners not to fall into a post-coital coma, perhaps she could knock him out with a fallen branch or something. Although she doubted if she could bring herself to do so. After all, what if she killed him?

She sank onto the rough grass under a tree on the edge of the grove nearest to the farmhouse and smiled at him invitingly. He lay down next to her, his young body lithe and lean as he stretched out on one elbow.

She was just about to bend down and kiss him when she heard the sound of a car approaching, out of sight around a bend. Like a shot Gino leapt to his feet and dragged her to hers, before pulling her out of sight behind the tree.

She knew he was afraid it might be the police. If it was she'd kick him on the shin and make a run for it.

She groaned silently when she saw Marco, crouched malevolently behind the wheel of the second car, returning after a night spent elsewhere.

Sod it!

She daren't try it now because as soon as they heard her drive off, they could chase her in the second car. They'd undoubtedly be able to run her off the road before she reached other traffic. She was a bad driver at the best of times. In an unfamiliar car with left-hand drive and in a panic, she'd probably be killed.

Unfortunately Gino wanted to go back to the house, so Sue had no option but to return. Marco was in the kitchen with his back to the stairs so she slipped silently up them and went to her room.

It was a long boring day and she passed the time by thinking up new concepts for the hotel group's advertising campaign, but she was well aware that even if she thought of something brilliant, if she didn't write it down she wouldn't be able to remember it tomorrow.

Gino brought her up some bread, ham and wine in the afternoon. He also brought her a large, ripe plum tomato which she fell on eagerly – she usually ate a lot of fruit and salad and already had withdrawal symptoms from almost two days without.

Scar-wrist paid her a visit in the late afternoon, bringing the sun-cream with him. She was so bored that she welcomed the diversion and threw herself into the proceedings with an appetite which obviously surprised him.

She masturbated him with her hand covered by her silk

panties then took the tube of cream from him and massaged some into his dick, stimulating the swollen end with the ball of her thumb, while he groaned deep in his throat.

He screwed her on all fours with her dress still on, flipped up over her waist at the back and pulled down at the front so her heavy breasts hung out. Afterwards she wouldn't let him fall asleep, but kept him awake by nipping and biting at him gently and handling his flaccid, sticky cock until renewed life returned.

When she'd coaxed a reluctant erection out of him she led him over to the table, lay on it on her back and wound her legs around his waist. At the sight of her lying wantonly there, her swollen deep-pink nipples thrusting towards the ceiling, her golden hair spilling out around her head, he was suddenly beset by sheer animal lust and rammed into her like a bull.

She cried out, then tightened her legs and began to move sinuously under him. She kept him hard at it, whenever he showed signs of flagging she gave him a few skilful squeezes with her internal muscles, keeping him labouring above her until she'd come again.

He was exhausted and sweat-drenched when she finally released him. He staggered from the room to go and take a much needed nap, his cock clutched protectively in his hand.

She suspected he didn't want to fall asleep in here in case she woke him and demanded servicing again.

It felt good to have had the upper hand for once.

Chapter Nineteen

There was an altercation taking place when Sue descended the stairs that evening. She poured herself a glass of red wine, wondering why there was never any white. It wasn't that she didn't like red – it was just that she'd drunk an awful lot over the last couple of days and would have welcomed a change.

She listened carefully all the while, trying to understand what they were arguing about, but it was difficult when they talked so fast.

It obviously wasn't her – no one had even glanced her way when she came downstairs, except Gino who gave her a fleeting half-smile.

She gathered that two of them were going back to the hotel to try and ascertain what was happening, but there seemed to be some dispute as to which two.

She rummaged in the fridge, found the tomatoes and ate three while they continued to shout at one another. They were very good tomatoes – much better than you ever found in London, she thought absently, while she waited to see what the outcome of the dispute would be.

If only two of them were left it might present the ideal opportunity to escape.

After a lot of shouting and banging on the table it seemed to have been decided that Scar-wrist and Marco would go, leaving Gino and Ricardo to guard her. Sue heaved a sigh of relief – she wouldn't have been too happy about having Marco around without Scar-wrist there too.

They all ate stew, which tasted exactly the same as last night's – Gino's repertoire was obviously limited, though not as limited as hers.

Just before leaving, Scar-wrist pulled her against him and kissed her hard, his teeth mashing into her full lips. She was about to brace herself for the inevitable pinch, but decided to take the initiative instead. She groped for his groin and squeezed, smiling provocatively. She suspected from his sharp intake of breath that she'd hurt him, but he had too much machismo to show it in front of the others.

'*Arrivederci.* Hurry back,' she murmured, loudly enough for them all to hear. He smirked at her, then he and Marco got into the car and roared off down the hill.

Two down, two to go.

She sauntered back into the farmhouse, hips swaying, and curled up on the wooden settle with her glass of wine. First she needed to split them up – but how?

Gino solved that one for her by going upstairs. Sue glanced swiftly at Ricardo, who was playing with his dice again, then went upstairs herself.

She hung around in the doorway to her room until she heard the flushing of the chain in the other bathroom. When Gino emerged she was posed seductively against the doorframe, one hand on her hip. She smiled at him and beckoned, then with a twitch of her hips went slinkily into the bedroom.

He followed her, looking uncertain. She immediately wound her arms around his neck and pressed the length of her curvaceous body against his lean, hard one. His arms went around her automatically, but he looked nervous.

Presumably he was worried about Scar-wrist's reaction if he discovered that something had happened between them.

She pulled his head down and kissed him, and was soon gratified to feel him hardening against her stomach. When she pulled away he was no longer looking uncertain – arousal had blanked out all emotions other than lust.

She sat him on the edge of the bed, then slowly and seductively removed her dress, leaving her clad in only her strapless bra, panties, suspender belt and stockings.

She went into the bathroom and turned the hot tap on full. When she came back she undid his shirt, kneeling beside him on the bed and dropping kisses on his thick, black chest hair as she undid each button.

He reached behind her and undid her bra, then caressed her breasts eagerly as she pulled his shirt out of his tight-fitting trousers and threw it on the floor. She reached for his zip and he bent down and impatiently tore his shoes and socks off, then stood up and stripped off his trousers and boxer shorts.

His member sprang proudly from the thick curly nest of hair around his groin. Sue had never known men as hairy as these Italians and suppressed a shiver of carnality as she touched his cock tentatively with the tip of her forefinger. Gino stood with his hands on his hips and his head thrown back as she closed her hand around it and felt it throbbing hotly against her cool palm.

It was big.

Not as huge as Scar-wrist's, but big nevertheless.

Still holding it, she led him into the bathroom like an elephant by the trunk and pointed to the bath, now half full of warm water. She indicated he should get in and he looked puzzled, then took her wrist and tried to take her back into the bedroom.

But that didn't suit Sue at all. She needed to immobilise him and although the bed had a headboard, it was solid wood and it would be difficult to tie him to it. Whereas the bath had two large brass taps at the top which would lend themselves to her purpose very well.

She broke free and picked up the soap, working up a lather before reaching for his cock. He grinned and obviously decided to humour her. He climbed in and lay back in the water, his shaft breaking the surface like a periscope. Kneeling by the bath she washed it thoroughly, working it in her hands until it was covered in thick foam. She lathered his chest too, then his legs, before returning to his cock and working him up to boiling point.

He reached for her and tried to pull her into the bath with him, but she eluded him and skipped into the bedroom, returning with his belt. He looked taken aback when she pulled his wrists above his head and started to lash them to the taps, but to her relief he seemed to accept it as a form of erotic love-play.

As soon as he was secured she stood back, ready to pull her bra and dress back on and go and deal with Ricardo, but something stopped her.

Maybe it was the sight of his ramrod-hard virility rearing up so temptingly.

Maybe it was because in caressing him into arousal she'd become aroused herself.

Or maybe it was the surge of power she felt at the delicious contradiction between his arrogant member and his helplessly bound wrists which made her suddenly decide to avail herself of his impressive erection before she went.

It needn't take long after all.

She stripped off her stockings and suspender belt and climbed into the fast-cooling water and straddled him. He grunted appreciatively as she lowered herself and took his dick in her hand. She used the swollen, plum-like head to stimulate herself, rubbing it backwards and forwards along her clit, bending to kiss him as she felt butterflies of lust spiralling in her groin.

It felt great to be so in control after having been kept prisoner for almost forty-eight hours. She only wished it was Scar-wrist lying helplessly beneath her, not because he had a bigger cock – his was definitely on the borderline of being too large – but because she would have liked to have him at her mercy.

She soaped her own breasts at the same time so that only her pert, deep-pink nipples were peeping through the suds. As she did so, beads of sweat stood out on Gino's brow and he strained impatiently at his bonds.

She used his shaft selfishly for her own pleasure, although she knew she was pleasuring him too. She stimulated herself almost to the point of climax. Then, when she was suffused by the nerve-tingling wave of heat which preceded it, she sat down hard. She felt his cock spearing right into the heart of her as she came with a low-voiced cry, her full cunt adding to her wanton excitement.

As soon as the waves of hot, carnal satisfaction had receded she began to ride him. It was difficult keeping him inside her in the buoyant, waist-high water and she had to bear down hard on each stroke, keeping her internal muscles partially clenched. He bucked beneath her, driving his hips vigorously upwards, panting with the effort, his eyes riveted on her bouncing breasts.

Faster and faster she rode him, with the water from the tub splashing over the side at each movement until the floor was drenched. Sue had almost forgotten she was planning to escape and was in fact wasting valuable time, so great was her absorption in what was taking place.

At last with a low growl, Gino made one last powerful thrust with his hips, nearly throwing her off, and came with an eruption like a long-dormant volcano bursting into renewed life.

Sue held him tightly inside her, rapidly fluttering her pelvic muscles to trigger her own orgasm.

She gasped and moaned as she came for the second time. Then when the nerve-tingling pleasure subsided, she reluctantly let him slip out of her and climbed out of the bath.

Gino pulled at his bonds and asked her in Italian to untie him. She bent over and kissed him on the mouth, then dried herself off on the threadbare towel. She went into the bedroom to dress, ignoring his pleas. When he raised his voice she was afraid Ricardo would hear and returned to the bathroom to gag him with his own shirt.

A look of total bewilderment crossed his face as she stuffed some of the material in his mouth, then tied the shirt around his face with the sleeves.

She let the water out of the tub and after one last kiss on his forehead said, 'Sorry about this,' and left him alone. In the bedroom she fished his car keys out of the pocket of his trousers and transferred them to her bag.

She went downstairs to find Ricardo moodily playing patience.

'How about a game of cards,' she suggested innocently, joining him at the scarred table still cluttered with the remains of their meal. He brightened up and nodded. 'What shall we play?' she asked.

'Poker,' said Ricardo, leering at her. 'Clothings off poker.'

'You mean strip poker,' she corrected him. 'Okay.'

Ricardo looked like he could hardly believe his luck as he dealt the cards. Sue knew the rudiments of the game, but it didn't really matter whether she won or not, in fact the sooner she lost the better.

The real name of the game was distracting him.

She lost the first hand and immediately removed her dress. No point shilly-shallying about with her shoes. The sight of her luscious breasts thinly veiled by her strapless bra made Ricardo go to pieces and he fluffed dealing the cards.

He lost the next game and removed his shirt, revealing a thick mat of wiry hair and no less than five gold chains of differing thicknesses.

Sue deliberately threw away the next hand and unclipped her bra, throwing it carelessly across his bare shoulder and smiling playfully.

She was horrified when he grabbed her breasts, squeezing painfully and nearly pushing her off her chair. She hadn't bargained for such a rough assault and tried to fend him off, but he dragged her to her feet and threw her on her back on the table, sending couple of dirty plates tumbling to the ground where they shattered into dozens of pieces.

Wincing, Sue tried to sit up, but he shoved her back down and kept his hand on her chest, ripping her panties down her thighs so impatiently that they tore in two.

She'd planned a similar scenario to the one with Gino, except that she hadn't intended to let Ricardo actually screw her.

Now it looked like she wasn't going to get the choice.

Her plan had backfired.

He spread her legs and jammed his hand between her thighs, jabbing at her with his fingers, trying to locate the entrance to her pussy. He managed to get two hard fingers inside her and she cried out as he jiggled them roughly around. He took his other hand off her chest to unzip his trousers and brought out an angry, engorged cock, already oozing moisture in anticipation.

Sue hit wildly out at him and missed. He grabbed her wrists and held them over her head. Leaning over her, so she could smell his wine-sour breath, he stabbed at the entrance to her honeypot with his organ.

Her hand closed on something cylindrical and smooth and out of the corner of her eyes she saw it was the handle of the cast-iron frying pan which had held their stew.

This was no time to be squeamish.

Grasping it, she used all her strength to break free from his grip and hit him with it hard on the side of the head.

An expression of astonishment crossed his face and then his eyes closed and he slid slowly down her body and slumped to the floor.

Shaking, Sue managed to get to her feet and bent over him. There was no blood but he'd gone a terrible colour. Her hands were trembling so much that she could hardly do up her zip, but somehow she managed to get into her dress, not bothering with the bra, and then had to sit down as the room whirled around her. She seized the bottle of wine from the table and drank from it, needing the alcohol to steady herself.

She tried to breathe deeply and evenly. She didn't have time to hang around recovering, she needed to get out of here before the other two returned.

At last, when she felt her legs might just support her, she picked up her bag and tottered weakly towards the door. The Fiat opened easily, but once inside she couldn't find the mechanism to bring her seat forward so she could reach the pedals. She scrabbled frantically around, then dropped to the floor on her knees and at last located it.

She switched on and sighed with relief as the engine leapt into life. The control for the headlights was equally difficult to find, and when at last she succeeded they were so bright that she suspected she was on main beam.

It was a long time since she'd last driven and her heart was in her mouth as she tried to shift the gear lever into first. It wouldn't move and it took her a few seconds to remember that she had to depress the clutch before she could get out of neutral. Once in first she pressed the accelerator cautiously and let her foot lift off the clutch, then was thrown into a panic when the car began to bunny-hop forward like something possessed.

The handbrake.

She needed to take the handbrake off – where the hell was it? She couldn't find it. Then she remembered the car was a left-hand drive, so it would be on the right, rather than the left.

She released it and moved off slowly with a noisy crunching of gears as she changed into second. The road was dark, winding and narrow and it took all her concentration to keep the car on it and not run off into either a gorge or a wall of rock.

It was terrifying.

How come Gino and Marco roared down here at what sounded like about sixty miles an hour? She was only going slowly but even so it was hard to tell which way the road wound through the dark, sticky night.

Her hands were sweating so much that they kept slipping on the steering wheel. It felt like one of those endless nightmares from which you awoke drenched in perspiration and with a deep sense of relief that it wasn't real.

Except that it was.

She didn't pass another car as she headed interminably downwards, the engine screaming, but she was too overwrought to realise she should be in third. By the time she reached the coast road she felt like she'd been driving all night.

Here was a new terror.

The traffic was all flashing past at what seemed to be the speed of light. She didn't know how she was ever going to work up the nerve to join it. But there were no bars or restaurants nearby and she was afraid to get out of the car and flag down a passing motorist in case she fell into the hands of more potential rapists.

She thought she spotted a gap in the traffic and shot out, then realised there was a car coming straight at her. With a deafening blast on his horn the other driver swerved round her.

Fuck!

She'd forgotten they drove on the right over here. She had difficulty changing gear again and several cars overtook her, also sounding their horns, as she lurched along at about fifteen miles an hour.

At last she got it into third and kept on going, looking neither left nor right, nor in the mirror.

If the Italians were such bloody brilliant drivers they could all damn well avoid her.

She could see the lights of a town up ahead and the traffic got heavier. She followed the car in front and found herself sucked into a confusing one-way system. A car cut across her and she swerved, then stalled, blocking the road.

Immediately every driver in the vicinity hit the horn. In the din which followed she was dimly aware of people eating at pavement trattorias looking curiously up, then she saw the most wonderful sight which had met her eyes since she'd been kidnapped.

A taxi rank.

She swung out of the car leaving the door open and the keys in the ignition, walked across to the rank and climbed into the first cab, giving the driver the name of their hotel.

She didn't register anything about the drive back, just lay there with her head on the back of the grimy seat with her eyes closed.

She almost wept when the taxi pulled up outside the familiar facade of the hotel. She doubted if she had enough money on her to pay the fare and she didn't feel equal to trying to count out foreign money in her current state, so she simply strode into reception intending to get them to sort it out.

The first sight that met her eyes was Joe and Gemma talking to Paulo, the deputy manager.

'Hi guys,' she managed to say brightly, then she threw herself into Joe's arms and burst into tears.

Chapter Twenty

The ferry cut through the blue-green waters of the bay of Naples en route to Capri under a perfect, hyacinth-blue sky.

Leaning over the rail, her hip pressed close to Joe's, Sue was hoping to see the dolphins which she'd read sometimes accompanied the ferry on its journey.

It was their last day in Italy and although a large part of her didn't want to leave, part of her was looking forward to the comforting familiarity of her scruffy flat and her chaotic office in the advertising agency.

It was a week since she'd done her hair-raising drive down the rocky mountain to the coast road and she seemed to have spent a good part of that time enduring countless interviews with the police, going over and over the sequence of events.

The good news was that although none of the gang had actually been captured yet, they'd all been identified by the fingerprints left at the farmhouse and she'd been able to provide verification by looking at police photos.

When she'd led the police to the farmhouse the following day, not surprisingly they'd all fled. At least she knew that

Ricardo wasn't dead, he'd been treated for concussion at the hospital in Naples. The police were confident that they'd track them down soon and she had to be content with that.

When she and Joe arrived at Marina Grande they took the funicular railway up to the pretty little town of Capri and wandered round exploring, stopping to drink frothy cups of cappuccino in a pavement café near the church of Santo Sefano.

Joe sat with his hand on Sue's thigh, tanned now to a rich, dark, honey-gold, enjoying the admiring glances she was attracting from the passing Italians and tourists. She was wearing a tight pair of khaki shorts with a sleeveless tee-shirt in a lighter shade of khaki, which moulded itself lovingly to the generous contours of her breasts.

They were both a little tired – they'd been up half the night screwing among a tangle of damp, crumpled sheets – but he was already hot for her again.

'What do you say we buy a picnic and find somewhere secluded to eat it,' he suggested.

She looked up at him from beneath her long lashes.

'Good idea,' was her reaction.

They bought crusty olive-oil bread, cheeses, ham, tomatoes, peaches and beer and headed out of the town with the sun beating so strongly down that the road shimmered in a heat haze.

After passing through the fragrant, leafy shade of orange and lemon groves and a precarious scramble down a steep cliff, they found a grassy plateau edged by camellia bushes, with a walnut tree providing a respite from the broiling sun.

About a hundred yards below them the indolent sea

lapped gently at the jagged rocks at the foot of the cliff. The air was redolent with the scent of salt and wild herbs.

They lay on a blanket under the tree and Sue dozed while Joe lay on his back with his hands clasped behind his head, brooding. Today, for the first time since arriving, the proximity of their return forced him to confront a problem he'd been able to put to the back of his mind for a while.

Mandy.

And, as if the memory of her behaviour wasn't bad enough, there was also the memory of his own.

He went hot and cold when he recalled the lengths she'd goaded him to. If his aunt and uncle hadn't arrived when they did, would she still be tied spread-eagled to his bed, her bare backside showing the marks of repeated spankings, her pussy oozing with his juices from repeated fuckings?

He had a horrible feeling she would.

She'd turned him into a half-crazed creature who understood only revenge and lust.

And tomorrow he had to return to confront the same problem. He might see now that his actions and intentions had been far from rational, but who was to know whether, after a few days back in the flat with her, he might be driven to even greater extremes.

He might think he could find her a new place to live and move her into it but, let's face it, to date his attempts to dislodge his cousin had been spectacularly unsuccessful.

In his worst nightmares he saw her provoking him to even more desperate measures.

It didn't bear thinking about.

With a sickening feeling of certainty he knew she'd

somehow manage to split him up from Sue – just when he'd got her safely back. He'd been frantic during the two days she'd been missing, harassing the police relentlessly to do everything humanly possible to find her.

He groaned and rolled onto his stomach, his face buried in his hands.

'What's up?'

Sue, eyelids fluttering sleepily, turned onto her side and touched his shoulder in concern. Taking a deep breath Joe sat up and looked at her.

'There's something I've got to tell you.'

'Then I'd better open a couple of beers.'

Deftly, she wrenched the caps off two bottles of the now tepid beer and passed one to him. When he hesitated, uncertain how to begin, she prompted him. 'Let me guess – you're married?'

'No. But it's not a hundred miles from what I'm going to tell you.'

In graphic detail he related the living hell his life had become since Mandy had taken up residence, uninvited and unwanted, under his roof.

She interrupted only once to say in an awed voice, 'And you didn't push her off the terrace? I can't believe you had so much self-control.'

At the end of his account, culminating in the arrival of his aunt and uncle, Joe was astonished to have Sue burst out laughing. As she'd just taken a mouthful of beer she immediately choked and he had to bang her on the back.

'That's just . . . that's just so funny,' she spluttered.

For the first time, Joe saw the humorous side and laughed too.

'I'm glad you think so,' he told her.

'I do, I do. Poor Joe – why didn't you tell me before?'

'I couldn't – I didn't think you'd believe me.'

'You couldn't possibly be making it up – the question is what do we do now?' She mulled it over for a while then said, 'Actually it's going to be really easy – I'll pretend I'm moving in with you permanently.'

'How will that get her out?'

Sue shook her head, 'You obviously know nothing about women, Joe. From the way you've described her she's a spoilt, self-obsessed little madam who won't be able to stand the attention being off her and on me. And I've got two younger sisters so I'm wise to any tricks she might pull. I'd give her a week before she'll be out.'

'Do you think so?' Joe saw a light at the end of the tunnel for the first time.

'I guarantee it. She won't dare pull all those stunts with me around. I promise you that she'll find me much more unbearable to live with than I will her. Now – how about some lunch?'

Stretched out on her stomach on a towel on the balcony of their suite, Gemma was treating herself to a day of total self-indulgence.

When she'd woken up she'd rung room service for her breakfast, which she'd enjoyed very much – but not as much as she'd enjoyed the lithe young body of the waiter who'd brought it.

Around mid-afternoon she'd rung for coffee. A different waiter had arrived with it, another boy she'd already had several times. As soon as he'd poured it, hot and steaming, he'd unzipped his trousers to reveal his tumescent dick, also hot and if not actually steaming, well along the way to being so.

She'd heard that the hotel staff practically fought with each other to serve their suite. She wasn't sure whether she'd worked her way through them all yet, but she was certainly giving it her best shot.

Now it was time for lunch.

She went inside and sat alone at the table in the sitting room, wearing only a lemon bikini. As the youth unloaded the tray of delicate nibbles, Gemma caressed his taut young buttocks, only stopping when the strength of his hard-on made the already tight fabric of his trousers tauten to ripping point.

She fed herself titbits as he silently moved behind her and undid the ties of her bikini top. It fell to the floor and he reached around her and stroked her breasts, teasing her large caramel-coloured nipples to heavy points. He poured half an inch of dry white wine into her glass, then fitted it delicately over one small, pert breast.

A perfect fit.

As the icy liquid sluiced over her heated skin, tiny goose bumps formed and her already swollen nipple hardened. He took the glass away, drained it, then bent over her and licked the wine from her smooth orb.

He repeated the procedure with the other breast, then slid under the table and knelt between her legs. Two tugs on the ties holding the bikini closed over her hips, and the material fell away, exposing her mound to his hungry gaze.

While Gemma proceeded to calmly eat her lunch, he parted her thighs and gorged himself on her. He licked, nibbled, lapped and sucked until at last she was squirming with pleasure, a sticky puddle forming beneath her luscious backside.

She came suddenly in a hot, shuddering spasm which made her lose interest in the food. He crawled out from under the table and seated himself opposite her, his trousers unzipped and his thrusting cock rearing invitingly up from his hairy groin.

Gemma left her seat and went to stand in front of him at the table. He bit her buttocks softly, sliding his fingers into her from behind and finding the honeyed juices flowing copiously from her velvet interior.

He pulled her down onto his cock, letting her take it slowly into her overflowing pussy. Her foot slipped on the tiled floor and she sat down more suddenly than she'd intended. She gasped as his cock jabbed sharply upwards to be swiftly engulfed by her warm folds.

She felt as if she were being pierced by something with a life of its own as it throbbed there, and she rocked herself backwards and forwards on it, enjoying the pressure on the walls of her honeypot.

She held onto the arms of the chair and moved up and down, helped by his hands on her hips, slowly at first, then with gathering speed.

At last, after a dizzying ride, he slammed her down on his cock one last time and came with a hoarse cry, spurting high up inside her.

A few minutes later he prepared to take his leave. He poured her another glass of wine and murmured solicitously, 'Will there be anything else, signorina?'

Gemma, still naked, smiled sweetly.

'Not until I ring for afternoon tea.'

At Sue's suggestion she and Joe ate their picnic in the nude. He wanted to screw her before they ate, but she made him wait, cruelly ignoring the massive hard-on rearing up between his thighs at the sight of her voluptuous, naked beauty.

To finish the meal she chose a succulent, ripe peach and bit into it with her small white teeth. A flood of peach juice ran down her chin and dripped onto her breast. Joe couldn't stand it a moment longer and rolled her onto her back. He licked a drop of sweet juice from where it lay poised on the end of her nipple, wrapping his tongue around it and making her squirm with pleasure.

It tasted so good that he squeezed another peach over her stomach, letting it run into the golden floss of her bush. He lapped up every drop, making her wriggle with delight as he followed the trickles over her belly and down between her thighs. He sucked her clit, probing beneath the tiny fold of the hood then flickering along the side until she was trembling with lust.

When he'd licked it all up he plunged into her urgently and fucked her with a heat and passion which made her moan out loud. Every searing thrust drove her onwards and upwards, closer to a mind-numbing climax.

Every nerve-ending in her body was crying out for release when he suddenly stopped and pulled out of her.

'Don't stop!' she gasped. 'Not now!'

But Joe wanted to finish it from behind. He pulled her up and onto her knees, then ran his hands over her gorgeous backside. He impaled her again, thrusting inside her so strongly that she almost came, even after the break in stimulation. It only took a few vigorous thrusts and she cried out, her whole body spasming as she climaxed.

Joe continued to pump in and out of her, fondling her breasts and smacking his balls against her curvaceous bum so hard that her buttocks quivered. His last thrust had such force behind it that she fell forward onto her hands and knees, while he clasped her tightly as if he'd never let her go.

When they'd recovered enough, they scrambled down the steep cliff and dived into the clear blue water, washing off the sweat, dust and, in Sue's case, peach juice.

They fucked again on a ledge just above the water, then were forced to hide behind a rock, still joined at the groin, when a boat sailed past a few hundred yards out to sea.

'I hope you stay as insatiable as this when we're back in London,' Sue told him, as he moved his cock in and out of her, both of them uncomfortably cramped against the cliff.

'Only if you stay as gorgeously, temptingly fuckable as this,' he grunted, revving up for the last lap.

It was raining in London. Dreary, grey drizzle which told them very plainly that summer was over and winter was on its way.

As he fitted his key into the lock of his flat, Sue just behind him, Joe found himself perspiring nervously. However reassuring Sue was, he was still half-convinced that Mandy was destined to be the permanent cuckoo in his particular nest.

The door swung open and he was met by the sight of a strange man, overweight and middle-aged, holding Mandy's suitcase in one hand and several carrier bags in the other.

From behind him Mandy emerged from the bedroom expensively attired in a new pink, raw-silk suit.

'Oh, so you're back,' she greeted him reproachfully. 'I'm amazed you have the nerve to show your face here again after taking off so rudely and abandoning me to entertain my parents all by myself. Anyway I'm leaving. I was going to write you a note – not that you deserve one after the way you've treated me. This is Hooper.'

Hooper dropped the suitcase and shook first Joe's hand and then Sue's, saying, 'Pleased to meet you, folks.'

His accent was decidedly American.

'This is Sue,' Joe introduced her, not to be outdone in the politeness stakes.

Mandy stared at her for a few moments, then said haughtily, 'Well, I just hope he treats you better than he treated me.'

She held out her left hand to Joe, fingers extended, waggling an enormous ruby ring nestling next to a wide, plain gold band.

'Hooper and I got married this morning,' she announced. 'No – it's no good saying anything,' she continued, as Joe's jaw dropped. 'It's too late now to regret your horrible behaviour. Hooper's a millionaire and he buys me clothes much nicer than the tat you thought was good enough for me. I've already got a whole new wardrobe in the limousine waiting for us outside. I just stopped off to pick up what I'd left here. We're flying to Houston today.'

'Congratulations,' said Sue, beaming. Joe's larynx seemed to have seized up.

'Do . . . do your parents know?' he managed at last.

'No. You can ring them for me and tell them,' she said airily, adjusting a large ruby earring and looking disdainfully around as she added, 'Hooper has a mansion which makes this place look like a rabbit hutch – he's shown me the photos. And he's got servants so he won't be expecting me to scrub the floors on my hands and knees like you did.'

'We'd better get going, honey,' said Hooper, smiling at her indulgently. 'We don't want to miss our plane. I'm just dying to get my honey-lamb back home and take her shopping in Houston. London ain't got nothing to compete with the shops there.'

Mandy slipped her hand into his arm.

'I can't wait. Goodbye, Joe. I may forgive you eventually, but not yet.'

With a last twitch of her pert backside she left the apartment, and hopefully his life, forever.

'I feel like an enormous weight has been lifted from my chest,' he said to Sue as soon as the door had closed behind them.

He reached up and under her skirt and slid her panties down her thighs.

'And what do you think you're doing?' she asked sternly.

'Mandy leaving has had the strangest effect on me,' he told her. 'Feel.'

A selection of Erotica from Headline

SCANDAL IN PARADISE	Anonymous	£4.99	☐
UNDER ORDERS	Nick Aymes	£4.99	☐
RECKLESS LIAISONS	Anonymous	£4.99	☐
GROUPIES II	Johnny Angelo	£4.99	☐
TOTAL ABANDON	Anonymous	£4.99	☐
AMOUR ENCORE	Marie-Claire Villefranche	£4.99	☐
COMPULSION	Maria Caprio	£4.99	☐
INDECENT	Felice Ash	£4.99	☐
AMATEUR DAYS	Becky Bell	£4.99	☐
EROS IN SPRINGTIME	Anonymous	£4.99	☐
GOOD VIBRATIONS	Jeff Charles	£4.99	☐
CITIZEN JULIETTE	Louise Aragon	£4.99	☐

All Headline books are available at your local bookshop or newsagent, or can be ordered direct from the publisher. Just tick the titles you want and fill in the form below. Prices and availability subject to change without notice.

Headline Book Publishing, Cash Sales Department, Bookpoint, 39 Milton Park, Abingdon, OXON, OX14 4TD, UK. If you have a credit card you may order by telephone – 01235 400400.

Please enclose a cheque or postal order made payable to Bookpoint Ltd to the value of the cover price and allow the following for postage and packing:

UK & BFPO: £1.00 for the first book, 50p for the second book and 30p for each additional book ordered up to a maximum charge of £3.00.
OVERSEAS & EIRE: £2.00 for the first book, £1.00 for the second book and 50p for each additional book.

Name ....

Address ....

....

....

If you would prefer to pay by credit card, please complete:
Please debit my Visa/Access/Diner's Card/American Express (delete as applicable) card no:

Signature .... Expiry Date ....